Abby opened a cupboard and put away a jar of honey. "He's hardly my soulmate."

"I may not have the gifts you have, but I can see what's in front of my eyes." Her best friend made a face. "Wake up and smell the Guinness, babe."

She made a face back. "He's just a nice man who can help us, Lynne."

"He's a nice man who can help us, who is hot. He also cares about you a lot and you've barely met." Lynne held up a finger. "And he's *hung*, by the way."

Yeah, she'd had a sense of that when they were pressed against each other. "I don't know that he's my soulmate," Abby repeated.

"You would if you tuned in." Lynne folded her arms, her cheeks flushed rosy, looking more alive than she had since the attack. "Don't be stubborn about this. The Universe is handing you a love buffet on a platter. What if this is why we came to Ireland?"

"We came to find Finn so he could help your leg heal."

"No, we came so we could *both* heal, so that we could *both* go back to living our life's purpose. Don't piss me off. I'll run you down with my wheelchair."

PRAISE FOR KATHIA

"Put simply, Kathia's novels are like a glass of champagne – heady, addictive and leaving one with a taste for much, much more."

— THE LITERARY SHED

"I simply adore Kathia's novels. Her series are fun and delightful to read. She knows how to add enough drama to the story to make it interesting, while at the same time making it something that could happen in real life. I love how she takes beautiful strong women and makes them even stronger by falling in love."

— A NOVEL GLIMPSE

"In truth, Kathia's super power is creating very real, very relatable characters that sort of just suck you in. Her secondary super power is inserting those characters into fun scenarios and situations that keep the plot moving along quickly and most interestingly."

— ROLO POLO BOOK BLOG

"Kathia is a professional writer who knows how to craft a well-structured story."

"I can't help the ear-to-ear smile I have plastered to my face when reading any of Kathia's books... She makes me laugh out loud, even on a crowded bus!"

"[Kathia's] writing is fluid, with a touch of sexiness and loads of romance, just what you need to relax after a long, hard working day."

"If you haven't read any of Kathia's books, start now. She's great storyteller, and a talented writer."

"Reading Kathia's books is my favorite way to spend an afternoon. (Well.. Okay, my second favorite way, the husband insists I clarify.)"

PRAISE FOR THE IRISH HOPE SERIES

"So fun, unique, and has a lovely Irish setting perfect for St. Patrick's Day. Overall, it's a great read, and I am looking forward to more marvelous stories from Kathia."

— THE KINDLE KWEEN

"A new paranormal voice has hit the market, one that is sure to only get even better as the years go on!"

— THE BOOK QUEEN

"Keep an eye on this author and series."

— ROMANTIC TIMES BOOK REVIEWS

"If you're a sucker for a HEA you have to read this!"

— HOME IS WHERE THE WINE IS BOOK BLOG

"If you have not started reading this series, what are you waiting for?"

— AS YOU WISH REVIEWS

PAINTER OF SOULS

AN IRISH HOPE NOVEL

KATHIA

PAINTER OF SOULS

ACKNOWLEDGMENTS

This book was made possible by...

You, who said, "Kathia, I really miss your stories."

Ava, who said, "Maybe you should write a book set in Ireland."

Martha, who said, "I find artists fascinating."

Kimberly, who said, "I'm on this book like a lion on a hunt!"

Shannon, who said, "Dragons would visit me if I wrote as much as you in a day."

The liquor store clerk, who said, "Is all this wine for a party?"

Thank you with all my heart.

BEFORE...

The first time my mama gave me paint and a canvas, when I was six, I felt like I'd been handed the world.

I knew exactly what to paint—the vision was right there in my head: a man in a funny black floppy hat and a white floofy thing around his neck, holding a dead rose. At the time, I hadn't known that it was a scene from a past life of my mama's, or that the man had been her in that seventeenth century existence. I'd only known it needed to be done in shades of blue, even the skin.

"Remember, Abby, blue is the color of voice and vision, and when you marry them together you can make miracles," Mama used to say to me.

At six, I didn't know what that meant, but I'd known it was important.

So I painted that scene in all the blues: turquoise eyes, ash-blue skin with deep accents, ultramarine clothing. The background was in midnight blue interspersed with Payne's gray, a gray color with mysterious blue undertones that I loved from the first moment I'd rubbed it between my fingertips. And because light was essential, a dash of white around the neck and eyes.

But I changed the scene a little—something told me I needed to. Instead of the sadness in the man's eyes, I painted cerulean love. Instead of the dying rose, I painted it alive, its pink petals vibrant and dewy and lush.

When I finished the painting, I gave it to Mama because she was sick, and on the inside, I knew this painting would make her better.

At six, I hadn't understood what pneumonia was. I just knew it was bad and Mama hadn't been able to play with me for days, and the coughing made her so tired. Mama had looked gray all the time—the muddy kind of gray when you mixed a lot of colors together, not pretty like Payne's gray.

I also hadn't understood how incredible it was that my mama's illness had disappeared immediately after I'd given her the painting.

Neither did I understand what I was doing—that I was healing a persistent karmic wound or scar from a past life. In painting a new, improved version of that moment, I edited that lingering hurt out completely, healing the person of it in this life and every life thereafter.

Mama had understood, though, because she had gifts from the Divine too. When I handed her that first painting, she'd looked at me in wonder and said, "Abigail Angevine, you have a rare gift from the Divine."

I'd felt good about that. Being like her made me happy. I understood then that blue wasn't just the color of voice and vision: it was the color of connection and love, and those two together healed every illness and malady. In my mind, blue brought the promise of sun and warmth and laughter.

It brought hope.

I held on to that, even in those moments when no amount of painting could fix the situation. Like when Mama died when I was eight and I had to go live with the nuns in the orphanage. Or when my best friend, Lynne, went to New York to pursue her dream of becoming a dancer and left me alone in New Orleans.

Or when I fucked up six months ago and destroyed not only my life but Lynne's too.

1

"Everyone is a color, baby," her mama used to say. "And all the colors are beautiful."

Gripping the steering wheel with her good hand, Abby glanced at her best friend sitting in the passenger seat next to her. Normally, Abby agreed with her mom's wisdom, but her mom wasn't there to see Lynne.

Her best friend's color was far from beautiful lately. It was the sort of flat pasty gray that Abby never used in her artwork. All of her was that shade of gray—from her physical body to her soul. Lynne was pale and drawn, inside and out: her normally bouncy golden hair lank, her clothes sagging on her too-thin body, her spirit just as colorless and limp. Abby bet Lynne's leg was throbbing in pain because that was how Abby's sprained wrist felt.

"I don't want to do this," Lynne said, staring out the window.

Frankly, Abby didn't either.

At the moment, thousands of miles from home in Ireland, exhausted after four months of caring for Lynne in her small Manhattan apartment, jet-lagged from the long-ass flight and then the three-hour drive from Dublin to Tullaghan in County Leitrim, Abby just wanted to crawl under a comforter and cry. She imagined Lynne felt the same.

But she needed to be encouraging because coming to Ireland was her idea in the first place. So she put on a cheery smile that took all her reserves to muster. "It's going to be great, going to physical therapy."

"It's going to be painful," Lynne said, rubbing the top of her leg where the brace ended. "Like always."

"I talked to the physical therapist yesterday. He sounded nice, and you like meeting new people."

Lynne said nothing.

"Maybe he'll be cute," Abby added. "He definitely has a sexy Irish accent."

Lynne sighed and said in a whisper, "I can't imagine anyone wanting me like this. Have you seen my leg?"

Of course, she had. She'd never say it out loud, but each time she rubbed salve on it, each time she helped Lynne on and off with the brace, she wanted to cry.

After being broken in three places and reset with surgery with all the torn ligaments, after weeks in traction, it wasn't healing. Still much too swollen, it'd also atrophied.

Abby understood energy, so she got that the hot swelling was a result of suppressed anger and it atrophying so badly was a manifestation of trapped grief.

Which was why they were here in Ireland, because after six months, two surgeries, and trying everything to heal Lynne's leg, the doctors in New York were at a loss for how to proceed. They said they'd tried everything, and the fact that Lynn's leg wasn't responding to treatment made the prognosis bad. They had doubts she'd ever walk again, much less dance.

Abby wasn't willing to accept that.

But she needed to be upbeat, to keep Lynne's spirits up, until they found Dr. Carrick Fionnlagh. The moment Abby had read about him—they called him the Miracle Worker—she knew he was the one. She could see colors of blue swirling around him, highlighting his eyes.

Good Lord—his eyes were so striking. Even on her phone's browser, in tiny low-res photos, his soul reached out to hers, like it was reassuring her that he'd be able to help Lynne heal.

As bad as her leg looked in this moment, as much as it hurt, they were going to find Dr. Fionnlagh and get Lynne up and dancing again. So now with Lynne, Abby kept it light. "That's ridiculous. You're beautiful and smart and funny. Of course anyone would want you. If I liked girls, I'd totally bang you."

That brought a ghost of a smile to her best friend's lips. "Thanks," she said with some of her old humor. "But you're not my type."

Hearing that glimmer of Lynne's old self sent a pang of hope through Abby's chest. She *missed* her best friend.

She should have been used to missing her. Lynne had been living in New York for the past fifteen years working as a professional dancer. Since Abby had stayed in New Orleans, she was used to physical distance between them.

It was the emotional distance between them since the accident six months ago that Abby couldn't quite bridge.

The doctors said it was normal—of course Lynne was going to experience depression since she couldn't dance.

But it wasn't all Lynne. It was Abby too, because she'd been hurt that day as well.

Worse: it'd been her fault.

"I thought it'd be dreary and rainy in Ireland, even now in July, but it's beautiful," Lynne said, staring out the window. "If you did landscapes, they'd look like the passing scenery."

She wondered if Lynne was trying to distract her. Lynne may not have gifts like Abby did, but she was very intuitive.

"Maybe being here will be as healing as your paintings. There's just so much blue," Lynne added.

"I know. I hadn't expected that." Everyone raved about the greens in Ireland, but no one had prepared Abby for all the blue. So many shades of it, from high intensity saturated tones to subtle and soft. The baby blue of the sky. The deep azure of the Atlantic. The bright cheeriness of the denim-hued hydrangeas... Even the grassy knolls were a blue shade of phthalo green.

Blue had always been the color of hope to her. It was a healing color, the color she saw banded around people with healing abilities, the primary color she used in all her paintings. It was like someone was trying to hit her over the head with it, encouraging her to recall that.

As if reading her mind, Lynne said, "We were right to decide to come here, even if I'm tired and need to be reminded. Ireland feels right. Thank you, Abby, for bringing me here."

The sincerity in Lynne's voice made her throat close

with emotion. She blinked the sudden tears back ruthlessly, forcing herself to focus on the road. How could Lynne be thanking her when it was her fault that they were in this situation?

She flexed the fingers of her sprained wrist around the brace she wore, wincing at their puffy soreness. Suppressed anger, indeed. And just like Lynne's leg, it wasn't getting any better.

Abby still wasn't sure where she went wrong. Lynne had needed help to get over a roadblock with her dance company and had asked her for a painting to help her ascend to greater success. Given that Lynne was thirty-four—older for a professional dancer—Lynne had said she needed all the help she could get.

No biggie. Abby was commissioned to do paintings for that purpose all the time, and this was Lynne.

But the past life scene that she'd seen had perplexed her. It was from maybe the thirteenth century, where Lynne had been a girl in love with a man who was domineering and disapproving. Abby had been her brother in that life, but she hadn't been able to defend Lynne against that man. In the scene, the man who had been Abby in that life was standing to the side, unable to do anything as Lynne's husband beat her.

Abby had no idea how that scene correlated to what Lynne needed in this life. Yet it'd been so clear that she'd gone with it. In her painting, she'd edited the scene so she stepped in and defended Lynne against that man.

Despite her niggling doubt, she'd done the painting quickly and eagerly, and before it had even dried completely, she delivered it to New York herself.

That was when everything backfired.

Abby had been doing her healing paintings since she was six years old. She'd done hundreds of them without any mishaps. Sure, not everyone healed all the way, but she knew that was a choice that had nothing to do with her work.

This was the first time something had gone so bad. It didn't escape her awareness that it was also the first time she'd ever painted herself into a scene.

Now she knew it was going to be the last time too.

Lynne's boyfriend Kevin had been in their apartment when Abby arrived with the painting. It was the first time she'd met Kevin—Lynne had met him a few months before and immediately moved in with him. He'd looked excellent on paper: the director of a charity for homeless kids, doing good in the world. Lynne seemed happy with him. Abby thought Lynne had finally gotten past the string of jerks she usually dated and found someone worthy of her.

But the second she saw Lynne, she knew something wasn't right. Lynne looked nothing like herself—kind of hazy at the edges, her color diffused, like she was overlapped with someone else. Now, Abby would have waited to give Lynne the painting, to look at things deeper, but at the time she'd thought the painting was the way to get her best friend back to normal. Hindsight, right?

Kevin flipped out the second Abby had unveiled the painting.

Literally *flipped out*, in the Jekyll and Hyde way. Gone was the nice guy he presented on his résumé. In his place was a monster, his hands striking out in his rage, yelling at Lynne about what a bitch she was and that he couldn't believe she'd waste her money on a painting by a charlatan. He screamed that Abby was a bad influence and that he never wanted her to step foot in their apartment ever again.

Because she'd always done it, from the time they'd met at the orphanage where they'd grown up, Abby stepped in to deescalate the situation and protect Lynne. That was when Kevin shoved her.

She fell on her wrist. For the span of a long breath, she'd felt something give and was afraid that something had snapped, and her heart had stopped because she was afraid she'd never paint again.

Then he turned on Lynne, charging her, and Abby's fear amplified to encompass her best friend too.

Abby could still see the red crawling up Kevin's neck and the bulge of his black gaze as he tried to grab Lynne. She still saw the yellow cast of fright on Lynne's face as she backed up with her hands out to ward him off. She heard the terror of Lynne's scream as he lunged for her and the thumps after she "tripped" and fell down the stairs.

Abby could still see Lynne lying at the bottom of the stairs, her leg at an impossible angle. The silence of it echoed in her nightmares.

The doctors had said it was lucky Lynne had only broken her leg and torn musculature, implying that she could have been paralyzed—or worse.

Swallowing the bile rising at the memory, Abby clung to the steering wheel of the rental with her good hand

and reminded herself to drive on the left side of the narrow road as a car approached. The last thing she needed was to get them in an accident. They'd dealt with enough the past six months, what with Kevin moving out and her staying in New York to take care of Lynne twenty-four-seven since the accident, trying to get both of them back to normal.

But it wasn't working. Lynne's leg wasn't healing—the continued swelling and limited mobility concerned all the doctors while it defied them by not responding to any treatment. And Abby's wrist...

She couldn't focus on that now. She knew it was linked to Lynne's injury, and she also knew that if Lynne got better, then *she'd* get better.

Which was why they were here in this small Irish surfing town in County Leitrim. They were both looking for a miracle, and that miracle's name was Dr. Carrick Fionnlagh.

As if reading her mind once more, Lynne said, "How hard do you think it'll be to find that orthopedic surgeon?"

"I'll find him." She had to. He was their last hope, especially since she was out of commission and couldn't help Lynne herself.

Normally, she would have meditated until she saw the right scene from one of Lynne's past lives, and then she'd have painted it and Lynne would have healed. But there were two problems with that.

First: Abby was positive her painting had been what triggered Kevin. It was stark, the change that came over him when he saw it. Most people became peaceful and relieved, definitely hopeful. Some cried. He became furious, a black rage that infused his whole soul.

The only thing that was different with that painting was that she'd painted herself into it. But that had been part of the vision she'd seen. She was at a loss as to why it went so wrong.

Needless to say, she'd burned the canvas the day after Lynne fell down the stairs.

The second problem: Abby couldn't do another painting to heal Lynne. Her wrist was too injured.

She'd tried, even though she was scared of fucking things up worse. She couldn't *not* try to heal her best friend. Lynne was the only family she had. So she'd made herself paint, forcing herself to hold the brushes and palette knives. She'd painted past the point where her wrist was painful until she couldn't hold anything in her hand.

It'd been months, and she still couldn't hold a paintbrush for longer than five seconds before her right hand seized up. Her doctor had said she'd made her injury worse, but he couldn't offer any advice on how to remedy it other than to stop using it for a period of time and to take ibuprofen.

If she couldn't paint...

Well, she couldn't think about it, because the idea of never painting ever again made her want to weep. Much like Lynne not dancing made her close in on herself.

Abby gingerly closed her fingers as much as her brace would allow, wincing at the pain in her hand and wrist. It just wasn't getting any better; it was getting worse.

Some healer, huh?

The thing was, Lynne's injury had persisted so long that even if Abby could do something to heal her energetically, the physical repercussions would take longer to reverse. Abby could do all the healing on Lynne's etheric body, but Lynne's physical body needed a doctor's expertise to help her get back to healthy. Abby was conscious of the fact that every day that passed made Lynne bouncing back that much more difficult. Time wasn't on their side.

Lynne faced her, angling her body as much as she could without straining her leg and with the restriction of the brace. When Abby glanced at her, Lynne had her hand wrapped around the shungite pendant Abby had given her after the accident, to ward off afflicting energies.

"You really think this doctor is as great as they say?" Lynne asked.

"Yes," Abby said with full conviction. She remembered seeing his picture and his eyes—that color of bright hope—and the instant feeling of comfort she felt, and she nodded. "One of the nurses raved about him from working with him in Dublin before moving to New York. She said there was no one like him. He's the one. He doesn't have a perfect track record, but I'd be suspicious if he did."

"And Bro Paul confirmed it?"

Abby pretended to focus on the car passing her. Maybe if she didn't reply, Lynne would drop this subject.

"Abby, tell me you talked to Bro Paul about this."

Maybe not. She wrinkled her nose. "I told you I'm taking a time out from talking with him."

"Abby, he's your *guide*."

14

"More is the pity." Some people thought guides were guardian angels, but she knew they weren't always angelic, per se. They were spirits who worked with the living in hopes of ascending to higher levels of spiritual evolution. The thing was, he was a *guide*, meaning he should have *guided* her. But he hadn't warned her that her painting was going to ruin their lives.

You didn't ask me, Bro Paul's voice sounded in her head.

She gritted her teeth, because he was right, and that was on her too.

Regardless, since what happened, she and Brother Paul, the Franciscan monk spirit that was assigned to her, weren't on speaking terms. Her decision—Bro Paul continued to harass her despite her recent strict "leave me the fuck alone" policy.

She didn't know how other guides interacted with their charges, but she had a suspicion they didn't tell fart jokes, encourage brandy drinking, and throw their rough brown robes up to moon people. She'd asked him about his unorthodox ways one time; he said that he'd needed to learn how to better connect with his charges in these modern times, so he'd binge-watched *Buffy* for the download. That Bro Paul was her guide was proof that the Divine had a sense of humor, one that Abby no longer shared.

Lynne groaned. "Abby, we concocted this crazy idea to come thousands of miles to find this doctor, despite all the best doctors in New York saying my leg was a lost cause, because we felt that this guy could actually help us—"

"To help *you*," Abby clarified. Her wrist would be fine once Lynne was healed. She hoped.

"—and you didn't ask Bro Paul for confirmation?"

Abby winced. She hadn't asked for confirmation with Lynne's painting either, assuming she knew what she was doing, and that had been disastrous. Maybe she needed to reconsider the standoff.

Lynne threw her hands in the air. "You've got mad gifts. Healing, channeling, seeing ghosts... If I had gifts like that, you can be damn sure I'd be using them right now."

Gifts. Abby snorted.

When she was little, she'd thought everyone saw ghosts. Her first memory was of her grandmother leaning over her crib, bestowing a blessing on her with soft fingertips. Abby didn't realize until much later that her grandmother had been dead for over twenty years. To her, spirits and ghosts were just as solid as real people. She could hear, see, and touch them the same way she could Lynne. Or they could touch her. Chicken, egg.

That sort of gift—and others—ran in her family. Her mother had had gifts, as did her grandmother and her great-grandmother and every woman before her. It was only on the feminine side, and that's how Abby also knew God had a sense of humor. However, Abby was the first one who expressed them through art.

She knew the power of her paintings; that was never a question in her mind. Even that very first painting she'd done when she was six, as rudimentary as it'd been stylistic, was mighty in its power. After all, it'd healed her mother.

Living in New Orleans had been good for Abby. People believed in all things woo-woo there. Outside of it, anyone else might have called Abby crazy to believe that she infused healing into her paintings, but Lynne, like her mother, had never doubted her.

Obviously, Lynne drank the Kool-Aid. And look where it got her.

The maps app directed Abby to turn left into the parking lot of the physical therapy center. She concentrated on pulling into the circular drive at the front of the center.

Apparently, Lynne wasn't finished with their conversation. "It's bad enough that you can't paint right now, but cutting yourself off from Bro Paul isn't the answer. Talk to your guide."

"The only answer I have right now is Dr. Fionnlagh." Abby put the emergency brake on, grabbed Lynne's crutches, and went around to help Lynne out of the car.

Lynne shook her head as she eased herself out, wincing in pain. "Don't think you're off the hook, Abigail Angevine. We're going to talk about this later."

She kissed Lynne's cheek. "Trust me."

"Of course I trust you." Lynne rolled her eyes. "But the entire point of finding the Miracle Worker is so that we can go back to being who we are, not to deny more pieces of ourselves. The past six months we've been living in a haze, Abby. I know a lot of it's my fault—"

"Nothing's your fault," Abby protested.

"—but we need to start living again or figuring out what's next, regardless of whether he can help us or not."

Lynne paused. "You know I'm not going to be able to dance again."

"No, I don't know that. And he'll help us." She knew it in her soul, because while she may not want to talk to her guide, she wasn't completely closed off to the Divine.

Lynne shifted shakily on the crutches. "Provided we find him."

"I'm going to find him," she promised. She'd thought he'd be easy to track down in Dublin, where he had an office. It'd thrown her that he'd left town for a sabbatical in Tullaghan, his hometown, and that no one knew for how long.

Fear turned Lynne's eyes a cloudy sort of gray-green. "And how long are we going to give it?"

"As long as it takes." She had plenty of money saved—her paintings had been in great demand; she owned her place in New Orleans outright, and the only thing she spent her money on was more art supplies and to visit Lynne in New York. "Don't worry. I've got this. I have a plan."

Lynne's lips quirked with a hint of a smile. "Of course you do."

She ran a hand down Lynne's back, trying to brush away the anxiety that had settled on her since the accident. "While you're in there kicking PT ass, I'm going to visit the hospital here where the Miracle Worker did his residency. Someone's got to know how I can reach him or his family. I read in an interview online that said his family owns a farm nearby."

Lynne groaned again. "Stalker, much?"

"I'm not stalking. I'm searching." She stepped back so Lynne had room to maneuver. "Have a great session."

Her best friend muttered under her breath and she painfully made her way inside, her body hunched over the crutches. Abby waited until she couldn't see Lynne any longer before getting back in the car.

She put her head on the steering wheel, her hand cradled against her body, giving in to the exhaustion.

Then she took a deep breath and forcibly set it aside. She didn't have the luxury to fall apart right now—not when she was here. She was so close she could feel it; she just had to hang in there. She'd find Dr. Fionnlagh and get him to agree to help Lynne. And then Lynne's leg would heal and she could go back to dancing.

And then Abby's wrist would heal too, somehow, because she was positive it was linked to Lynne's leg healing. And then she could paint again. Because without painting—without healing people—she had no reason to exist.

2
_____

F inn lay in the small bed of his youth, staring up at the ceiling like he used to when he was a kid.

Back then, he dreamed of all the places he was going to go and everything grand he was going to do. Now, he lay sideways to accommodate his big body, but his feet still hung off the end and the old springs poked his sore muscles.

Now, his dreams and his nightmares merged into one.

Back then, he'd wanted to be an adventurer, going around the world, meeting people, seeing exciting sights. He'd planned on setting off on his first quest when he was eighteen, just after secondary. He'd just bought his ticket and new backpack the day his twin Fiona was hit by a car.

He shifted on the mattress, that day like an ever-present thistle around his feet. He'd come home excited to show her the new bag she'd helped him pick while she was in the hospital being told she'd never walk again.

Her accident had changed the course of his life. He'd

watched the frustration and anger she'd had, the apathy of the doctors who didn't believe she'd ever stand on her own two feet. Under their care, she wilted until her determination became depression. She hadn't been tough enough to defy them or believe they could be fallible. They'd killed her spirits as surely as the reckless driver had killed her future.

He'd been the one to find her, overdosed on her pain meds, in her room, the one next door to where he was sleeping even now.

Closing his eyes against the image, he fisted his hands to stop their shaking. It was the worst day of his life, like the other half of him was rended from him.

So instead of leaving for parts unknown, he'd changed course and gone to uni, to become an orthopedic surgeon. A damn good orthopedic surgeon. The great Dr. Carrick Fionnlagh, who helped the people other doctors had given up on.

If he'd been his sister's doctor, he'd have helped her walk again.

That was what he did now. He helped people who had no other hope. It made him pleased to know that he'd taken Fiona's tragedy and turned it into wins. He thought Fiona would have been happy about that too.

That was what made what had happened with his patient that much worse.

"Carrick!" he heard his mom call from down the hall. "Come for breakfast."

He wasn't hungry, but he knew his mom well enough to know she wasn't going to let him molder in his room.

He sat up and swung his feet to the floor, wincing at the achiness in his body.

The doctor in him knew it was from depression. He could catalogue the symptoms and list any number of medications to help alleviate the malaise.

The man in him couldn't do it. He'd fucked up, and he wasn't ready to let it go. He certainly wasn't going to take the easy way out and numb it all. He owed more to Jaime Walsh. If Finn had been paying better attention, he'd have noticed the anesthesiologist had been high. If he'd listened to his nurse's warning, he'd have called in another anesthesiologist instead of forging ahead with the surgery.

Instead, the anesthesiologist had botched the epidural. Instead, Jaime Walsh, a young man who should have recovered nicely from an easy knee surgery, woke up to find himself partially paralyzed from the waist down. Instead, one of Manchester's brightest football stars lost all hope of not only winning a World Cup but going back to the thing he loved most.

Instead, Jaime Walsh had killed himself.

Like Fiona.

"Carrick!" his mom called again. Molly Fionnlagh was nothing if not relentless, especially in her love.

He reminded himself that this was why he'd come home to them—to surround himself with his parents. Despite their own grief, they'd lifted him up when Fiona's death had left him devastated. He knew he could count on that now too.

Not to mention that being at home buffered him from the reporters who wouldn't leave him alone. The press coverage alone was enough for the hospital to ask him to lay low—to take a sabbatical until it calmed down. Not that the medical review had found him at fault, but there were haters who wanted someone to blame for their golden boy footballer being gone.

A sabbatical. He hadn't had a leave in so long, he didn't know what to do with himself. He ran a hand over his hair and left his room before his mom came and dragged him out.

His mom was at the table in the kitchen, pouring coffee into a cup. She took him in with her all-seeing gaze, lingering on the unfamiliar scruff shadowing his face. He watched her mask her concern with a slightly put-out look.

He could have kissed her for that grace. Sympathy would have broken him down, and he wasn't sure he'd be able to pick up the pieces.

"Lollygagging won't cure what ails you, Carrick Fionnlagh," she said, setting the press pot on the table with a *thunk*.

"What do you think will?" he asked with none of his usual curiosity, lifting the coffee to his mouth out of rote habit.

"Do you need me to put together a list of chores for you?" She eyed him. "You're good at sewing. Maybe you can make new curtains for my office."

"I do bodies, not curtains," he replied dully.

"Or maybe I should find a woman for you. Someone to care about instead of yourself."

He gave her a flat look. The thought of caring for

someone else made the coffee he'd just swallowed burn in his esophagus.

"A little loving will set you right," she said, her hands on her hips. "Love always makes everything right. Why, your father and I—"

"Mom, please." He put his hand out to stop her before she could draw him the picture. It was an ongoing skit between them: whenever she talked about her love life with his dad, Finn would feign being embarrassed.

Not so secretly, because his parents and he all knew it, it was their love that had brought Finn back from blackness after Fiona's death. He loved seeing their affection, even if he pretended otherwise. It surrounded him, grounded him in what was important.

It was why he'd come home.

Sighing, his mom came over and ran a hand over his head. "It'll pass, son. Things happen for a reason."

"Things don't happen in *my* operating room," he said, regretting his harsh tone but unable to curb it.

He could tell she wanted to say something more, but instead she turned to the stove and began filling a plate with sausages and eggs and rashers. There was absolutely no way he could eat any of that, but he let her put the plate in front of him.

His dad trudged into the kitchen, giving him a worried look before going to his wife and kissing her soundly. "I moved the cows to the south pasture," he said as he sat at the table and reached for the coffee. "They got away from me and ran up Matthew McGuire's driveway. Tore his turf up something good," he added gleefully.

His mom set an equally laden plate in front of his

dad, shaking her head. "And you're not sorry in the least, are you, Conall Fionnlagh?"

"Of course I am," he said, the playful light in his eyes belying his words. "They trampled his prized posies. Now maybe I won't have to listen to him ramble on about them at the pub."

"The pub!" his mom exclaimed. She faced Finn. "That reminds me. Dermot called, looking for you. He said you weren't answering your phone."

He had it turned off because of the barrage of calls about Jaime's death. "What did Dermot want?"

"He's in Tullaghan and—"

"Dermot's in Tullaghan?" Finn frowned. "He hates coming back here."

His dad shrugged. "Bought that property up the coast, didn't he? It's a nice one too. Good land."

"He said to tell you to meet him at Hairy's tonight," his mom said. "Seven. You'll be going." She lowered her chin, giving him a look that brooked no argument.

"That's not a question," he pointed out.

"No, it's not," his mother replied firmly.

He nodded, too tired to argue. He'd go, only for his mom—not because he didn't want her to nag him to death but because it'd ease her a little to see him do something normal.

3

Abby sat in the hospital's parking lot, watching people in scrubs and masks come out of the entrance's sliding doors.

She fucking hated hospitals.

Except one of those people could be Dr. Fionnlagh.

She hugged her wrist to her chest, staring at each person, but none of them felt like him. She and Lynne had looked him up online, and she knew she'd recognize him. He was one of the most compelling men she'd ever seen. Yes, he was physically handsome—she had a thing for blue eyes like his—but in all his photos she'd felt his will to heal others, a tangible force, and that was what she found most attractive.

She willed him to walk outside so she wouldn't have to go in.

She'd only been in a hospital twice that she could remember: when her mama died and the day Lynne tumbled down the stairs six months ago.

Her mom had died when she was eight. Abby had

come home from school to find Mrs. Toulain from next door waiting to take her to the hospital where her mama was. When they arrived there, all Abby saw was ribbons of black swirling around the building. She'd been sure they'd wrap around her and squeeze her to death.

That time, she hadn't been in the hospital long; her mom died minutes before she and the neighbor arrived. A brain aneurysm, they told her, though at the time she had no idea what that meant, except that she was alone.

The second time was the day Lynne's boyfriend, Kevin, lost it.

Which led to today.

She watched the bands of black swirling around the building and shuddered. She told herself that those bands wouldn't touch her, but they still creeped her out.

When her mom was alive, she used to say, "The Divine directs you right to where you need to be."

Abby undid her seat belt and took a shaky breath. "I need more direction, please."

The air shifted in the car, almost like a breeze had blown in through an open window, and something settled in the seat next to her. "Direction is here."

This voice she recognized.

She turned to find Bro Paul's large Franciscan monk self wedged into the passenger seat. Despite not understanding why he hadn't warned her about the painting she gave Lynne, she felt an overwhelming relief having him here now. He'd been a constant presence in her life since that first day in the orphanage, and he was the only mentor she'd ever had. When he hadn't said anything six months ago, that was the first time they'd had conflict. Part of her knew she needed to forgive him because he hadn't done anything wrong, but part of her couldn't let it go yet because then she'd have to take all the blame, and she wasn't sure she could handle that.

He sighed because, of course, he knew what she was thinking. "The longer you stick to blame, the longer it's going to take to find a solution to this predicament."

"Is this where you tell me to forgive is Divine?" She held her wrist against her chest as it started to throb.

"Fuck Divine. Forgiveness is the easiest path to moving forward." He leaned forward, his voice low and intent in a way that she'd never heard before. "I would never do something to harm you. *Never.* It hurts that you'd even think that."

She looked at him, at a loss, feeling his hurt as well as her own. "Then what happened?"

"What do you think happened?"

She shook her head. "To help Lynne, I painted what I saw in that vision. But when I took it to her, everything went sideways."

"Uh-huh."

She glared at him. "You don't sound surprised."

Instead of answering her, he asked, "What did you paint?"

"The scene I saw," she repeated. "With the person I'd been back then added in it."

Bro Paul leaned in. "Are you sure that's what you *should* have painted?"

She felt something oily and sick in her stomach. "What are you talking about?"

"I'm asking if you looked at what Lynne needed to

heal." At her puzzled silence, he sighed, a gusty exhalation of exasperation. "I'm going to start calling you 'rocks for brains.' Ask the right questions, get the right answers. If you don't ask them, I can't tell you. I love you, kid, but I'm not your parent. I'm your guide. I don't tell you what to do. I counsel you when you ask me to. That's what we heavenly folk call free will. I help direct you to the answers, but you have to want to go there."

"I want to fix Lynne's leg," she said, her voice hoarse with desperation. "And I want to paint again."

"Then go in there." He pointed at the building.

She turned her attention back to the hospital. "Are you saying I'm going to find the doctor in there?"

"Find a doctor in a hospital? Seems crazy." He rolled his eyes. "You've all the tools, kid. Use them."

Lynne had said the same thing. Abby hugged herself, careful of her wrist. "That's what I'm worried about. That I'll use them wrong again."

"That's always a possibility. Like I said, free will and all. But I have faith in you."

"That was mostly reassuring," she muttered, that tendril of fear in her gut wrapping around her like a tentacle.

"Well, I can't lie to you." He scrunched his face. "Look, kid, you're at a crossroads. Given what you've done with your life, it was time for you to uplevel. Did you screw up this first pass? Yeah. Now figure out why. You'll get a second pass, and a third, and so on, as long as you keep trying. So you gonna give up, or are you gonna do this?"

It wasn't even a choice. "I'm going to do this."

"Then trust your instincts. Trust that you and Lynne are where you need to be."

Trust wasn't her forte; that was Lynne's department. And Bro Paul's.

"If you're going to go into the hospital, now's the time," he said.

"Okay." She picked up her purse and took a deep breath. "Okay."

"You got this." He gave her two thumbs-up as he vanished.

She didn't feel like she had this.

She fucking hated hospitals.

She pushed herself out of the car, lowered her head, and strode with determination to the front entrance.

4

Dermot Farrell loved hospitals. Even the astringent smell in the air got his heart pumping. Here, there were all manner of people in various stages of miracles, being born to passing on. Here, they controlled chaos in a way that he'd never found anywhere else.

He envied it. He studied it.

Walking down the corridor, he nodded to the nurses, hiding the jittery feeling that was crawling up his back. He knew most donors didn't get an all-access pass to the patient areas, but they made an exception for him. He'd been born here, and he'd donated quite a large sum of money to the hospital every year for reasons they all well knew. If that wasn't enough, he'd subtly encouraged the director to let him roam the floors so he could see the good his money was doing.

Though he already knew exactly what he was buying. This was as personal as it got for him.

He had no choice but to come here, because it helped control the chaos within *him*.

Just being here helped calm him. He stopped sweating under his suit and exhaled deeply as he turned down a quieter hall, drawn inexorably toward the room at the end. Inside that room, there was a man who'd just had his second heart attack, according to the nurses.

Dermot could feel death waiting in the wings for the right time to take the man. He felt a shock of sadness for the man even as his own system revved up, getting ready. He hated the feeling of excitement that surged in him—he wanted to resist it. He just couldn't.

So he focused on the bright spot: the man's soul.

It was open and loving and filled with a deep abiding love for his family. It had called to Dermot the moment he'd entered the hospital.

Dermot tried to resist it, but he couldn't. He never could.

Just a piece, he told himself, straightening the tie at his neck. And he would help the man transition to the afterlife in peace instead of continuing to suffer in this one. This man wasn't going to live despite the hospital's best efforts. Dermot's role was an act of mercy. He made it so, every time.

Except that first time, with Fiona.

He refused to think about that, though, because it'd been an accident and he hadn't meant to hurt her. He couldn't bear to think that Fiona died because of him. She'd been his first love, and he'd wanted to be with her forever.

At least he had the piece of her soul with him, what he feared had led to her accident. He touched his solar plexus, over his suit, on the spot where he could feel that piece lodged. That was where all the soul pieces he was given were housed.

They felt *good*.

He walked into the man's room and stood in the doorway. With Fiona, he'd been infused with her passion for life. With this man, Dermot would feel the unconditional love he had.

The dying man was asleep, his family probably taking the opportunity to have lunch. On the surface, this man should have been like any other average middle-aged Irishman Dermot had known his entire life: without purpose except to have another pint with his mates. Like Dermot's dad had been.

That was why this man was so surprising. Dermot looked at the family man's soul, intrigued by the way it surged protectively around his heart. This man had no selfishness, no false manly bullshit most men had. It wasn't corrupted by alcohol, and there was no malice or bitterness. His deep abiding love for his family filled his whole being. This man's soul had a purity of love that Dermot had never seen in a person like him.

The need in him rose up, urging him to feel that love for himself.

Dermot fought it for a moment, sweat breaking out on his forehead. In the beginning, he'd fought each time he was presented with a new soul piece. The struggle didn't last long these days.

Some soul pieces broke off easily, coming to him almost eagerly. Some put up a fight. He picked a spot close to the man's heart, where it was the weakest, to make this easy and fast.

But still this soul piece wasn't cooperating, and Dermot felt whatever it was in him that caused this to surge up and use the force of his will to rend it. At the last moment, when it finally tore loose, the man in the bed opened his eyes, a startlingly vibrant emerald green as he reared up in alarm.

And then the machines at his bedside began to frantically beep.

Holding the soul piece in his hand—oh, it felt deliciously airy—Dermot looked the man in the eye and bowed in respect. "Thank you," he said gravely before he stepped back into the hallway and waited for the staff to come tend to the man.

They came rushing, fast and efficient. He heard someone say, "Cardiac arrest." He waited in the hallway, concerned, a part of him wanting to see the death unfold. He gave a little prayer for the man, that he be at peace.

Inside the room, the machine's beeping went flat.

One of the nurses who often flirted with him came to stand next to him, tears in her eyes. "This is so sad, Dermot. We were hoping he'd made it past the critical point and would recover."

Dermot took a handkerchief out of his pocket and handed it to her. He couldn't remember her name. "I'm sorry to hear that."

She dabbed at her tears. "It's such a shame. He was a good man. So loving to his family. It's almost like his heart was too big for his body."

Yes, that was exactly it. His hand tightened on the soul piece, eager to finish this. "I should get out of the way here. Please accept my condolences."

"Thank you, Mr. Farrell." She managed an innocent flirty smile despite her grief.

He turned and headed to the chapel.

There was no one inside. Not that it mattered—no one disturbed a person here.

He sat in the front, closest to the stained-glass window. He looked at the soul piece he held and then pushed it into his own soul.

He felt the other soul pieces he'd collected over the years shift. There was the moment of disorientation and discomfort, and the pressure cut off air to his lungs. He struggled as the piece fought him, wrestling with the pain, until suddenly, like always, it settled into place with an orgasmic rush. He moaned with the surge of ecstasy.

And then there was euphoria.

And the love...

He lifted his head to the stained-glass window above, his hand on his heart, feeling the full weight of the new piece he'd collected. It felt more buoyant than the triumph of closing a hard-won deal, more blissful than any drug he'd ever tried. Better than any sex he'd ever had, and he'd had plenty of good sex.

For the first time, he understood what the unconditional love of family felt like. He closed his eyes and savored the unfamiliar sensation.

The sun broke through and illuminated the window, showering him with shards of color.

He basked in the afterglow that blanketed him. As he inhaled, he swore he could smell a hint of the coconut shampoo Fiona used to use.

The moment he integrated a new soul piece into

himself was a rush like no other. It jolted him awake —*alive*—filling that perpetual ache inside him. It filled him with the essence of the soul piece, and he experienced firsthand what that soul offered.

But each time the rush, the feeling, slipped away faster, fading much too quickly, leaving him edgy and desperate for another soul piece to boost him again, enliven him again. Lately, it barely lasted beyond a week.

If it were up to him, he'd stop. He wanted to stop—he just couldn't. He hadn't asked for the first soul piece, or the second, or any after that. They'd just come to him. He'd tried everything to keep himself from taking them —from studying with Buddhist monks to talking to Catholic priests about exorcism. Nothing had worked.

And so he made sure that he expressed his gratitude for the gift.

But, when he was being honest with himself, he was afraid of the next time. What if he lost control? He made sure the soul pieces he collected were from people already dying, but what if the next time it wasn't? What if what had happened with Fiona happened again?

And he couldn't stop it.

He put his hand over his chest, feeling the surge of all the soul pieces he'd taken over the years. Some days, he wasn't sure he wanted to stop it.

Once his legs had stopped shaking, he stood and went to find the hospital's director for their meeting. He intended to add to the sizeable donation he'd planned on giving her today for the expansion to the wing he'd donated in Fiona's name ten years ago. And he needed to send flowers to the family of the man who'd just died.

5

It hit Abby the second she entered the hospital: the cry of all the people who had died there who hadn't crossed over.

It happened that way sometimes. Not with cemeteries, but places where the loss of life was catastrophic—like battlefields or sites of tragedies. Abby avoided the World Trade Center site categorically.

In places like hospitals, the spirits had a potpourri of needs. Some were in pain, some were angry, some implored her to help them. They all pulled at her. They all wanted to talk.

Ghosts just did not shut up.

Abby had good boundaries. She knew how to close them out; otherwise, she would have heard their incessant chattering in her head. But the more persistent ones had a way of making their presence known.

It was always the same—she'd feel a bit of pressure above the bridge of her nose. Her mama had taught her that there was nothing to fear; the press on her forehead just meant they wanted to say something to her. "Spirits aren't so different from people, baby," her mama would say. "They just want to know someone's listening to them."

She didn't want to listen to them now. It was bad enough that she'd had to enter the hospital. So she envisioned a Provence blue bubble around herself—the warmest kind of blue she knew—pushing out the energy until she had a nice buffer between her and the spirits.

Once their cries died away, she became aware of the smell of the hospital: death covered by antiseptic. She tried not to gag. Gathering more of that blue bubble around herself, she blocked out what didn't serve her and headed to the woman at the reception desk.

The lady looked up, purple fatigue circling her eyes. "Can I help you?"

This was it. Abby crossed her fingers. "I'm looking for Dr. Carrick Fionnlagh."

"Oh. Dr. Fionnlagh." The woman seemed to melt, her cheeks coming alive with rosiness. "He's a lovely man. But he no longer works here except for rare occasions, and I haven't seen him in months."

Abby wilted. *Damn it.* "Are you sure?"

"Oh yes, I would know if he was here." The woman blushed deeper. She cleared her throat, professional again. "He has an office in Dublin. I can give you the number there."

"I have it, thank you." She looked around. Someone had to know him personally, right? Or at least know where his parents lived. "It's really important that I make an appointment with him."

The woman's gaze dropped to the brace on Abby's wrist. "Oh, you poor thing. Is it a recent injury?"

It was on the tip of her tongue to correct the woman and tell her she wanted the doctor for Lynne, but she just asked, "Is there an administrator or another orthopedic doctor I might speak to, who might know him?"

The woman looked apologetic as she shook her head. "I can take your name and number and give it to the director, but that's all I can do."

"That would be fine." Abby quickly jotted down her info. She added a little light to it, so that it'd find the right person, and pushed it across the desk. "Thank you."

"There's a board commemorating his service over there." The woman pointed to the right. "If it's of interest. He's a hometown legend."

Murmuring her thanks again, Abby made her way over to the board, as the lady called it—slowly, feeling anticipation build with each step. It looked like a shrine, in some respects, with quotes and photos of previous patients, before and after, and from the media about Dr. Fionnlagh's greatness. She skimmed over them quickly, and with each one, her heart expanded with more conviction that she'd picked the right man.

In the center, there was a large picture of him.

Abby leaned in, touching the edge of it instead of his face like she wanted to. He pulled at her in a way she didn't fathom yet. It was his eyes, surely, but his gift was also palpable. She understood the charge of a gift, and she recognized even from the photo that he didn't take it lightly. In this photo, up close, just like every other picture of him that she'd seen, his eyes seemed to look right into her soul, reassuring her that everything was going to work out.

She needed to believe that.

She *did* believe that. She'd find him. Tullaghan was a small community. Someone would know his parents if they still lived there.

Turning around, she booked it toward the sliding doors. She couldn't get out of there fast enough.

In her haste to exit, she walked straight into a man who was also leaving.

They both exhaled at the collision. She would have bounced backwards but he caught her arm and steadied her.

She started to excuse herself but got distracted by the ghost clinging to his back, an older man with great anger in his emerald-green eyes and a big hole in his chest, like a part of him was missing.

It was *not* normal for a spirit to cling to someone like that. She silently asked the spirit to leave, to give herself space to think. It hesitated for a second and then disappeared.

She took a relieved breath and focused on the man holding her. Handsome, a head taller than her own five-six, with burnt umber hair and dark, dark eyes—a color more layered than simple black. Successful, based on his bespoke suit and the gold watch that cost more than most people made in a year. Tasteful, given the way the rich maroon of his tie pulled out the red woven through his suit.

Out of habit, she softened her vision to see his soul. It was how she always saw souls—overlapped with a person's physical body. Most people's souls were a uniform gradient of whitish or golden light; some had gray or black sections—trauma from the past, either in this life or other times—like those she painted to heal.

This man's soul was uniformly white except for an amazing kaleidoscope of color that wound through it, like a spiraling band around its center. She realized it started from his solar plexus.

She'd never seen such a thing. She wanted to reach out to touch the colors, but she caught her hand at the last minute. "Excuse me," she said, stepping back.

Withdrawing his hold, he stared at her as intently as she'd been staring at him, as if looking deeper than what met the eye, like she had. Her curiosity perked up; she knew what she looked for, but she always wondered what other people did.

"Have we met before?" he asked, his voice deep and refined with an accent that was somewhere in between Irish and British.

She raised her brow. "That's what you're going to lead with?"

The interest in his dark gaze sharpened, with a hint of humor added to it. "Sometimes the tried and true is best." His gaze searched her again, sharper this time, but without any male appreciation. "You're American. Are you here visiting family? Or are you a patient?"

He'd noticed her wrist. "No." Then because she had nothing to lose, she added, "I came for a certain doctor. A specialist."

"Of course. We have fine doctors in this hospital. Which one are you here for?" He tipped his head, glancing at her wrist again. "I'm a donor here, and I know most of the staff. Maybe I can help you find who you're looking for."

"Dr. Carrick Fionnlagh," she said, barely daring to hope.

The man smiled slowly. "As luck would have it, Finn and I grew up together. He's one of my closest friends."

6

Dermot studied the woman in front of him. Though he'd just taken a soul piece from the family man, a hunger for the next one rose in his throat, and she called to that hunger.

He stepped back to distance himself from it. She was hardly at death's door and, therefore, off-limits.

Physically, he was unmoved by her. She wasn't like the women in his circle that he usually dated. She was earthy, a bit bohemian in her clothing with all the colors that rather impossibly flowed together. Curvy and average height, with long hair that would have thrilled most men.

Not him, though. He favored elegant women who were tall and stately.

But her soul... It called to him. Strong. Dedicated. Talented, though he couldn't read how. Odd, that. He could always pinpoint what made a soul special. The predator in him wanted to investigate in more depth. It urged him to bend his rule about taking only souls that were close to death.

But he would never do that. He had better self-control than that. That had only happened once—the first time—and it had hurt Fiona, whom he'd loved, as well as Finn and his parents, who'd done more to rear him than his own mother had.

He felt a surge of emotion in his chest as he thought about the Fionnlaghs. It took him a moment to realize it was a result of the family man's soul piece—a tide of unfamiliar warmth. Love?

He frowned. What an odd sensation.

He'd never felt anything like it, certainly not from his mother. She'd told him he'd be nothing.

In the end, she'd been wrong. With the other soul pieces, he could be anything—a brilliant businessman, an engineer, a poet, a king.

A loving family man.

With other soul pieces, he could experience anything, feel anything. It was a high that couldn't be replicated anywhere else, not even inside a woman's body.

Not touching this woman's soul would take all his self-control, because the predator in him craved it. He forced his hands into his pants pockets—the better to resist temptation.

There was something so familiar about her... It had sounded like a clichéd line, but he really thought he'd met her somewhere before.

Although he'd have thought that he would have remembered. A man didn't forget a woman with such expressive dark eyes, especially when she looked at him like he'd just given her the best gift ever.

Not that *he'd* classify Finn as a gift, he thought with a

smile. He'd known Finn since childhood—they'd shared too many antics to see each other as anything but mates.

"You know Dr. Fionnlagh?" she asked now in disbelief, bringing him back to the moment.

He tried to place her charming accent. "Where in the States are you from?"

"New Orleans," she replied, not veiling her impatience. "And Dr. Fionnlagh?"

"Finn is from Tullaghan. We both are. I spent most of my youth running around his parents' farm." He took a moment to feel the upwelling of emotion that caused before focusing on her again. Why did he feel like he recognized her? "I've been to New Orleans once."

"I hope you had a good time." She pushed her hair over her shoulder. "If you could give me Dr. Fionnlagh's contact info, I'll get out of your way."

He should let her go because her soul was very tempting. Despite how her injury weighed on her, it was the brightest, strongest soul he'd ever encountered, and part of him wanted to figure out what made it special.

Part of him wanted to tell her to run so she wouldn't get hurt.

He glanced at her wrist again. That was obviously why she wanted to see Finn. He wondered how she'd injured it. More emotion rose in his chest, and he put his hand over the spot where he felt it, reveling in it.

Something behind her moved.

Dermot raised his gaze to find the faint outline of a monk standing behind her. The large man had his arms crossed, scowling fiercely.

A ghost? Dermot certainly believed in them, though it

wasn't often he encountered them, despite living in Dublin. If one were going to encounter ghosts, a hospital seemed like place enough for it, he supposed.

The monk pointed at the woman. Dermot heard very clearly in his head, *She's your redemption. Help her.*

He startled. How peculiar. *That* had never happened before.

Then the words registered. *Redemption...* Could it be possible? He studied the woman closer, feeling a clean excitement that wasn't fueled by the need that had been driving him for the past twenty years. "Tell you what," he said, glancing at the monk who lingered behind her. "I'm meeting Finn for a drink at the pub tonight. Meet us there and I'll introduce you to him."

She frowned, her suspicion palpable. "That's convenient."

Grinning, he reached into his pocket for his business card. Finn was going to like her. He wrote Finn's number on it and passed it to her. He blinked as the monk gave him a thumbs-up and then disappeared.

Shaking off his bemusement, he returned his attention to her. "What's your name?"

"Abigail," she said, cautiously taking the card. She studied it and then frowned at him. "What is this?"

"Finn's mobile." He put his hands in his pockets and smiled. "You can call him yourself, though if he doesn't recognize your number, I doubt he'll answer."

She narrowed her gaze at him. "This is his real number?"

"I wouldn't give you a fake one. You obviously need to

see Finn, and I find myself wanting to help." He nodded at her wrist.

She cradled it protectively against herself. "Why?"

"I fancy myself a good Samaritan." And because a monk told him to for redemption. If she could lead him to a way of not taking soul pieces, then he'd lay his kingdom at her feet. "Finn will be more inclined to talk to you if I make the introduction myself, so I encourage you to join us at Hairy's Pub this evening, seven o'clock. It's public, and there will be other people around. You'll be safe."

"My safety isn't what I'm concerned about," she murmured, looking at the card.

She would be there—he was certain of it. He hadn't gotten to where he was in business without understanding how to pinpoint what people wanted and figuring out how far they'd go to get it—and knowing when they'd caved. "I hope to see you tonight, Abigail, but if I don't, I hope Finn helps you with what you need."

He smiled again and walked out of the hospital into the parking lot, knowing she was watching. Before he reached his Aston Martin, he looked up and met Abigail's gaze one more time before he got in and drove off.

She'd be there. He knew people, and she was bent on meeting Finn.

He also knew Finn wouldn't talk to a new prospective patient—not after what had happened with his patient last month. His patient's suicide had rocked him. Of course it had. It'd been very much like Fiona's suicide.

A wave of guilt washed over him at the thought.

He cleared his throat and put his car in gear. Abigail would need him to get to Finn, which would give Dermot the opportunity to figure out why she was his redemption and what she had to offer. Being around her soul would torture him, but he'd control his urges. He had so far.

7

Abby had Dr. Fionnlagh's number—in her non-sprained hand!

The relief staggered her. She exhaled, trying to keep herself together. Now wasn't the time to fall apart—she could do that after she picked up Lynne and told her that she'd found him. After she'd called him.

Once she felt like her legs wouldn't collapse, she hurried to the car. Lynne would be getting out of PT soon. Abby didn't want Lynne to have to wait, especially on crutches, which sucked the energy out of her.

She had his number.

Her hands shook as she started the car. She wanted to call him right then and there, eager to get him to see Lynne, but she thought it might be better to call once she'd calmed down, after she'd figured out what the most persuasive thing to say was.

Of course, she could just meet him and Dermot at the pub.

Normally, she wouldn't have hesitated—she would

have been there early, eager to meet the esteemed doctor. But something about Dermot caused her to pause—his soul, she realized. How did it come to be that way? It was beautiful, but it didn't feel right.

The last time she'd had doubts, she'd pushed them aside, and look where that had gotten her. She wasn't about to rush into anything.

She could ask Bro Paul.

Except what if he told her not to go? She wasn't sure she was willing to miss her chance to talk to the Miracle Worker in person.

She'd feel it out—she had until evening, after all, though she knew she'd rather meet the doctor and face whatever consequences arose from it. Lynne deserved that much and more. Abby slipped the card into the pocket of her jeans and went to pick up her best friend.

Lynne waited for her outside, leaning on her crutches, her face ashen, her hair barely moving in the breeze as though her pain weighed down the strands. Abby got out of the car, checking her pocket for the tenth time to make sure the card was where she put it. Touching it, she could feel a ribbon of azure hope surround the two of them. "Guess what?" she said as she hurried to help Lynne off her feet.

"You met the doctor," Lynne said with a groan as she hobbled to the car and plopped into the passenger seat.

"No, I met his childhood friend, who gave me his number." Abby smiled, and for the first time in six months, it didn't feel like she was forcing it. "We'll call him when we get home."

Lynne froze, gaping at her as Abby stuffed the crutches into the back. "Are you being serious?"

"Yes." She put her hand over her pocket, trying not to feel the tendril of fear that this was too easy and bound to be a disappointment. She didn't tell Lynne about the invite to the pub yet—not until she felt more sure about it. She was probably being overly cautious, but after screwing up so badly with Lynne's painting, she wasn't taking any chances.

"Holy shit, Abby," Lynne whispered, shock and awe adding a tinge of pink to her face. "Get us home and let's do this."

She rushed home as fast as she dared; she still wasn't comfortable driving on the opposite side of the road. She helped Lynne into the white stone cottage they'd rented for the month and helped her ease into the wheelchair Lynne preferred using around the house, which had only one floor, with wide enough doorways to accommodate it.

Then Lynne held out her hands. "Let me see the phone number."

Abby took the card out of her pocket and handed it over.

Lynne held it reverently, reading it out loud. "Dermot Farrell. Dermot Farrell is the friend?"

"Yes." Feeling nervous, Abby decided to make tea. Tea was calming, right? She went into the kitchen and flipped the switch on the electric kettle to boil water.

"Expensive cardstock," Lynne called from the living room. "Elegant font. It doesn't say what Dermot Farrell does."

"I don't care what he does," she called back. "I only care about Dr. Carrick Fionnlagh."

She heard the halting creak of the wheelchair on the old wood floors and turned around as Lynne stopped awkwardly in the kitchen's threshold. "Are we going to call him now?"

"Yes." She bit her lip. "After I have some tea and we talk out what I'll say."

"You know what to say." Lynne stared at the card in her hand some more. "Call him now."

"Now?" she said, hoping her friend didn't hear the way her voice cracked. She only had one shot to make this happen. She had to make sure she was gathered enough to get it done.

"Abigail," Lynne said in a Mother Superior tone, "we've come thousands of miles just to meet this man. You can't tell me you're going to wait another second to call him."

"Right." She nodded and took the card Lynne held out to her. Taking out her cell phone, she dialed the number, her heart pounding. He'd be able to help Lynne, she assured herself. *Please let him help Lynne.*

After several rings, his voicemail clicked on. She listened to his recording, understanding why the woman at the hospital had melted when she talked about him. Hearing his voice, Abby was melting too.

So were her panties.

Good Lord—she needed to pull herself together. She took a deep breath as his recording was coming to an end, focused her will, and waited for the beep to signal her turn.

Clearing her throat, she said, "Hello, Dr. Fionnlagh. My name is Abigail Angevine. Dermot Farrell gave me your number, and I wondered if you'd have time to chat with me regarding a potential case." She bit her lip against adding *You're my only hope, Obi-Wan* and ended the call with her number and a polite "I look forward to speaking with you."

She hung up and wilted against the counter, her heart pounding, sweat between her boobs. *She'd done it.*

"Way to go, Abs!" Lynne held her hand up for a high five, looking more like herself than she had in months. "Let's have tea and you can tell me about this Dermot Farrell."

Her hands still shaking, Abby put the teacups on the small tray she'd been using because she couldn't hold anything in her right hand. Balancing it with one hand, trying not to slosh the hot liquid, she asked, "Want to have it in front of the window so we can watch the waves?"

"And the surfers." Lynne backed right into the dining table. She rolled forward and then backed into the table again. "Damn it."

Abby rushed forward, spilling tea, cursing under her breath as the hot water just missed her hand. Feeling frustrated and helpless for both herself and Lynne, she said, "Here, let me help."

"I can do it." Lynne waved her off and then painstakingly turned herself around, her movements jerky but determined.

Call me back, Dr. Fionnlagh, Abby urged again, hating to see Lynne struggle so much. She schooled her expression because it upset Lynne to see her upset and set the tray on the table by their sitting area.

Lynne rolled herself to a stop next to the table as Abby sat down. "So now we wait, huh?"

Abby picked up the teacup, trying not to think about the doctor not calling her back.

As if she read her mind, Lynne asked, "What happens if he doesn't call us back?"

"I'll still find him." She bit her lip, thinking about Dermot asking her to meet them tonight. If the doctor had answered the phone now, she'd have let that go, but since he didn't, she needed set her reservations aside and be there.

One thing she was sure of: nothing was going to stop her from convincing the doctor to help Lynne.

Lynne gazed at Abby for a long time. "Promise me when you talk to him you'll let him look at your wrist too."

Abby shook her head. "You're the priority here, Lynne."

"You're equally important." Lynne held on to the necklace, staring at Abby's wrist like she was trying to X-ray it with her vision. "You sprained it worse by trying to paint me another scene. It's that bad because you were trying to help me. Now I'm helping you, because you need to paint."

Abby stared out at the ocean. She didn't want to think about painting—it *hurt*. It hurt physically and it hurt emotionally. It hurt because something that she did with such joy caused the person she loved the most to lose everything. She wasn't taking a chance on hurting Lynne again, or anyone else.

She took a sip of tea, hiding her face behind the cup. The last thing she wanted was for Lynne to see how upset she really was. She was the strong one here. She's always been Lynne's rock. She wasn't going to let her down—not again.

So she decided then and there. "Actually, Dermot Farrell is having a drink with him at the pub tonight. He invited me along. I'll go and talk to the doctor."

Lynne sat up, suddenly alert. "You buried the lede, Abigail. You're supposed to start a story with a tidbit like that. It's not every day you get asked out."

"I didn't get asked out. I was invited to meet a doctor." She made a face. "Besides, I didn't find Dermot Farrell attractive."

Lynne held her hand out. "Give me your phone."

She did so without asking. She watched Lynne swipe and tap furiously. "What are you doing?" Abby finally asked.

"Looking up Dermot Farrell."

"Seriously?" Abby rolled her eyes. "What for?"

Lynne looked at her like she was incredibly dim. "I want to see what he looks like."

She tried to recall what he looked like, but the only thing she remembered about Dermot was the strangeness of the spiral kaleidoscope around his soul. "And what's the verdict?"

"Hot. Successful. Generous. He's some sort of business tycoon. Acquisitions and mergers." Looking up from the screen, Lynne frowned at her. "He asked you out?"

"No, he invited me to meet his friend."

"Did he want to ask you out?"

Abby thought back to that morning. "He seemed interested, but not like that. He was more curious about me."

"Maybe he recognized that you're *Angevine*."

Abby remembered he'd been to New Orleans.

"He's the sort who'd have an art collection, even if he didn't know anything about art." Lynne frowned at the images on the screen. "What did you see when you looked at his soul?"

She recalled the mosaic of pie-shaped colors and shook her head. "I've never seen anything like it."

That stopped Lynne short. "In a good way, or bad?"

She thought about that. "I'm not sure. It was weird. Unnatural."

"I'm not sure a soul should seem 'unnatural.'" Lynne frowned as she returned to her web search.

"Come with me tonight. You can meet him yourself."

Lynne glanced up again. "Me?"

"Of course you." She had a moment where she wanted to take it back and leave Lynne at home. She had a habit of protecting her—she always had from the first minute she met the scared girl in the orphanage. But it was probably okay, and Lynne, a social creature, hadn't been out since before the accident.

Lynne returned her attention to the images on the screen. "Dermot Farrell is hot. Also, *hung*. You can just tell."

Abby snorted, but her heart smiled because Lynne hadn't declared a man *hung* in longer than she could remember. She used to say it was because she was around men all day in tights and it wasn't something a man could hide. Abby said she had a sixth sense.

It was like having her old friend back, bit by bit.

"You seriously didn't like him?" Lynne asked incredulously. She held up the phone. "Look at this photo. He's superb."

"Come with me tonight and *you* can go out with him," Abby said, setting her empty cup down. Though after she said it, she wondered if she hadn't been hasty. She wanted Lynne to go out and date and have fun again, but after Kevin, Abby wanted to make sure Lynne was safe, and Dermot's abnormal soul didn't inspire confidence in her.

Some of the light that had infused Lynne dimmed. Smiling sadly, she handed the phone back. "I don't think so, Abby. But thanks for the offer."

Then again, was it bad to have her meet the guy just for an evening? If meeting him put the smile back on Lynne's face, Abby could overlook the wonky soul for one night. "Just come with me. We haven't gone for a drink in ages. You can flirt a little. You haven't flirted in forever."

"I'm not going to flirt when I'm like this." She gestured to her wheelchair.

Abby took her hand. "He won't care. You know why?"

"Why?"

"Because there's no one in the entire world more beautiful or interesting than you. And no one has a bigger heart. Of course he's going to want that."

Lynne turned her face away, her hand reaching for the pendant. "I'm tired. I think I'll go to my room."

Just like that, a pallid gray shadow fell, eclipsing all the good they'd accomplished today.

Watching Lynne awkwardly wheel herself down the short hall to her bedroom, Abby managed to keep the tears at bay until after she heard the sound of the door snapping shut.

8

Everyone in Tullaghan knew everyone else's business, so Finn had no delusions of privacy. He figured everyone knew what had happened in Dublin. If they hadn't seen it in *The Irish Times*, they'd heard it from one of his mother's friends.

He also knew that in Hairy's Pub, he was safe. It was as home as his parents' farm was, since he, Dermot, and Niall Ferguson, who owned the pub now, had grown up together. They'd spent as much time in the Fergusons' pub as they had at his family's place. More than that, Niall would punch anyone who dared harass him. Loyalty was as much a part of Niall as his DNA.

Funny how he was still worried about what Niall would think, especially given Fiona. Niall had to have heard about Jaime Walsh. As publican, Niall liked to think of himself as father confessor and Tullaghan as his parish. He knew everything happening in the county.

Trying to blank his mind, rather unsuccessfully, Finn wore a cap low over his head. He hadn't bothered to shave. As a surgeon, he kept himself clean-shaven, but since he'd gone on sabbatical, he'd grown facial hair. The better to hide. And, to be frank, he didn't have the energy to shave.

He parked his car down the street—he figured the short walk would fortify him—and slowly made his way toward the pub. He had to force himself to push open the door and walk in.

Not much had changed in Tullaghan since he'd moved away. He only came home to visit a couple times a year—his parents came to him most of the time due to his schedule—but he could set his watch by certain things: the sheep being sheared in the spring; the surfers flocking to the Black Spot in the summer, hoping to catch the perfect wave; and Mrs. Kelly making marmalade in the fall.

As his eyes adjusted to the dimness of the pub, he realized more than he had ever before that nothing had changed in there either. There was the requisite old man slumped over a pint in one corner, a table of tourists—all women—in another.

There was comfort in that constancy.

The only thing that was different now was that instead of Mr. Ferguson shining a pint glass behind the bar it was Niall.

There was little of the boy Finn had grown up with in the man Niall had become. Large and broad where he'd been scrawny, wisdom in his eyes where there'd been the devil. Finn had been surprised when Niall decided to stay in town and run his family's pub, but Niall had very simply said, "It's the last place someone who doesn't have anything to live for would go before they did something tragic. I'm going to be there for that moment, like I couldn't be for Fiona."

That Niall would be always be there was reassuring.

"Well, if it isn't the prodigal son, home again," Niall said. And then he grinned, set the pint glass and rag down, and rushed out from behind the bar to give him a bear hug.

Finn had been home in December for Christmas, so he knew the demonstrative hug wasn't because Niall missed him. He could feel the concern in it, and it almost brought him to his knees. He closed his eyes, emotion choking him as Niall clapped him on the back.

When they separated, there were tears in Niall's eyes too. "It's going to be all right, Finn," his friend said gruffly. "Pint?"

Finn nodded, swallowing the feelings back down.

Niall nodded and ducked back behind the bar.

Keeping his cap on, Finn pulled out a seat at the far end of the bar and slouched into it. "Your parents good?"

Niall huffed as he began to build the Guinness. "Mom convinced Dad to rent a camper and go around the countryside this summer. She said it's the honeymoon they never had. Happy as clams, they are." His friend looked at him over the tap. "They're stopping through in a few weeks on their way north. You here for long? You can see them."

"I'm not sure yet."

His friend looked up from behind the tap. "It wasn't your fault."

Finn stiffened. It was his patient—he was responsible by default.

Niall topped off the beer and slid it across the bar toward him. "I learned a long time ago that another person's decisions are his own. You couldn't have done anything about it, the same way we couldn't have done anything about Fiona."

That wasn't true. Finn was Jaime Walsh's doctor, and he'd failed him. He picked up his beer and took a long drink so he wouldn't have to answer. Then, to redirect things, he said, "Pour one for Dermot. He's coming to meet me."

Niall's disposition soured immediately. "Can't that bastard stay in Dublin?"

"Can't you two just kiss and make up?" he asked, glad for the change in topic, even if it was the not-so-subtle enmity between his two oldest friends. "I don't even understand where this bad blood came from."

"It came from Dermot." Niall set the glass under the tap and began to pour, too good a pub owner not to serve a customer, even if it was Dermot Farrell. "Something's not right with him. It started with Fiona's accident and it's just gotten worse since."

Everything started with Fiona's accident. He wondered what she'd make of everything going on. "Fiona wouldn't have wanted the animosity between you two."

"She also wouldn't have wanted him to capitalize on her death," Niall retorted.

Finn raised his brow skeptically. Dermot was rich as

Croesus, but as far as he knew, it was all through buying and selling businesses. "How is he doing that?"

"The wing he gave the hospital ten years ago in her name. He's expanding it."

"And that's bad?"

Niall whacked the counter with his towel. "He's doing it for show, for the press coverage."

Finn lifted his brow. "I doubt that."

Fiona's death had led Finn to become an orthopedic surgeon. It'd led Dermot to funding hospitals and mental care facilities after he'd made his money. Which Finn appreciated at the fundraising times of the year when his hospital needed donations.

Dermot Farrell of today was a far cry from the Dermot Farrell of their youth. Back then, Dermot had been in threadbare secondhand clothes, not custom-made suits. Given where Dermot had come from—a leaky, crumbling cottage without heat—where he'd ended up was miraculous. Dermot had always said that he wouldn't give his mother the satisfaction of ending up a piss-poor drunk like her, and he hadn't. His life was at the complete other end of the spectrum now.

A fact that Niall, apparently, took exception to.

"He's showy and selfish," Niall decreed, pointing at him. "He may have been an okay kid, but something happened to him in uni. He's not all he seems. You wait. He'll show his true colors."

What happened in secondary was that Dermot and Fiona fell in love. Finn had always wondered if Niall hadn't harbored feelings for Fiona himself, hence the hostility between him and Dermot. Regardless, it should have dissipated over time, but the two men were determined to hold on to the grudge even though twenty years had passed.

Knowing the conversation would go nowhere, Finn lifted his beer and casually tried to change it. "You seeing anyone these days?"

Niall chuckled. "No, but I hear there's two American women who just moved into the Sea View Cottage down the way."

He couldn't even imagine meeting a woman now, despite what his mother thought. But he didn't need to reply, because the front door opened, and by the acidic look on Niall's face, it was Dermot who walked in.

He turned around as Dermot walked toward him and clapped him on the shoulder. "Good. You started without me."

"If I'd waited for you, I might have died of thirst," he pointed out.

Dermot laughed.

The group of women got quiet, and Finn could feel their interest radiating all the way across the pub. Not surprising. Women had always found Dermot irresistible. Him, too, he supposed, but he owed that in large part to being a doctor. No one would mistake him for a doctor dressed as he was now.

Not that he cared. He'd always been focused on his career. He casually went out, but it was never anything permanent, much to his mother's dismay.

"I met a woman earlier today," Dermot said, bringing him out of his thoughts. He pulled out the seat next to him and sat down. "I invited her to join us."

Finn turned and gave him a flat look.

"This one is different. She wants to meet you."

Before Finn could curse his so-called friend, Niall plunked down a pint in front of Dermot with a glare and stalked off to the other end of the bar.

Dermot shook his head. "Why do we still frequent this place?"

"Because it's the only pub close to home, and because Niall is an old friend."

"Old friend? Speak for yourself." Dermot's face sobered, and leaning in, he lowered his voice. "How are you doing?"

"Holding up." Barely.

Dermot put a hand on Finn's shoulder. "It wasn't your fault. I talked to the medical board and they say the same thing. Tragic things happen, and the mistake wasn't yours. I know it's been only three weeks, but I'm worried about you."

He almost wished Dermot didn't know what had happened so he could have some space, but some quirk of fate had his friend at the hospital in Dublin that day, meeting with the hospital's director regarding a charity gala. "You been talking to my mom?"

"Molly is a smart woman." Dermot sat back. "Talk to Abigail when she comes in."

"Abigail?"

"The woman I invited, who wants to meet you."

He bristled. Leaning in so Niall wouldn't hear, he said, "I swear, Dermot, if this woman is some journalist masquerading as—"

"She's not a journalist," Dermot cut him off. "Her wrist is hurt."

That shut Finn up. He felt that part of him that wanted to save people rear up, and he pushed it back ruthlessly. He wasn't in the space, mentally or physically, to take on a new case, no matter how simple it was.

As he reached for his pint, he saw his hand was shaking.

Tucking his hand out of sight next to his leg, Finn focused on his longtime friend. "You like her."

"I'm intrigued by her," Dermot corrected. "And I couldn't help feeling like our meeting was appointed by a higher power."

Dermot had always believed in things like that—that there was a great hand that moved the chess pieces of people's lives. He believed in psychics and ghosts and whatnot. An Irish trait, Dermot liked to say.

Fiona had been the same. He remembered how Dermot had given her tarot cards for her sixteenth birthday. She'd shined like she'd been given a diamond tiara.

Finn no longer believed in any higher power or mystical things. He'd lost faith in anything like that the day he'd found Fiona dead.

"I don't know that Abigail will actually come," Dermot was saying now, "but I'd like you to meet her."

Finn looked at his friend in disbelief. "You asked her to come and she didn't jump on it?"

"No."

"But she wants to meet me?"

"Yes." Dermot took a sip of his beer. "That's why I gave her your phone number."

"You what?"

Dermot turned to him. "You heard me."

As a surgeon, he didn't normally get into fistfights, because his hands were sacred, but he was willing to make an exception tonight.

As if sensing conflict, Niall came over and pointed at him. "You good, Finn?"

Finn understood that he was asking about more than drinks. He wondered if he shouldn't have Niall hit Dermot. "I'm fine," he muttered, reminding himself he was a healer and not someone who destroyed.

When Niall was gone, he hissed at Dermot. "You gave her my mobile?"

"I know you're taking a break, but you're here, and she's here..." Dermot shrugged. "I figured you wouldn't mind hearing her out. She's probably already called you."

"I haven't checked my voicemail." He'd been avoiding all calls since he'd left Dublin. He'd directed his reception to tell all patients that he was on an extended sabbatical and that they'd be contacted when he returned.

"I didn't think it'd hurt for you to talk to her," Dermot continued. "Maybe you could refer her to someone else if you can't help her."

If he'd had his mobile with him, he'd have checked his messages then and there, but he'd left it buried in his sock drawer. He'd promised the hospital he wouldn't engage, but truthfully, the last thing he needed was the aggravation of the media and all the fake well-wishers—

they all just wanted the sensational gossip. They hardly cared that a young man's life had been wasted.

Dermot's phone beeped. He pulled it out and looked at the screen. Wincing, he put a hand on Finn's shoulder. "It's the office. I need to answer it. Be right back," he said, already heading out the front door.

Finn took a token sip, out of deference for Niall more than anything. He didn't have a taste for it. Getting lost in alcohol was no more appealing than taking antidepressants. Getting lost wasn't going to fix what was wrong.

The pub's door opened.

He would have expected Dermot, but somehow he knew it wasn't his friend. He didn't have to turn around to know who it was, either. He just knew.

Dermot's Abigail.

He went to pick up his pint, but his hand was shaking too much, so he abruptly got up and went to the loo. Inside, he turned on the faucet and doused his face with cold water. He didn't have to talk to her. He didn't have to do anything.

If only the window in here opened, he'd have gone out the back, but it'd been nailed shut decades ago.

He closed his eyes and told himself he needed to calm down. But behind his closed eyes he saw Jaime Walsh's face.

He barely made it to the toilet before he threw up.

9

Lynne refused to go with her, so Abby decided to walk to the pub. Her maps app said it was a twenty-minute walk from their rented cottage. If Lynne had come with her, she'd have driven, but since she was flying solo, she opted for the movement and fresh air. It wasn't raining for once.

She left at ten to seven so she wouldn't arrive before Dermot or the doctor. Sitting at the bar by herself, waiting for two men she didn't know, was too nerve-racking.

Hairy's stood out, a beacon among a cluster of houses, with a big red and black sign. There were a few cars parked around, and the lights glowed warm from inside though the sun was still high in the July sky.

This was it.

Taking a deep breath, Abby stood straight and strode inside.

The first thing she noticed when she walked in:

Dermot was not there, nor was any man who looked like Dr. Fionnlagh.

She checked the time. Had she missed them? Something that felt like panic rose up her throat.

No need to panic, she assured herself, trying to breathe it out. If she'd missed them, she'd just call Dermot. She had his number, after all. She'd have a drink and wait, in case they were late, and then go home if they didn't show.

But—*oh*—she wanted them to be here tonight.

Once she calmed enough, she noticed how clean the pub was. Not in a sanitary way, but of spirits and other dark things. Having lived in New Orleans where ghosts were part of life, she always had an appreciation for spaces that were as clean as this.

How did they manage it? By the look of the building and wood bar, she could tell the place was old.

Behind the bar, there was a man shining a pint glass, watching her, weighing her.

She studied him too. He was close to her age, maybe a couple years older, with broad shoulders that could hold up under any sort of weight.

Then she looked at him like her mom had taught her to do—not at his physical presence but at what was beneath the surface. "Look at their energy, look at their soul," her mama had instructed her.

The bartender's energy was as clean as the pub, and his soul was intact, without any sort of tear or missing piece. Abby exhaled, relieved.

He came over to her, a smile on his handsome face. "You must be the American who moved into the Sea

View Cottage. I'm Niall Ferguson, and this is my family's pub."

"I'm Abigail, and I love it here," Abby said genuinely. If circumstances were different, she would have come here to sketch.

A twinkle lit his eyes. "In Tullaghan? Or my pub?"

"Both."

He laughed and gestured to her to sit at the bar. "Can I get you a pint? Or something stronger? On the house, to welcome ya."

"A pint is great," she said, pulling out a stool and taking a seat.

He set the glass he'd been wiping under the spout and began a careful construction of a pint of Guinness. He glanced up at her. "So you're an artist, I hear, Abigail."

She blinked in surprise. "You heard that?"

His lips quirked. "Everyone did. We have a love of artists and writers in Ireland, and a fondness for Americans too. Especially pretty ones. My pub is going to be overcrowded with the gents if you start coming here."

"You're exaggerating." Lynne had always been the beautiful one. Whenever they'd gone out together, she was the one men gravitated toward.

"You wait and see." He slid the pint across the bar to her. "I should be buying all your drinks for the money you'll bring in."

Snorting, she lifted her glass in salute. "You're exaggerating."

"Exaggerate? An Irishman? Go on with ya."

"Can I ask you a question?" She leaned closer. "Why is the pub named Hairy's?"

Niall's face lit in a devilish grin. "Now that's a story for ya. My granddad, Harry Ferguson, opened this place sixty years ago. One night, before he opened the pub, he had a disagreement with Seamus O'Callahan, down the way. Seamus is the sign maker, you see."

Abby wasn't sure she did, but she nodded.

"Don't get into an argument with the man who's making your sign," Niall said in a wise tone. "Good thing Granda's name wasn't Bob, I always thought. Boob's Pub could give people the wrong idea."

She laughed, relaxing into her seat. She took a sip of the Guinness Niall had poured for her, feeling more surefooted. Worst case scenario, she'd ask Niall about Dr. Fionnlagh. He had to know him, being the publican here.

He picked up a rag and began polishing another glass. "Have you talked to Sarah?"

"Sarah?" She had no idea who he was talking about.

"The woman who lives in the cottage next to yours, with the yellow door. She has a little girl, Claire, who's six. They're both lovely."

Abby heard a hint of longing in his tone. "You know her well?"

"We went to school together." He set the glass down and began pouring another beer. "She went off to university but moved back just a few weeks ago."

The light changed in the bar. Abby turned, seeing a door open on the far side, from where the restrooms probably were.

A tall, broad man walked into the main room from there. She couldn't see his features for the cap he had pulled low over his head and the thick scruff over his face, but his manner was manly and attractive. She could see his hair was dark, a rich mink that curled around the edges of his hat. He looked like he was made at the same factory as Niall, but instinctively she knew they weren't related.

Something about him was so familiar.

She softened her gaze to look at his soul. At its essence, it was clean, gold, though large areas of it were tarnished. Lynne's soul was that way too: normally bright but mostly dulled because she was mourning the loss of what she loved most.

Abby frowned. What was this man mourning? She had the oddest compulsion to comfort him.

He stopped short of the spot at the bar and stared at her. His gaze fell to her arm, the one she'd hurt. She felt it throb in response to his attention.

Then he raised his gaze again and met her eyes.

She felt the *zap* between them, and then his soul changed, lighting up, beaming in bright pinks and golds, reaching out to her. She knew she was gawking at the transformation, but she couldn't help it.

His eyes.

Cerulean—the same passionate color that blazed in the spring sky back home. Her favorite shade of blue. The kind of blue that made one's heart race and expanded one's spirit. That perfect shade that artists over centuries labored to achieve.

Her fingers ached to paint them.

Her fingers just ached.

That's when it hit her: she was looking into Dr. Carrick Fionnlagh's eyes.

"Finn, meet Abigail," she heard Niall say.

Carrick Fionnlagh—Finn—didn't acknowledge Niall's introduction.

Niall didn't notice. "She's my new friend. Abigail, Finn and I grew up together. I can vouch that he's not normally as disreputable as he looks right now."

"How does he normally look?" Abby asked, her heart beating so hard in her chest that she was surprised no one commented.

Niall turned to Finn and studied him. "Boring," he said with an insouciant grin.

"I find that hard to believe," Abby muttered, trying to ignore the unexpected way her panties seemed to have lit on fire. She wasn't here for *that*. She wanted to talk to him about Lynne.

No one said anything for what seemed like a long time.

Niall was the one who broke the silence. "I've been behind this bar all my life, and I have a sense about things."

That drew Finn's attention. "What?"

Leaning across the bartop, Niall pointed at his friend. "How often do you come back to Leitrim?"

"Not often," Finn said, his brow furrowing. "Holidays, a few days here and there."

"Exactly." Niall crossed his arms, looking satisfied.

Finn shook his head. "I have no idea what you're talking about."

Truthfully, Abby didn't either.

"Abigail just moved here. You just came back." Niall

raised his hands. "I recognize an important meeting. I know fate when I see it."

Finn turned to her, frowning. "I don't believe in fate."

"I do," she replied. Over the years, she realized fate was the opportunities the Universe offered, but will was what you made of them. Things didn't just happen—there was a reason in everything, but what became of those openings was up to you.

She knew there was a reason she found Finn online. Meeting Dermot, who led her here to him, was confirmation. Fate, such as it were.

Niall broke into her thoughts. "Finn's never been one to appreciate whimsy. He needs help believing in magic."

"I don't know how you can live in Ireland and not believe in magic," she said.

"Life happens," Finn said grimly, his soul dimming again.

She couldn't debate his response—she felt the same, in some respects. Still, it made her sad. She wished she could do something to help him, but her wrist...

Without warning, like it always happened, in her mind, she began to see a scene: the moment she would have painted to heal whatever it was that weighed on his soul. It was from another time though she couldn't tell how early. There was a stone cottage with a thatched roof, small and cozy-looking. By the door, there were roses—dying blooms, once scarlet that had turned an ash black, smothering the walls of the house. Golden fields stretched out to the sea.

He stood in front of the house, wearing rough trousers and a white shirt open at the collar. At his feet, there was a worn leather doctor's satchel on its side, almost like it'd been cast away. He had the same blue eyes, sadder here with tears streaming down his face, and his hand rested on a tombstone.

My tombstone, she realized with a jolt.

Next to it was a smaller headstone, and she knew instinctively that it was for a baby.

Abby felt mourning for that child like a sharp stab to her heart, the sorrow of its loss shocking her with its potency. *His fault*, she heard from somewhere, though somehow she didn't believe it.

She knew that to heal this moment in Finn's past life, she'd need to paint the baby alive in his arms and the woman she'd been laughing into his smiling eyes, her long dark curls blowing in the wind.

She shook her head, trying to clear the vision, but it persisted. She fought to pull out of it—this wasn't for her to deal with. She *couldn't* deal with it, even if she *could* pick up a paintbrush. The last time she painted herself onto a canvas for someone else had been disastrous.

Niall's voice penetrated her fog. "Abigail, you okay?"

She shook her head again to clear it, trying to plant herself back in the present, but the pull of that old time was strong, beckoning her, wanting to share more details.

Finn was suddenly at her side, his hand on her back. "Breathe," he said in a low, reassuring voice.

Nodding, she tried to wave him off, but he took her injured hand with his other one, cradling it to his body protectively. His touch felt solid and grounding despite its slight shake.

Which was shocking, on so many levels. First: she

couldn't remember the last time she'd touched a stranger's hand. Since the pandemic, things like that had changed in the States. New Orleans had been hit hard by the virus, and people were rightfully cautious. If you didn't know someone, you didn't risk touching them.

County Leitrim had barely been affected by the virus. Abby hadn't known that when she'd decided to bring them there, but now she realized that of course it would be, if Bro Paul was to be believed. If the Universe set you up to succeed, then of course the place where they needed to go would be safe for her and Lynne with their stress-compromised systems.

But, truthfully, safe was the last thing she felt right now. She was on fire. His hand on her back burned hot through her shirt. The one holding her hand was slightly callused and very manly while gently strong and offering security.

It was *wonderful*.

It also freaked her out.

Most of all, she could feel her heart. She hadn't felt the energy of her heart this strongly since before Lynne's accident. It felt like it was expanding, rising up tight and painful, like it wanted to burst free.

What would it feel like if his hands explored her, focused and intent? Not that she would go there. Her focus had to be Lynne.

She cleared her throat, trying to disengage before any line was crossed.

"Give it a moment," he murmured to her, keeping her hand. "Do you get fainting spells often?"

She made a face at him. "I wasn't going to faint."

"Have you eaten?" he asked, his tone conveying his disbelief on that.

"Yes." Sometime. Maybe. But she didn't need to tell him that.

"Are you pregnant?" he asked brusquely.

"You have to have sex to get pregnant," she replied without thinking. She winced. "Forget I said that."

"Not a chance." The corner of his mouth twitched, and his soul lightened and sparked pink again.

She glanced up at Niall, hoping if she focused on him the spinning would stop. "Did you hear that?"

"I heard nothing about sex," he said with a publican's diplomacy.

She groaned. "Is all of Tullaghan going to know by sundown?"

"They won't be hearing it from me," Niall assured her. "I wouldn't be able to handle the stampede in here from neighboring counties wanting a chance to help you out."

She groaned.

Almost absently, Finn rubbed his thumb along her knuckles, uncovered by the brace she wore on her wrist. "All the men know about Abigail?"

Niall laughed. "Have you been gone so long that you don't remember how quickly news travels? Especially when it's of a beautiful woman."

Abby snorted. She wasn't beautiful—that was Lynne.

Finn gazed at her intently, whether it was to assess her health or what, she had no idea. But whatever he saw made him let go of her hand.

A relief—at least that was what she was going to

believe. She exhaled. The feeling of loss probably just had to do with her still-swimming head.

"Can I get you some water, Abigail?" Niall asked.

"I'm taking her home," Finn said.

She blinked at him. "What?"

"I'm taking you home."

She didn't know what to say. She should have jumped at it, so she could talk to him about Lynne. But she was totally shaken and needed to regroup.

Also, *him*. She looked up at him, and he was so unexpectedly tall and broad and delicious. If Lynne were here, she'd say, "*Hung*," but Abby was *not* going to think about that.

"I'm driving you home," he said. He leaned in. "And then we can discuss why you wanted to meet me."

She gasped. He knew. She looked around for Dermot.

Finn shook his head. Turning to Niall, he said, "When Dermot comes back from his call, tell him I took Abigail home."

Niall raised his brows. "You sure you want me to say that?"

"Yes," Finn barked, taking Abby's arm—her good one this time—and leading her out of the pub. On the street, he said, "My car is this way."

Abby let him guide her for a way before she finally said, "Dermot told you about me."

"Yes," he said bluntly.

"I know this isn't the way to do it, and I know I shouldn't tell you that I'm desperate, but I am."

He glanced at her injured wrist but didn't say

anything, marching her toward an opulent dark-blue SUV parked on the street.

She blinked at the color of the car, so symbolic. It was like a sign. Feeling a surge of strength, she looked up at him. "My friend Lynne needs help."

He stopped abruptly, right next to the car. "What?"

"My best friend Lynne fell down some stairs and broke her leg in three places." Abby pushed back the sight of Lynne lying unconscious at the bottom of those stairs. "The doctors put her leg back together, but she isn't healing. Her leg is more swollen than it should be and it's not making it easy to rehabilitate, so it's atrophied alarmingly. She's not responding to their treatments, and they've said there's nothing more they can do."

His gaze flickered at her wrist again. "And you?"

"My wrist is just sprained. It'll be fine. I want you to help her." Should she be impassioned or professional? She had no clue how to reach him, so she just decided to be herself. "Lynne's a dancer. It's all she's ever wanted to be."

He frowned at her. "And what does that have to do with you?"

She frowned right back at him. "She's my best friend, the only family I have. I can't just sit by and watch her fade away into depression and worse."

Something flickered behind his gaze, but she couldn't decipher what it was.

So she went on. "If I could do something to help her, I would, but I can't." She ignored how her voice cracked. "I researched doctors and found your name."

He stared at her for a long silent moment. Then he opened the car door. "Get in."

Confused, she did what he said.

He waited until she was settled and then closed the door. He went around to his side, got in, and sat there staring out the windshield.

"Do you need me to drive?" she asked, feeling much more settled now that she was in his car. It smelled like him. It made her feel safe and secure.

He shot her a look. Then he pressed the ignition and gingerly put his hand on the gearshift. "You're at the Sea View Cottage?"

She frowned. "How do you know that?"

He rolled his eyes. "You're in Tullaghan," he said, as if that explained it all.

He drove her in silence all the way home. Fortunately, it was only a few minutes.

Unfortunately, it was only a few minutes.

A flash of that past life vision flared in her mind again. *His fault*, she heard again. It had something to do with the sadness weighing down his soul now. Except whatever responsibility weighing on him had to have happened before he met her this evening. She shouldn't figure into it.

She *couldn't* figure into it. She couldn't take a chance and insert herself into another painting—not until she figured out why it'd gone wrong six months ago, or what she'd tapped into. Living in New Orleans, she'd known a few healers and spiritualists who'd tapped into dark things when they hadn't meant to, without understanding why. Was that what she'd inadvertently done?

No, she heard Bro Paul answer her.

She sighed. Inside, in her heart, she hadn't believed that she did, but hearing confirmation was reassuring.

Trust your instincts, kid. They're never wrong.

Easy for him to say.

Unbidden, the edited scene flashed in her mind, and she felt the rightness of it down deep. More, the longing for it was so powerful that it stole her breath. She sank in the leather seat, hugging herself.

"What?" he asked.

She glanced at him. "Nothing."

He raised a brow imperiously. "It didn't sound like nothing."

"Look, I just want to talk about Lynne and how you can help her."

"I'm on sabbatical," was his mumbled reply.

"You won't be on sabbatical forever."

"It doesn't feel that way," he said so softly that she wasn't sure she heard him right. Before she could ask him to repeat it, he pulled in front of her rented cottage.

She looked at it. Lynne was inside. Her friend was expecting a miracle. She *needed* him to give them a miracle.

But when she faced him, she saw all the sadness in his soul. She felt the urge to fix it, strong, like she always felt when Lynne needed her.

Except she couldn't fix it. And on some instinctive level, she knew if she pushed him to help Lynne in the current state he was in, it would break him.

As much as she needed help for Lynne, she couldn't do it at his expense. She just couldn't. It went against everything she was as a person and a healer.

You made contact, kid, she heard Bro Paul's voice say. *That's all you can ask for.*

Was it? Because she could already see the crestfallen expression on Lynne's face, much like the one on Finn's, and this didn't seem like enough by a long shot.

It killed her to open the door, but she did it. She hesitated, glancing back at him, seeing the pale-green sadness blanketing him.

How was she going to help Lynne? How was she going to help herself? And—good Lord—why did she feel a pressing need to help Finn too?

He said nothing, only watched her with haunted eyes.

She shut the car door.

10

————

By the next morning, Finn had listened to Abigail's voicemail a dozen times.

He lay in his small bed, listening to his mother bustling around the kitchen, and he couldn't help playing it again.

"Hello, Dr. Fionnlagh. My name is Abigail Angevine. Dermot Farrell gave me your number, and I wondered if you'd have time to chat with me regarding a potential case."

He listened to her recite her number and the faintly desperate "I look forward to speaking with you" at the end. He kept picturing the way she'd favored her wrist, the puffiness of her fingers, the tightness around her eyes that signaled pain, and he couldn't figure out why she hadn't pressed him for help. Instead, she'd talked about her friend who needed help.

It did not compute.

When people found out he was a doctor, they felt entitled to him. They asked him for medical advice, told him about all their aches and pains, and begged him for assistance.

She hadn't.

Reverse psychology? Playing hard to get?

He didn't think so.

Neither had he figured out what to do about it yet. A part of him wanted to confront her and ask her what she was about.

He got up because soon his mom would come drag him out of bed. Splashing water on his face, he put on a shirt with buttons for the first time in days and thought about Abigail and the way she'd cradled her wrist.

The doctor part of him that wanted to fix people wanted to know what had happened to her and to help her get better. He wasn't just morally obligated to do it because of his oath; his soul required it.

And then there was the larger part of him that wanted to know what she tasted like and how her hair felt clutched in his hands.

He paused as he brushed his teeth. That was the surprising part. He hadn't been interested in anything— not even life—the past weeks and suddenly he wanted a woman he didn't know.

It had to be some sort of white knight syndrome, where he needed to save her. Although he never dated patients—he'd never been tempted to. Though with Abigail, he was less interested in saving her and more interested in getting to know her. Why had she sought him out, and who was the friend who needed help so badly that Abigail came all the way to Tullaghan to find him? If her friend was that hurt, the journey to Ireland would have been difficult.

He left the sanctuary of his room to brave the kitchen and his mother.

His mom looked up from the table with a frown. "Lollygagging in bed won't cure what ails you, Carrick. Unless you're in there with a woman."

In the days since he'd come back home, she'd vacillated between hovering around him to get him reengaged in life and wanting to throttle him. Apparently, today she was leaning toward the latter.

"So, were you in there with a woman?" she asked, her tone hopeful.

"I would hardly dare," he replied. He went to her, dropped a kiss on top of her head, and set to making himself a cup of tea. He could feel her eyes following him. He knew she was worried about him—*he* was worried about himself. "Where's Dad?" he asked to distract her.

"With his cows, where do you think? I keep telling Conall we should sell the farm and buy one of those recreational vehicles and travel around like Niall's parents have done, but he's a stubborn man." She gave him a look. "You get that from him."

"Do I?" he asked mildly, stirring honey into his tea.

"How are you?"

He knew it wasn't a casual question. It was, in fact, very bold, because he'd been home for several days and this was the first time she'd asked him so directly. That had to be a good sign. He examined his state of mind. His concern for Abigail had replaced some of the guilt he'd been feeling about Jaime. He wasn't sure that was a good thing. He frowned. "Better, I think."

"You don't sound happy about it," his mom observed hesitantly.

He sat across from her at the table. "Is this where you ask me to go to yoga with you at the community center?"

She huffed, waving her hand. "If I thought some sun salutations would cure you, I'd have dragged you down there by now."

He felt his lips curl in what might have qualified as a smile. "Dermot sent his regards. He said to tell you he's going to stop by soon." He'd texted yesterday night to apologize for abandoning him, but he had an emergency with a deal that was going through.

Her face lit up. "How is my boy? I didn't know he was back in town. He comes home so rarely these days."

Dermot's home life being what it was, he'd often taken sanctuary here on the farm. Finn's parents had always looked on him as another son. But after Fiona's death he'd stayed away for the most part, seeing Finn's parents when they visited Dublin. It'd surprised Finn when Dermot bought a house in Tullaghan, but he figured maybe Dermot was finally moving on. "He's having the wing he donated to the hospital in Fiona's name expanded."

His mom's eyes flooded with tears. "Well," she said brusquely. A few escaped before she managed to blink them away. She swiped at them, clearing her throat. "That boy needs to let the past go. He needs a woman too. Maybe your new friend has someone for Dermot."

"New friend?" he asked suspiciously.

"Don't try to tell me you haven't met a woman, Carrick Fionnlagh."

His gaze narrowed at his mother. He knew better than to believe the "mother's intuition" shite. Molly Fionnlagh always knew everything because of the vast web of gossip she was plugged into. "What did you hear?"

"What do you think I heard? That you left the pub with a woman you couldn't keep your hands off and drove her home?" She rolled her eyes. "Would that be too much for this old mother to ask for?"

He cursed under his breath. "I came home minutes after I dropped her off."

"Is that all the time it took, then?" she asked in affronted shock. "I need to have Conall talk to you."

"For goodness' sake." He took his teacup, kissed her head again, and started to stride out of the kitchen only to get blocked when his dad stepped in.

"Oh good, you're back," his mom said. "Conall, talk to your boy."

His dad raised a brow at him with the silent question *What did you do now?* He dropped a kiss on Molly's cheek and poured himself a cup of tea. "What does he need talking to about?"

"Women."

Conall scoffed. "Now, Molly, you always say what I know about women would fit on the head of a pin. Why would I be talking to him about it when he likely has things he could teach me?"

Finn groaned. Knowing better than to think he could get away, he dropped onto a seat.

"Carrick left the pub with a woman last night," Molly pronounced.

"I didn't," he corrected his mother, giving her a look. "I took her home because she wasn't feeling well."

"Shannon O'Leary said he was *looking* at the girl." Molly waggled her eyebrows.

His dad frowned at him. "You were looking at the girl? Who is she?"

"The American that just moved into the Sea View Cottage," his mother said with authority. "They say she lives with her sister, but the poor girl rarely leaves the house. She's in a wheelchair, I've heard."

Finn winced. Of course she was in a wheelchair. He tried not to picture her. He tried not to wonder if he could help her.

He tried not to think of how Abigail looked when she left his car last night.

He was unsuccessful on all counts.

"Humph." His dad stood with his hands on his hips. "You recall what I told you about love, don't you, boy? Love comes when love is ready, no matter if you are or not."

His dad had talked like this for as long as Finn could remember. Finn teased him from time to time, saying there was a poet in there that needed to get out. Truth be told, when his dad talked like this, Finn loved it. He himself wasn't a whimsical man, but he appreciated that an old-time farmer like his father was.

His dad pointed at him. "When love comes to you, boy, you take it, with both hands, and you hold on forever, because it's the most important thing. Love makes everything possible."

Finn was positive nothing would bring Jaime Walsh back, not even love. And what he felt—if anything—for Abigail had nothing to do with love. You didn't fall in love the moment you met someone, no matter what his parents believed. "Love doesn't come to everyone, Dad," he pointed out.

"It does if you're paying attention." His dad pointed a finger at him. "Pay attention. I didn't raise an eejit."

"Invite her to dinner." His mom made it an offhand comment but the demand behind it was clear.

"Have you kissed her?" his dad asked. "No woman can resist a kiss from a Fionnlagh."

His mom turned a stern glare toward him. "Is that so?"

"You know my kisses are only for you, Molly." Pulling her from her seat, he grabbed her around the waist and twirled her before lowering his lips to hers. She played hard to get for a few seconds before she gave in.

Shaking his head, oddly reassured just like every time he caught them affectionate, Finn stood. He always recognized his cue to leave.

As comforting as their love was, Finn had never imagined having a relationship like theirs. It hadn't been a focus—becoming a surgeon had commanded all his passion. But as he left the kitchen, he thought about Abigail and wondered what it'd be like to reserve all his kisses for her, the way his dad had pledged.

He stopped in his tracks, caught off guard by the uncharacteristic thought. He went out with women—he was hardly a monk—but romance had never factored into his brief relationships. They were functional.

It had to be his mom putting ideas in his head.

She was really good at it, he realized, because he was still thinking about kissing Abby hours later.

11

———————

Last night when she'd gotten home, Lynne had already been asleep—her physical therapy had worn her out yesterday. So Abby hadn't told her yet that she'd met Finn but didn't get anywhere with him.

This morning, Abby slipped out of the house before Lynne had roused. She needed to figure out what to do now that she couldn't ask Finn to help them. She just needed to regroup, and she didn't want to say anything to Lynne until she had a plan.

But, yes, she was probably a coward too.

Abby sat in front of the rose bushes that lined the side of the property, wondering if they were supposed to look as tangled as they did. Not that she was going to do anything about them—they were very thorny. Were they supposed to be that way? It seemed inhospitable having plants like this around your property. "Like they were warding something off," she said to herself.

"Is she talking to fairies, Mom?" a young voice asked.

Abby turned around as a woman and a little girl came

up the walkway. The woman murmured something to the girl, who had to be her daughter—they were carbon copies of each other. Same coloring: pale ivory skin with red hair that glinted with copper in the sunlight. Same features: fine-boned and delicate. Same fashion sense: plain jeans with a light sweater. The only difference was that the girl's hair was a mass of wild curls in a lopsided ponytail while the woman had long, straight, controlled hair.

But everything about the woman screamed *controlled*, from her tall, thin frame to the way she held herself. Even her soul seemed contained, not radiating out the way most did but staying within its confines. It looked dingy, a sort of bathwater gray, with a big piece missing around her heart. A lot of times children filled up missing pieces of their parents' souls, but that wasn't the case here.

Abby almost expected her daughter's soul to mirror her mother's, but she was relieved to see it was that of a child's, still brightly golden from birth, though Abby could see where the tarnish of life was beginning to fray the edges of her light.

"Are you talking to the fairies?" the little girl asked her this time, apparently not satisfied with her mother's reply.

Abby smiled at the whimsy, happy to be distracted for a moment. "I'm talking to you. Are you a fairy?"

Her eyes got big. "No, I'm a girl. But sometimes my mom says that she wouldn't mind if the fairies took me for a little while. They say I'm supposed to stay here though."

"Claire," the woman said, shaking her head. She

turned to Abby with a warm smile. "I'm Sarah Connelly, and this is my daughter Claire. We live next door."

She remembered Niall mentioning them. "I'm Abigail, and my best friend Lynne is inside."

Claire gasped. "You live with your best friend?" she asked reverently, like it was the most incredible thing she'd ever heard.

It would have been incredible too, if it hadn't been for the circumstances. Abby smiled sadly. "I've known her since I was just a little older than you, so she's more like a sister."

Sarah put a hand on Claire's head but held her other hand out. "We came to welcome you to Tullaghan."

Abby noticed the wrapped bundle for the first time. She set down her cup and accepted it with her good hand.

"It's soda bread," the little girl said as Abby unwrapped the foil to peek at it.

"Thank you," Abby said with a smile at both of them.

"Do you like soda bread?" Claire asked. "It's best with marmalade. Do you like marmalade?"

Sarah chuckled, her hand on her daughter's shoulder. "She's excited to meet you. We haven't had anyone next door in ages. But we'll go now. Claire, we need to have lunch and then you need a nap."

"I'm too old for naps. I'm six," Claire said with all the indignation a little body could hold.

Sighing, Sarah shook her head. "I have a new appreciation for the school season now that I have a child."

Claire tugged on her mom's sweater. "Can I come play with Abigail later?"

"Abigail is busy, and we don't want to impose."

The girl faced Abigail. "Are you busy?"

"My mama always told me it was important to make time for some things," she answered, not wanting to go into detail about Lynne's PT or anything else they had going on.

"Like donuts?" Claire asked, her button nose wrinkling as she tried to understand. "Mom took me to have donuts once in Dublin and I loved them, but we can't go back there because we can't go on holiday because she's working."

Abby nodded solemnly. "Donuts are certainly important."

"We'll let you get back to things now. I'm sure you're busy, and I have a meeting in a few minutes. Come, Claire." Sarah smiled at Abby. "It was nice meeting you. If you need anything, we're just next door."

"Thank you." Abby waved because Claire kept looking back longingly, like she wanted to stay.

"She's a cutie," Bro Paul said as he appeared next to her. He looked around the rented property, nodding in approval. "I like it here. We did good, finding this place on such short notice during tourist season."

"You didn't have anything to do with the sudden cancellation the landlord had, did you?"

"*Moi?*" He batted his eyes in false innocence. Then he pointed to the rose bushes. "They're a tad neglected, aren't they? They could use some love."

"Can't we all?" she murmured, trying not to think about Finn.

"The women in your line don't find happily ever after, do they?" He frowned. "Perhaps it's time you changed that."

"Is that why you're here, to tell me I need loving?"

He pointed at the rose bush. "You know about Irish roses, don't you?"

Abby shook her head, confused by the segue. "Excuse me?"

"Irish roses bloom every year with the hope to attract love. It's the eternal hope of the Irish, that as long as the wild roses bloom, love is possible."

She remembered that vision of Finn's past life and the dead blooms strangling the stone house. Then she looked at this rose bush. There wasn't a bloom in sight. "I guess I'm screwed." She tried to joke to cover up how oddly upset the sight made her.

"Not if you stick with me." He polished his fingernails on his woolen robe, as if he had a modest bone in his ethereal body. "Miracles are us."

That just made her think of Finn all over again. The Miracle Worker, though not for her and Lynne.

"Oh ye of little faith." He clapped a big hand on her back, almost causing her to fall over. "I wouldn't let you down, no matter what you think. You've just gotta ask the right questions."

"I'm low on my faith in the Divine right now." It was a terrible thing to doubt your gifts.

"Kid, tell me something I don't know." He rolled his eyes. "But that's not the question here."

She frowned at him. "What's the question?"

"The question is, why don't you trust yourself when you know what needs to be done? Why don't you trust your gifts?"

She hated that he could read her mind. She hugged her hurt arm to her chest. "Because bad things happened!"

"Just this last time, and that's a judgment," he replied calmly. "Things happen for a reason. They've led you here, after all. They've put you and Lynne"—he waved a hand at the cottage—"on the right path."

"The right path?" She felt the bread begin to crumble under her furious grip. "This isn't the right path. The right path is Lynne dancing and me painting. This is the road to perdition."

"Do you know what her path looked like before?"

She frowned. "No," she admitted reluctantly.

He put his hands on his wide hips, his gaze narrowed. "Then how do you know she isn't exactly where she needs to be?"

"In a *wheelchair*?" She was still sputtering when she heard the front door open and Lynne call out.

"Abby? Everything okay?"

No, everything was not okay. She glared at Bro Paul.

"They told me you'd be a hard case before you were born. Good thing I like a challenge." He patted her back again. Then he sighed. "Abs, I have things to teach you, and you have things to teach me. We're in this together."

"Teach *you*?" she asked, incredulous. "You're the guide here."

"That doesn't mean that I'm not learning from you.

Otherwise, what kind of relationship would that be? I'd just lord my superiority over you all the time."

"Because you don't?"

He laughed. "Touché, kid." Grinning, he waved at Lynne. "Lynne needs you now, so probably you should go. And, hey."

She looked at him.

"You know the amethyst you brought with you?"

Frowning, she nodded. She always kept a few stones with her because they helped ground and focus her when she needed something extra.

"Keep it on you for a little while. I blessed it extra good."

"Why does that sound nasty?" she murmured.

She could still hear him laughing even after he faded away.

Knowing Lynne was waiting, Abby headed toward the door.

"Who were you talking to?" Lynne asked, rubbing her ear. "Local ghosts coming to check you out?"

"No, just Bro Paul."

Lynne perked up. "You're talking to him again? That's great. Did he have any words of wisdom for us?"

She didn't tell Lynne that according to him, Lynne was on the right path. That path didn't include dancing at the moment, and that was unacceptable. "He told me I should keep my amethyst on me."

"Hmm." She rubbed her ear a little harder.

"Are you okay?" Abby asked, concerned. With Lynne being laid up for so long and bordering on depressed, Abby worried about her getting sick.

"I'm fine. My ear has just been ringing a lot." Lynne rolled her wheelchair back so Abby could come in. "You didn't wake me up last night, so I guess meeting the Miracle Worker didn't go as planned?"

She remembered the intense pull she'd felt for him and the hurt in his blue eyes. "No, I met him. I asked him to help us."

Lynne screamed with joy. "That's great! What did he say?"

"I couldn't follow through. I decided I'd find someone else." Abby put extra certainty in her voice. "Don't worry. I'll find someone else. Today. Maybe Dermot Farrell might even know someone. We still have his card."

Looking disoriented and confused, Lynne shook her head. "What happened?"

"His soul is hurting. I couldn't burden him with this." She tried to smile reassuringly. "Don't worry. I'll figure this out."

"Of course you will. You always do, and you're not a quitter." Lynne rolled to the window in the living room and stared out at the ocean.

From the side, Abby could see a frown creasing her friend's brow. She swallowed back the surge of guilt, but she had to check. "You don't think I picked him over you, do you?"

Lynne turned to gape at her. "Of course not. I trust you. More than that, I know you. You wouldn't be able to hurt another soul, not even to help me. And besides, I wouldn't want you to."

Still, it didn't mean she hadn't failed. All this way from the States to be at a loss.

"What's that in your hand?" Lynne asked suddenly, probably trying to distract her.

Abby looked down at the loaf. "Soda bread. Our next-door neighbor and her daughter welcomed us to Tullaghan."

"Is it supposed to look crushed like that?"

"Blame Bro Paul."

Lynne rolled her eyes. "You're doing enough of that for both of us."

Word, Bro Paul said in her head.

Abby ignored them both, going into the kitchen to put the loaf away. She had another brilliant orthopedic doctor to find. A needle in a haystack? She hoped not.

12

"Did you know Rosserk Friary was built for an order of Franciscan monks and nuns who could be married?" Lynne shook her head, swiping the screen on her iPad. "Until a henchman of Queen Elizabeth burned them out. Can you believe that? I wonder what Bro Paul thinks about that."

Abby looked up from her seat by the window where she was Googling Finn. "Why don't we just go see this place? We can do a little day trip. It's not far, right?"

"No, it's not far," she replied noncommittally.

When Lynne didn't say anything more, Abby sighed. "Don't you want to see it?"

"Yeah. Someday."

Abby could all but hear Lynne think how hard it'd be to visit a historical site on crutches, much less in a wheelchair.

Which was why she should be continuing her search for another doctor. She'd put out a couple feelers, but they didn't feel right.

Finn had felt *right*.

Something prodded her to look him up again. The last time she'd Googled him had been weeks ago, and she hadn't seen anything to indicate he was on sabbatical.

Abby recognized the signs of depression—she saw it in Lynne every day—and the grief around Finn was so stark that she knew something had to have caused it. It felt tied to the reason he'd gone on sabbatical.

And there was. With a sinking heart she read about what had happened with his patient, Jaime Walsh, a few weeks before. The medical inquiry concluded that he hadn't done anything wrong, blaming the anesthesiologist. Walsh was apparently a big-time soccer player. Given the number of trashy articles about the situation, she bet Finn went on sabbatical to get away from the press.

"You know, I've been thinking," Lynne said, a little too casually.

Abby looked up from her phone. "About?"

"You said Finn's sexy friend had an in at the hospital. Maybe we should contact him and ask him if he knows of another doctor."

"You mean Dermot Farrell?"

"Hmm."

"That's the same sound you make when you see a delicious pastry," Abby pointed out.

"Because he's good enough to eat." She frowned. "Not that I could offer him much of a buffet in return."

"Maybe you should text him," Abby said.

"Maybe." Lynne dropped her chin, her hair hiding her face.

A knock sounded at the door. They both looked up.

"Who'd come to our house?" She got up and went to the door.

It was a man in a safety vest, holding a package in his hands. He looked at her with that clear searching gaze most Irish people had, like they really wanted to see you. "Are you Abigail Angevine?"

"Yes." She frowned.

"It's heavy." He eyed the brace, his gaze skeptical. "I'll bring it in before I get the rest."

"The rest?" she parroted, watching him go to the dining table. The box rattled as he moved, and when he set it down it made a heavy *thunk*. "There must be a mistake."

Lynne rolled her wheelchair over to where the postman had set the box. "It's for you. What is it?"

"I have no idea." She joined her. "I didn't order anything."

"Maybe it's from a secret admirer."

She made a face at her as she turned the box around to read who it was from. "It's from Marjorie," she said in surprise.

"What would your agent be sending?" Lynne asked. "It's too big for a contract."

Abby put her hands on the box. Her heart began to pound with the energy of what was inside. She could feel it pulsing through the cardboard. *Colors.* She'd recognize the feel of paints anywhere.

A longing shot through her chest, so powerful that she almost bent over with the pain of it. The fingers on her right hand twitched listlessly of their own accord, reminding her they wouldn't perform no matter how tempting the paints inside were.

"Where should I put this?" the postman asked from the threshold.

Discombobulated, Abby turned around and blinked at the long rectangular box he awkwardly balanced on his shoulder.

"There is great," Lynne said, pointing to the side of the living room closest to him.

He nodded and set it down where Lynne had indicated. "Three more. I'll just put them here too, shall I?"

"Yes, please," Lynne replied.

"Why would she send all this?" Abby demanded.

"Why don't you open it and find out?" Lynne said.

Abby began to carefully peel the packing tape off, barely aware of the postman delivering the last package and telling them goodbye. She lifted the flaps open, and even though she'd expected it, she gasped when she saw the contents.

Her favorite oil paints from France. Tube after tube of her favorite colors—St. Remy Yellow, Provence Blue, Eva Pink, Opaline Green... With them there were brushes and palette knives, all the sizes she favored, carefully bundled together.

She caught a faint whiff of the paint. Some people thought it stunk, but to her paint smelled like joy. She picked up a tube of Intense Turquoise and held it in her good hand. A longing to open it and feel the smear of paint on her fingers clutched her chest. The emotion rose up and almost choked her.

Slowly, deliberately, she closed the box. When she spoke, her grief made her voice so raw she barely recognized it. She put her hand on the amethyst she'd tucked into her bra, to keep it on her like Bro Paul suggested. "Why would Marjorie send all this?" she asked again.

Lynne watched her, pale, her hand gripping her necklace. "Beats me. Maybe you should ask her."

She turned at stared at the other packages lined up against the far wall. She didn't have to open them to know what was inside—she could tell by the size and shape of the boxes: canvases and other stuff that she needed, like her favorite gessoes and tools to put together the canvas. Probably an easel.

Marjorie had always been thorough. That was why Abby had signed with her to begin with—that, and the fact that, with the most successful gallery in New Orleans, with a branch in New York, Marjorie was one of the most sought-after artist representatives in the business.

As if on cue, her phone rang. She didn't have to look at the screen to know who it was.

Lynne stopped next to her and put her hand on Abby's back. "You going to answer it?"

Abby nodded and lifted her phone.

"I just got a text saying your packages have arrived," Marjorie said enthusiastically. "I know, I know. You aren't painting right now, but I was called to send them. I had a dream."

One of the other reasons Abby had picked Marjorie to rep her was because Marjorie came from a family long-entrenched in New Orleans culture. The woman understood the arcane, but she also knew how to market it so it wasn't cheesy. More than that, Marjorie had always been supportive of Abby's choices, even when Abby said she wanted to pick her own commissions.

Given how respectful Marjorie was of her decisions about her art, Abby shook her hand as she looked at all the boxes in the living room. "It must have been some dream."

Her rep laughed. "It was the first time I had a monk in a dream. That was a shocker."

She stilled. "A monk?"

"A monk!" Marjorie laughed again. "A big one, with a stein of beer in his hand. Can you imagine?"

"Yes, actually." Abby shook her head. "What did he say?"

"That I needed to send you art supplies, which I understand given the state of your wrist is insane, but he told me I needed to do it. For when inspiration strikes. So I did. Except instead of getting you stretcher bars and canvas, we thought it'd be easier on you to have ready-made canvases. I know you prefer to make them yourself, but desperate times and all that." Marjorie paused. "You aren't upset, are you?"

"You just followed your guidance," was all she said. Abby hugged the tube of turquoise to her heart, not sure how she felt. Angry, a little manipulated, but also comforted.

Most of all, hopeful. He wouldn't have had Marjorie send paints unless he thought she needed them. He could never be cruel. Even in her darkest moments, she hadn't believed that he'd set her up.

Marjorie went on, oblivious of Abby's quandary. "It was crazy guidance, but I felt good about it. How's your wrist doing? How's Lynne? Don't worry about anything here. That last article that ran in *The New Yorker* about you has gotten us more requests for commissions than I've had from all the other artists I represent combined. People are *clamoring* for an *Angevine* original. I've spun this healing period the past six months to our favor, so when you get back to painting, you won't have to worry about ramping up again."

She didn't think about what would happen if she couldn't paint again. She wasn't willing to accept that option. "Thanks, Marjorie," she said in a hoarse voice.

"Hang in there, kid. You've got this."

Abby blinked. Only one person called her "kid" and he had an enormous belly covered by a brown wool dress. Marjorie was definitely being influenced.

"Let me know if you need anything else. I'm here for you," her rep continued. "Tell Lynne I wish her the best."

Abby stared at her phone after the call ended.

Lynne cleared her throat. "I take it the Franciscan strikes again?"

Abby looked upward. "Bro Paul!" she yelled.

He appeared instantly, a snifter of brandy cupped in his big hand. "You rang?"

She gestured to all the boxes. "Explain, please."

He shrugged. "I will always want to surround you with the things that bring you joy. When you didn't listen to me about that, I went to a source you trusted to provide those things." He sipped his brandy with a satisfied sigh. "I think we did good."

"What is he saying?" Lynne asked, rubbing her ear again.

"This is what happens when you doubt yourself," Bro Paul said, focusing wholly on Abby. "That's why there are signs in the world, to help you when you don't trust yourself. You get confirmation that you need to move forward from people you trust. That would be Marjorie, in this case."

Lynne tugged Abby's shirt. "What is he saying?"

She shook her head, putting her hand on Lynne's.

"Always look for the helpers, kid. They show up when you least expect them." Bro Paul jerked his chin at the boxes. "This is your confirmation to trust in yourself and your gifts. In what you know deep in your heart. That's never been wrong. It's also a sign that you need to retrust in the Divine, because it is always trying to help you. We've got your back, kid."

He saluted her with his glass, and with that, he disappeared.

"*What's he saying?*" Lynne insisted.

Abby stared at the boxes. "I don't even know where to start."

13

The first thing Dermot had done when his mother died was raze the house they'd lived in.

He'd never expected to return to Tullaghan, but on a visit a few years ago to Dublin, Conall Fionnlagh had mentioned that a large parcel of land was available on the cliffs along the Atlantic, and Dermot had reconsidered. At the very least it'd be a good investment.

But when he'd set foot on the property, it'd felt right to renovate the existing house and use it as a holiday residence. That way, the people he'd grown up around would forget the poor boy of a drunk that he'd been and think of him as a successful man.

And so he'd returned to Tullaghan a king.

He sprawled on the white Italian leather couch, a tumbler of whiskey in the palm of his hand, and looked around at everything he'd built, everything he'd acquired: the house, the paintings, the expensive furnishings.

He hoped his mother could see him from her spot in Hell.

But as much as he had, he couldn't stop thinking about Abigail. He leaned back, and when he closed his eyes, he could feel the pulsing of her soul. She was injured—imagine how strong and vital she'd feel if she were completely well. Pain weighed on a soul. He'd known that since Fiona's accident.

The need to see Abigail rose again, like a wave of nausea. A bit of sweat broke out on his lip as he fought it.

How was she his redemption? Could she help him get rid of this need?

When he'd received Finn's text about missing Abigail at the pub, Dermot had felt oddly disappointed and relieved at the same time. He wasn't sure he could have spent an evening sitting next to her making polite conversation.

She'd texted him to thank him for inviting her to the pub, expressing her regrets that she'd missed him. He also knew where Abigail lived—everyone in town was talking about the two beautiful Americans in the Sea View Cottage. He just hadn't decided what his next move was.

Being close to her was not it.

The more he looked at it, the more he believed getting Finn to make the next move was the best course of action. Finn had a touch when it came to helping people rehabilitate. If anyone could get Abigail back to a hundred percent, it was him. Not to mention that it might help him get out of this guilt funk he'd been in since Jaime Walsh had died.

Most importantly, Finn would be a buffer between

him and Abigail while Dermot explored how she might be his redemption.

Dermot picked up his phone and dictated a text to his friend.

Are you going to help Abigail?

Finn never replied to a text right away, and since the loss of his patient, he'd been even more aloof. But this time, the response was immediate.

I'm on sabbatical.

That was tantamount to saying yes. With Finn, a noncommittal answer was the same as an affirmative—you just needed to reframe the question until it sparked the right response.

So Dermot said:

Aren't you returning to medicine after your sabbatical?

Finn sent:

Abigail asked the same question.

Deciding to cut to the chase, Dermot called Finn directly. He sipped his whiskey, knowing Finn would pick up.

Which he did. "This is unusual," Finn said. "Normally at this time of day you're busy amassing more wealth."

"I took a break today." He'd had his assistant cancel

all his meetings so he could focus on Abigail today. "About Abigail."

"Is she paying you to harass me?" Finn asked mildly.

"I keep thinking about her wrist."

There was absolute silence on the other end.

"Did she tell you how she injured it?" Dermot asked.

"No."

Dermot knew to stay quiet, to give Finn the opportunity to keep talking.

Which he did. Sighing, Finn said, "She said she wasn't here for herself, but for her friend. I should know better, because everyone treats doctors like public domain, but I find myself actually believing her."

"Would you say I have a good sense about people?" Dermot asked.

"Yes."

"She's not lying. If she says she wants to talk about her friend, then it's true." It was one of the things that made her intriguing to him. He wondered what was wrong with her friend. "The question is, are you going to let her stay in pain?"

Finn said nothing.

"I know you, Finn," Dermot said softly. "I have since we were six years old. I know you're hurting, but I also know that if you turn your back on her, you'll feel its guilt for the rest of your life. So think about it."

The silence stretched, and he didn't think Finn was going to reply. But then Finn murmured, "Thank you."

"It's what friends do," Dermot said. "I'll talk to you later, mate. Call if you need anything."

Hanging up, he closed his eyes and tried not to think

about the potency of Abigail's soul once she was fully healed.

He reopened his eyes when his mobile signaled a new text. Not recognizing the number, he clicked on it, expecting it to be rubbish.

To his surprise, it wasn't.

You met my friend Abby. I just wanted to say thank you too. Not many people care enough to help, especially strangers. Unless you're into damsels in distress. :)

Surprised, he felt the new soul piece in his chest pulse warmly. Putting a hand over it in wonder, he sat with the feeling for a few breaths before he sent his reply.

My trusty steed and I are at your disposal, Abby's friend.

She answered him quickly:

Heroes are few and far between these days. Your steed must be a unicorn.
And my name is Madelynne Broussard.

Grinning, he tapped back:

I only ride my unicorn on Sundays, Madelynne.

She replied:

LOL
That I'd like to see.

He sat back, feeling the lightness and calm she inspired, and he smiled.

Until the thing in him that was hungry swelled.

Surprised by its sudden insistence, Dermot swallowed it back. He struggled against it, resisting the way it encouraged him to touch Madelynne's soul to look for weaknesses. Breathing heavily, he finally wrestled the craving into submission again where he told it to stay.

It never did though.

14

Instead of another day of what his mother called *lollygagging*, that he preferred to call ruminating, Finn decided to go see Abigail. That Dermot was encouraging him to do so as well only solidified his resolve to talk to her.

He couldn't not ask what she and her friend needed. The doctor in him couldn't ignore someone in pain.

Truth be told, he didn't think he'd be able to ignore *her*.

Trying not to think about Abigail had proved futile. When he wasn't wondering what had happened to her wrist, he was remembering how she hadn't pushed him when he said he was on sabbatical despite her obvious need. He remembered the way she'd looked, certain of herself, elegant in her own unconventional way, like a gypsy stepping in from the wild.

He'd had more fantasies about wrapping his hands in her long hair than he'd ever had about anything since he'd hit puberty, including the Victoria Secret's angel he'd had a crush on as a teenager.

He wanted to see Abigail alone, in private—heaven help him.

Finn drove to the Sea View Cottage and pulled alongside the road between it and the house next door. He turned off the engine and stared at her place. It was a quintessential Irish cottage—white stucco with brightly colored window trimmings and door. Hers were red, while the one next door was yellow. The yard had seen better days, but he supposed that was to be expected in a rental property, which he assumed this was.

He got out of his car and looked closer. He caught a hint of movement in one of the windows. Frowning, he started up the walkway.

"Are you visiting Abigail?" a young voice asked him.

He turned and looked around but didn't see anything. Then he glanced to the left and saw a girl peeking out from over the stone wall that separated the houses. All he could see of her was curly red hair and large curious eyes.

"Are you the gatekeeper?" he asked.

Her forehead furrowed with a frown. "No. I'm Claire."

"Claire! Where are you?" a feminine voice called from inside.

"Uh-oh." Her eyes got even wider, and she ran toward her house and whoever was calling her. Then the little pixie turned around. "Abigail is my friend. I'm drawing her a picture, but don't tell anyone," she ordered before she disappeared inside.

He knew from years of being a doctor that children didn't just like anyone. They had better instincts than most adults he'd ever known. So for Claire to pronounce that Abigail was her friend, it meant something. He didn't know what, or whether it'd make a difference to him, but it was a check in her favor.

Determined to suss out her intentions, he strode the rest of the way up to the house and knocked on the door.

He was about to knock again when the door swung open. He lowered his gaze to the woman in the wheelchair who answered it.

She was lovely, with blond hair in that haphazard way women piled it on their heads. Her eyes were sad and clouded with pain and she had a colorful scarf wrapped around her shoulders. His training kicked in, and he assessed her pallor, thinness, and the slackness around her mouth. She looked wan and unhappy, though he bet the unhappiness was more depression than anything. He glanced at her legs. They were covered by a dark-green blanket, but he could see the outline of a brace through the wool.

But then she smiled, and she transformed into an angel.

"It's you," she said, her voice laced with a warm tinge of some accent that he couldn't place.

Then he registered what she said, and he shuttered himself. "Who are you?"

"Madelynne Broussard. Call me Lynne." She smiled even brighter. "You're here for Abby. She went to the store, but she'll be back soon. Come in."

She wheeled her chair backwards in an awkward manner that told him whatever reason she was in a wheelchair was a recent development. Shoving his hands in his pockets as they started to shake, he stopped himself from any further assessment.

"Are you going to introduce yourself or should I pretend I don't know who you are?" she asked with a teasing glance.

"Finn."

"Nice to meet you, Finn. Finn and Lynne. We're like the start of a limerick." Turning around slowly, she headed toward the kitchen. "Tea?"

He watched as she rolled into the kitchen to a station that looked designed to accommodate her disability and took out cups and the like for tea. Seeing the kettle, he picked it up and filled it with water for her so she wouldn't have to strain to reach the faucet.

"Thank you," she said with another brilliant smile.

He couldn't help returning his own, probably dimmed, version. "Is that your secret weapon?"

"What?"

"Your smile."

She blinked and then laughed. "Oh, I like you."

It seemed like she was about to say something more, but the kettle signaled that the water was hot. She shook her head again. "We'll take the tea into the other room and talk, okay?"

"I'll do this," he said, picking up the kettle and pouring the water into the cups.

They worked in silence that was oddly companionable, and he carried the tray of tea and nuts into the living area.

"Abby set up a sitting spot by the window," Lynne said as she wheeled her chair to a space that was obviously left open for her. "On good days, we can watch the surfers out there. I think she hoped I'd be encouraged by them."

"Do you surf?" he asked, setting the tray on the table next to her.

She laughed, a brittle sort of sound, waving at her legs. "In case you missed it, I can't walk."

"That doesn't mean you can't surf." He offered her a cup. "In fact, a lot of people with decreased mobility find swimming and water sports conducive to restoring some of the lost range of movement."

She raised her brow. "Is that your professional opinion?"

"What happened?" he heard himself ask. Knowing what happened didn't mean he had to do something about it.

"It was a random thing. My boyfriend got upset and in our, uh, argument, I tripped down the stairs in our apartment." She glanced away, occupying herself with serving him tea.

She wasn't being completely forthcoming. He recognized the signs: the way she averted her gaze, the hesitation in her speech, the tightening around her mouth. He'd witnessed it in enough patients over time to know there was some domestic abuse involved here.

Men like that should be castrated. But he kept his temper and his opinions to himself. Lynne was the important one at the moment. "That must have been terrifying," he said, accepting the teacup.

"I just..." She clutched the black stone around her neck, her expression worried. "Abby got caught in the middle. She shouldn't have been hurt."

"Where is he now?"

"I don't know. He left while I was in the hospital." She gave him a self-deprecating look. "He's obviously my ex now."

"Obviously," he said, feeling his lip quirk despite the severity of the situation.

She rubbed her thigh above the brace. "It broke in three places and I tore a bunch of ligaments."

That bastard ex deserved to be strung up. He heard stories like this all the time, or stories of senseless accidents like Fiona's, that left an innocent person debilitated, or worse, but he'd never gotten used to it. He doubted he ever would. "Can you use crutches?"

"It's easier to get around in this baby." She patted the wheelchair. Then her expression dimmed, and she gave him a stark look. "I was a dancer, you know."

He nodded, keeping his face impassive despite the emotions inside. "And your prognosis?"

"They said I was lucky it wasn't worse." She ran a hand over the green blanket, rubbing her thigh. Then she seemed to shake it off, sipping a bit of her tea. "I'm more worried about Abby."

He wanted to wring that bastard's neck all over again for putting his hands on this woman and Abigail. "How long ago did this happen?"

"Six months, but she keeps reinjuring her wrist trying to take care of me." She studied him steadily. "You know she's a healer."

The wariness came back a thousandfold. "Like a doctor?"

Lynne shook her head. "Like a healer. She comes from a long line of psychics from New Orleans."

He cocked a brow. "Voodoo?"

"No, they stayed away from dark arts."

He stared at her incredulously. She had to be putting him on. But her expression remained candid and clear, and he could see she believed what she said. "You're serious about that."

"Of course I am."

"I don't believe in psychics or any of that."

She tipped her head. "Aren't you Irish?"

"Yes."

"And you don't believe in fairies?"

"I'm a grown man." He'd stopped believing in shite like fate and magic the day he found Fiona. Then medical school had driven out any last vestiges.

"Even grown men need to believe in magic. Otherwise, where's the enchantment in life?"

"You believe in magic?" he asked, leaning forward.

"Yes."

"Yet you don't think you'll ever dance again?"

She looked stricken, and he cursed himself for it. Then she smiled sadly. "Touché."

"That was uncalled for." He grimaced at his own cruelty. "My mother would have my head. I apologize."

"Don't apologize for telling the truth." She sat forward too. "I'll make you a deal. I'll believe in more magic if you do too."

He shook his head. "I can't make that promise."

"Not even to help me?"

"I wouldn't lie to you like that."

Lynne smiled brilliantly again. "You really are perfect for her. How about if we both try to believe in more magic? You be open to possibilities, and I will too."

He considered her and then nodded, holding his right hand out. "Deal."

As she shook his hand the front door opened. They both looked up to find Abigail with two grocery bags, gaping at them.

15

The last thing Abby expected to see when she got home was Lynne and Finn having tea like two old friends.

She knew she stood gawking at them, but she honestly had no idea how to react. The first thought was confusion—what was he doing here?

Her second: happiness. She told herself it was because it'd been so long since she'd seen Lynne connecting with anyone, but seeing the two of them so obviously enjoying each other melted a barrier around her heart. It made her feel hope.

She stared at Finn, gratitude for him filling her chest.

She cleared the emotion from her throat twice before she could speak. "Are we having a party?"

Lynne laughed, like the way she used to, and Abby felt the threat of tears at the tip of her nose. Rubbing her nose to stop them, she glanced at Finn, who let go of Lynne's hand and stood like a gentleman. He really was a miracle worker.

"I was entertaining Finn until you got back," Lynne said with a knowing smile. "Pour yourself a drink and come sit down."

"Is it too early for whiskey?" she muttered.

Lynne laughed again.

"You shouldn't be carrying those with your wrist." Finn took the bags from her and headed to the kitchen.

"I can handle it," she said as rushed after him into the kitchen.

He set the groceries on the counter and turned on her, arms crossed.

She put her hands on her hips. "Why are you looking at me like *I* did something?" she asked in a low voice.

"You're going to hurt yourself worse," he replied in an equally quiet tone. He lowered his gaze to her wrist.

She watched his struggle, the way she had the night he'd brought her home, and she had the compulsion to hide it behind her back. She didn't want to be the cause of that; she didn't want to be another reason his soul lost color, adding to its lackluster.

He reached out and took her hand.

"What are you doing?" She tried to pull it away.

He held it gently but firmly. "Stay still or you'll aggravate it."

She watched as he unstrapped the brace and set it on the counter. He surveyed it, looking at the sickly green discoloration that wouldn't fade. Then he brushed over her skin with a slightly shaking hand.

She shivered, her skin rising in goose bumps with the caress.

It wasn't a caress.

She repeated that to herself another couple times, more forcibly, to drive it home.

"Lynne said this happened six months ago. It shouldn't be this swollen still," he said, a frown furrowing his brow.

She had a lot of anger at herself trapped in there. "The first time I injured it was six months ago."

"The first time?" He looked into her eyes.

"I overused it to the point where it got really messed up. That's a direct translation from my doctor."

Humor lit his eyes.

Good Lord, the color of his eyes. She lowered her gaze so they wouldn't distract her and saw his still-shaking hand. Nerves, she thought, wanting to gather him in her arms and tell him it'd be okay—wanting to heal all his hurts, emotional or otherwise.

She cleared the longing to help him from her throat. Lynne was her first priority. "I'm more concerned about Lynne's leg. Since you're on sabbatical, maybe you can give me the name of another doctor who can help."

"Lynne said you're a healer," he said.

She stilled abruptly. She couldn't tell what he thought of that by the tone of his voice. "You don't believe in that sort of thing."

"No, I don't," he replied simply. "But I do wonder if you're a healer why you haven't healed this. And Lynne's leg."

She swallowed thickly. "Did she tell you how me trying to heal her in the first place caused this whole situation?"

"No." His gaze sharpened on her, and he cradled her arm closer to his body.

"I heal through my paintings." Why was she telling him this? He was a skeptic. "Basically, I see a scene from a past life where things broke and fix it by painting the highest version of the person in that moment, empowered and moving from a place of self."

"Explain that to me."

She studied him, wondering if he meant it. She'd had plenty of people ask her about what she did, only to tell her she was full of shit.

But he watched her with interest. Even though she knew him to be skeptical, he felt open.

So she said, "Karma marks people when things go wrong or you make an ill-advised choice. It's like a wound or scar on your soul. Sometimes it shows up physically, like with a birthmark or a chronic illness. Sometimes it's more ethereal and gets imprinted on the person's soul itself. I see moments in people's past lives where karma left a wound or scar, and I heal it. I paint the best possible outcome of that past life moment."

"And how does that affect the person now?"

She'd expected him to sound doubtful, but his tone was just neutral. Her shoulders relaxed—she hadn't realized how tense she was. "It removes the energetic and physical obstacles in their way. For instance, my mother was prone to getting pneumonia and after I did a painting for her, she never got it again. She'd experienced a deep grief in another lifetime, and those tears manifested themselves as water in her lungs in this life."

He stared at her steadily. "You said that you trying to heal Lynne caused this situation. How is that?"

She swallowed again. If she told him, would he think badly of her? She usually didn't care what anyone thought of her—you couldn't be a successful artist and stay sane if you cared what people thought—but for some reason his good opinion mattered. "She asked for a painting to help her with her career, and it went horribly wrong. I don't know what happened. When I delivered it, Kevin, the guy she lived with, went postal. I had to have painted the wrong thing."

"Are you sure?" Finn asked.

She blinked in surprise.

Listen to him, kid, she heard Bro Paul say from a distance.

She shook her head. "What else could it have been? What I painted triggered the violent reaction from Kevin."

Finn opened his mouth and closed it. Then, after a pause, he said, "You're assuming that your painting caused the violence. How well did you know Kevin before?"

"I'd only met him that day, but Lynne seemed happy enough with him." She frowned. "You think Kevin was already abusive."

He shrugged. "It's difficult to see into someone else's relationship."

But this was Lynne. Lynne was her best friend—Lynne would tell her if something was wrong. Still, Abby could tell Finn measured his words carefully, and there was the historical evidence that Lynne dated a lot of assholes.

Like I said, listen to him, kid, her guide said. *He's onto something. But so are you. What about the scene was different than your usual work? You had your finger on it before.*

She'd painted herself into the scene. *Is that it?*

Bingo. Way to go, Abs. He applauded, his meaty hands making a loud clap that made her wince from the vibration. *Now you just need to understand why that didn't reap what you wanted it to.*

"Abby?"

She looked up at Finn and blinked to ground herself in the kitchen again. "What?"

"Are you okay?" He touched her temple. "Where did you go?"

She bit her lip. On top of everything she'd just told him, the last thing she needed to add was that she was talking to her invisible sidekick, the Franciscan monk with a fetish for modern vernacular. Finn would skip giving her an orthopedic referral and recommend her to the loony bin. "I was just thinking."

He studied her for a long moment, silently gauging. She felt the energy around her heart start to pulse harder with every passing second, reaching out to him. To her, it looked like silky ribbons of pink and green wrapping around him loosely, offering but not binding.

A flash of that scene she saw when she first met him in the pub lit in her mind. The longing to make that scene right was a deep ache in her chest. Her fingers twitched as though they wanted to close on a paintbrush.

She thought about all the boxes in the other room and she felt the colors of her heart fade with the futility of it.

Except his heart energy surged, strong, offering too. The colors of their energies mixed, the ribbons becoming the most beautiful, the most complex palette ranging from passion's red to love's pink and green's healing.

She watched the byplay in amazement. She'd never seen such a thing. She had to paint it—once her wrist healed.

His brow furrowed. As if reading her mind, he said, "Since your wrist is hurt, you wouldn't be able to paint, which means you can't heal anyone. Lynne or yourself."

Or him. "I feel like my wrist is tied to her injury. Lynne healing means I'll heal." She was positive of that.

He searched her eyes. "We're a pair, aren't we?" he murmured almost to himself. "Both feeling responsible for other people's choices."

She put her good hand on his chest. "You didn't cause that man to die, Finn."

He flinched as if she'd struck him. "And you caused Lynne's bastard ex to break her leg?" he asked in a low, harsh voice.

It was her turn to flinch, but something about what he said niggled her.

"That was uncalled for. I don't mean to tell you your business, Abby." He ran a soothing hand over the back of her hand, feeling around the swelling with the lightest touch. His hand, though still shaking a bit, felt warm and comforting.

"How much groceries did you get? It didn't look like

that much from the bags," Lynne said from the other room.

They jumped, both looking to the doorway as if about to get caught. Then they looked at each other again.

"I love her," Abby whispered. "I can't stand to think that because of me she won't be able to dance again. But I'm at my wit's end about what to do, because the doctors in New York couldn't explain why her leg isn't improving after treatment."

His swallow was audible. "I'll make you a deal. I'll look into Lynne's case if you let me help you. If I can't help Lynne, I'll help you find someone who can."

Abby wilted against his chest in relief, her third eye against his heart. "Thank you."

He stiffened.

Realizing that she was pressed against him, she froze. She lifted her head cautiously, knowing she should back off, but oddly reluctantly. One: he smelled good. Two: he felt *good*.

His gaze dropped to her lips, which parted on their own accord. His head lowered a little before he stopped. He searched her again before he pulled back.

Abby blinked a few times, trying to remember where she was.

"It's awfully quiet in there," Lynne teased from the other room.

Finn shook his head like he was trying to clear it, letting go of her reluctantly.

"Elevate your wrist tonight," he ordered. The doctor in him changed his entire bearing, making him no less caring but completely in charge. He picked up the brace and began tenderly rewrapping her wrist. "Do you have ice?"

"Yes." She'd bought a small freezable bag the first day they'd arrived. The cold soothed the heat in Lynne's leg.

"Put ice on it to help the swelling. Twenty minutes on, twice a day if you can do it." He gave her a look that brooked no argument as he checked the brace to make sure it wasn't too tight. "No carrying anything with it. If you need help, you call me. Promise."

She nodded, surprised by a surge of emotion. No one had wanted to take care of her like that since her mom, and she'd died twenty-seven years ago. "I promise."

"Tomorrow, text me her doctors' information. I'll ask them for her medical records. She'll need to authorize that."

"I'll take care of it," Abby promised, feeling her heart lift.

"Good." He nodded. With a last touch to her hand where the brace exposed her skin, he left the kitchen.

Abby drooped against the counter, listening to the low rumble of his voice as he talked to Lynne. Lynne replied, just as indistinct, like they didn't want her to hear. A moment later, she heard the front door open and close.

He was going to help them somehow.

He'd almost kissed her.

She put a hand to her forehead.

"He's gone," Lynne called out. "You can stop hiding now."

"I wasn't hiding," she said, joining Lynne.

Lynne wheeled her chair around to face her. "Did you even put the groceries away?"

"Oh shit." Abby rushed back into the kitchen, followed by Lynne's laughter.

She paused a moment, letting the bright sound surround her. She sent Finn a blessing, grateful for whatever magic he'd worked on her.

As she put the food away, Lynne rolled into the kitchen doorway. "So..."

She glanced at her friend. "So?"

"So, how do you feel?"

Closing the fridge, she stopped and checked in with herself. "I feel good," she said with a little surprise. Even her wrist didn't hurt as much as it had earlier.

"You should. It's not every day your soulmate just walks in the door."

"Ha." She opened a cupboard and put away a jar of honey. "He's hardly my soulmate."

"I may not have the gifts you have, but I can see what's in front of my eyes." Lynne made a face. "Wake up and smell the Guinness, babe."

She made a face back. "He's just a nice man who can help us, Lynne."

"He's a nice man who can help us, who is hot. He also cares about you a lot and you've barely met." Lynne held up a finger. "And he's *hung*, by the way."

Yeah, she'd had a sense of that when they were pressed against each other. "I don't know that he's my soulmate," Abby repeated.

"You would if you tuned in." Lynne folded her arms, her cheeks flushed rosy, looking more alive than she had since the attack. "Don't be stubborn about this. The Universe is handing you a love buffet on a platter. What if this is why we came to Ireland?"

"We came to find Finn so he could help your leg heal."

"No, we came so we could *both* heal, so that we could *both* go back to living our life's purpose. Don't piss me off. I'll run you down with my wheels."

Abby chuckled.

Lynne pointed at her. "I'm warning you now, Abigail, as your best friend and the only family you have, I will do everything in my power to make sure you don't fuck this up."

"Duly noted." She leaned down and kissed the top of Lynne's head. "You know I love you?"

"That's the only good sense you've shown today." Shaking her head, she wheeled out of the kitchen mumbling to herself.

16

While Lynne was taking a nap after a particularly brutal PT session, Abby had called and arranged for Finn to have access to Lynne's medical records.

She stood at the window and watched the gentle roll of the waves. The ocean was a deep blue today, as if reflecting the heavens.

It finally felt like things were going in the right direction.

She heard something outside the cottage door. Bro Paul wouldn't have encouraged Marjorie to send another care package, would he? Abby hurried to see so whoever was out there wouldn't wake Lynne up.

The little girl from next door, Claire, was on the threshold, leaning over. She looked up with her big eyes, a few pages of construction paper tied into a package with yarn in her hands. "I made this for you. My mom said to leave it here, because then it'd be like a gift from the fairies."

"That's very sweet. Thank you." Abby took it, seeing the pride on Claire's face. "Do you want to come in and have some juice?"

"Okay." Claire slipped past her before she could say anything. Inside the door, she toed off her shoes and went straight to the dining table. After a brief struggle to pull out a chair, she started to climb onto it. Setting Claire's gift on the table, Abby watched to make sure she didn't topple it on herself before going to fetch the refreshments.

When she came out with a tray of beverages and cookies, or biscuits as they called them in Ireland, she found Claire kneeling on the chair, looking into the box of paints that she'd left on the table. The girl looked up, guilt written all over her face when she felt Abby's stare. "It was open," she said like she was often caught in things she wasn't supposed to touch.

"It's okay." She smiled gently, setting the tray on the table with a little wobble. "It's just my paint."

"The whole box?" Claire asked, her eyes wide.

She sat on the chair next to her. "Do you like to paint?"

Claire nodded. "But I only have crayons right now, because my mom says paint is expensive."

Abby glanced at the box of colors. She might not be able to use them now, but that didn't mean that Claire couldn't. "If your mom says it's okay, you can come over and paint here."

"That's an excellent idea," she heard Lynne say from across the room.

She turned around as Lynne rolled into the living

area. Her friend looked not quite like herself, like the grayness she'd taken on since the accident was off-center, pushed over somehow.

But Lynne was smiling as she wheeled herself into the room, so maybe Abby was just being overly watchful.

Lynne pulled up to the end of the table where Abby had taken away a chair so she fit her wheelchair comfortably and set her phone on the tabletop. "I didn't know we were having company for tea."

"This is Claire. She lives next door. Her mom made us the soda bread."

"Why are you in that chair?" Claire asked Lynne.

Lynne's face went blank for a second, and then she smiled, albeit sadly. "I had an accident."

The thoughts were visibly churning in Claire's mind. Finally, the little girl picked up a cookie and asked, "Can I ride on one too?"

"Tell you what," Lynne said, also taking a cookie, "when you come to paint with Abby, I'll give you a spin on my fancy wheels."

Abby could have grabbed the little girl and hugged her.

"Okay," the little girl said, rocking excitedly in her chair.

Lynne's phone dinged with a text.

When Lynne didn't pick it up, Abby nodded at it. "I think you got a text."

"It's just Dermot."

"Dermot?" Abby asked in surprise.

"I texted him to thank him for his help. We've just been talking," her friend said, blushing.

Abby gaped. "Talking?"

"It's not a big deal. We're just chatting. It's nice to make new friends, and since he's Finn's best friend I thought I should make an effort," Lynne said, her voice lowered. "That's all there is to it, Abby. Don't make it out to be more."

Before Abby could say anything, Lynne picked up the construction paper gift and faced Claire. "What's this?"

"I made it for Abby." Claire smiled, pointing to it. "I wrapped it too."

"Abby always waits to open presents, so she can savor it." Lynne handed it over. "Why don't you open it?"

She gave Lynne a look to let her know she wasn't off the hook, but then she played along. As she pulled the string to untie it, Claire and Lynne edged closer. Abby set it on the table so everyone could see, and then she flipped it open like a book.

The drawing was on lined notebook paper. It took up most of the page: a big man holding a little girl's hand. The little girl, with red curls sticking straight out of her head and wearing a yellow dress, was obviously Claire.

The big man wore a dress too. It was brown and long, and he only had hair around his ears. His hands were proportionally huge and he had a large smile on his face.

Even in a child's stick figure drawing, Bro Paul was unmistakable.

Heart racing, Abby faced Claire. "Why did you draw this man?"

"Because he's my friend," she said simply, taking another cookie. "He said he's your friend too."

"Holy cow," Lynne said under her breath.

Abby exchanged a look with her friend. She set that drawing aside and then flipped over the next page.

Same lined paper, same sort of stick drawing. This time, there was only one person on the page: a woman. She had long blond hair and a sunny smile; her eyes were round green disks. She wore blue, and she had a necklace dangling from her neck with a big black stone. Around her shoulders was an open scarf in all the colors.

Like the scarf Lynne had on right now.

Lynne gasped, leaning forward to look closer.

Then Abby noticed it too: Lynne was standing on her two feet, a thing that looked like a brace discarded on the ground.

17

"What do you think it means?" Lynne asked the moment the little girl went home. She sat in front of the window, but instead of watching the surf, she stared at Claire's portrait of her. She hadn't let go of it since she'd seen it. "We should ask Bro Paul. Call him."

Before Abby could form a sentence, her guide appeared before her, looking pleased with himself. "You rang?"

"No, Lynne rang."

He shrugged. "To-may-to, to-mah-to. What do you need, kid?"

She pointed at Claire's gift. "I needed more confirmation?" Abby asked, barely daring to hope that the picture of Lynne walking meant what it showed.

"Yeah. You've got a lot of doubts. And who can discount a kid? Especially one with mad gifts like that one." He leaned over the page, studying it. "I think she did me justice."

"Claire has gifts?" Abby repeated. "She's so young."

"The same age you were when you healed your first person," Bro Paul pointed out. "Age has nothing to do with being open to your Divine gifts. Sometimes youth is a blessing, because things come easier when you're less jaded and think you know better." He raised his brows. "Ahem."

Abby ignored the obvious dig.

Bro Paul just kept talking anyway, as he often did. "The only other kid I've ever met to rival that cutie is you. And of course, Lynne."

"Lynne?" Abby gaped at him.

"What?" Lynne asked, rubbing her ear.

He waved at Lynne, though she didn't react because she didn't see him. Stopping, he shrugged. "What she closed down as a kid is about to open up, big-time. It's going to be a thing of beauty. Unless she fights it." He shrugged again.

"What?" her best friend asked again. "You're talking to Bro Paul, right? Did you ask him about Claire's drawing?"

He walked over to Lynne, bent down, and yelled in her direction. "Abby hasn't asked me jack shit yet." He gave Abby a thumbs-up over his shoulder before turning his attention back to Lynne. "Stick with me, kid. We're going to do great things."

Wincing, Lynne rubbed her ear harder. "I wish the ringing in my ear would stop. Maybe I'm losing my hearing?"

"More like it's tuning up," Bro Paul said, even though Lynne obviously couldn't hear him.

Her guide turned back to her. "Finn hit it on the head.

Talk to Lynne about Kevin. And you're going to want to remember that scene you saw when you met Finn. You remember it, right?"

The old version of Finn, standing over the graves, his heart broken, his doctor's bag discarded at his feet? "How could I forget that?"

"Trust me. You're going to want to work on healing what happened there."

"How?" She held up her wrist, brace and all. "I can't paint."

He snorted. "Yeah, you can. You have a left hand. Use it."

She frowned. "I can't paint with my left hand."

"Sure you can. It just won't be what you're used to, but what does that matter when it means you get to heal the man who can help Lynne." Then he winked at her. "Brace yourself, Abs. It's about to get real interesting."

Abby swallowed nervously. "Why does that worry me?"

He laughed, holding his big belly as he disappeared.

"He's gone, right? What did he say, Abby?" Lynne asked, angling her wheelchair to face her.

She shook her head, which was spinning. "I really couldn't say."

Lynne looked back down at the drawing in her hand. "Then what do you think it means?" she asked hesitantly, as if afraid to hope for the best.

"That you're going to walk unaided again." Abby didn't have to be psychic to know what was in Lynne's head. So she said, "And if you can walk like that again, you'll dance again. Finn agreed to help, so it's a done deal."

Her best friend didn't say anything for a long time, just staring at the picture.

Abby cleared her throat, trying to think of a gentle way to bring up Kevin. She knew Lynne was upset about him leaving after the accident. She didn't want to dredge up anything that'd make Lynne feel more upset than she was, but Bro Paul had also said she should ask about Kevin.

Before she could ask, a text pinged on Abby's phone on the table between them.

Lynne glanced at it and held it out for her. "Finn," she said in surprise and delight.

Abby grabbed the phone and swiped to read the text.

How is Lynne? How's your wrist?

She blinked.

"Well?" Lynne asked, rolling closer so she could see the screen. "Don't keep me in suspense!"

"He asked about you. And about my wrist."

Lynne smiled softly. "Of course he did. Write back and tell him he should kiss it to make it better."

Abby ignored her.

Lynne is hanging in there. I'm good. Less swelling. You have a magic touch.

His reply was immediate:

You've been good? Resting it?

"Tell him that you've been very good, but you can't wait to be bad," Lynne suggested.

Before Abby could answer, he added:

I have something for you. Meet me at Hairy's? I'll update you on my progress with Lynne's records then.

She didn't even have to think about it.

What time?

He told her he'd meet her there in an hour. The ellipses popped up after that text, and she waited to see what he was going to say, but in the end nothing else came through.

"Oh my God, we have only an hour," Lynne exclaimed, turning her wheelchair around.

Abby set her phone down. "What are you doing?"

"Helping you pick out underwear for your date," she said, the *duh* implied.

"It's not a date," she said, following the retreating wheelchair.

Lynne was already in the open door of Abby's closet, rifling through the hangers. "You're meeting a hot man for a drink. It's a date. Wear this." She passed a skirt over her shoulder.

It was one of Abby's favorites, pink and green patterned patches, shot through with shimmery gold thread. "I'm going to the pub."

"That doesn't mean you have to look like a slob." Lynne grabbed a dark-rose sweater and tossed it on the bed. "Get whatever color T-shirt you want. And your favorite underwear set, the one with pink lace."

"He's not going to see my underwear," she mumbled as she began to get undressed. If it weren't for the fact that Lynne was so engaged and animated, she'd have protested. But if wearing pretty underwear and letting Lynne believe that there was a chance Finn might see it made her happy, she was rolling with it.

She paused, thinking about Finn seeing her panties, and flushed a red so deep she bet it was darker than alizarin crimson.

All dressed, she turned around to find Lynne holding out a pair of heels.

"No way." Abby shook her head. "I'm walking to the pub. Also, if I wear heels in Tullaghan, I'll stand out more than I already do."

Lynne sighed. "Fine. Wear your boots then, the ones with the blue embroidery."

"It's teal and green," she corrected, going into the closet to find them.

She let Lynne fuss with her makeup and hair for another ten minutes. Finally, her best friend sat back and looked over her with a critical eye. "That'll do."

Abby rolled her eyes. "Thanks for the vote of confidence."

"Get going." Lynne moved out of the way. "You'll be late."

Putting on the sweater, Abby frowned at her. "Will you be okay till I get back?"

"Of course." She waved her hand. "Don't worry about me. I'm good watching the surfers on the waves."

Abby leaned down for a hug and then rushed out the door, excitement propelling her—and not just because she thought Finn might have a solution for helping Lynne.

Outside, Claire was running around, and Sarah was tending a profusion of lilies, marigolds, and roses in the yard. They both looked up and smiled at her.

Abby paused, studying the little girl's soul with fresh eyes. She saw what she'd missed the first time: bands of blue ringing around it. She often saw blue in the souls of people who had gifts.

Claire's blue was so light and crystalline, so pure, that it was barely distinguishable from the iridescent gold of her innocent soul. The blue was in stark contrast to the bit of tarnishing that had already started to happen at the edges of her soul.

Claire ran over and tugged on her skirt. "You look nice, Abby. Do you have a date? My mom doesn't ever have dates, but she said I can when I'm thirty. That's far away though, because I'm only six."

"It'll be closer than you realize," Abby said, brushing her good hand over Claire's flyaway hair.

Sarah sat back, clippers in her gloved hands. "You do look nice, Abigail."

"I'm just meeting a friend at the pub."

Claire began jumping up and down. "Mom, can we go too? Then we can see Niall."

Sarah flushed a delicate pink. "Not today, love. We'll go another time."

"And see Niall?" Claire asked enthusiastically. She turned to Abby. "Niall showed me how to pour beer."

"You've got all sorts of skills, don't you?" Thinking about the drawing, Abby had a sudden inspiration. She turned to Sarah. "I invited Claire to come paint sometime. I hope that's okay."

"Oh." Sarah blinked in surprise. "I wouldn't want her to bother you."

"It's no bother." She felt like it might even be good for her. She thought back to when *she* was six and how painting with her gifts had been filled with joy, not doubts. Maybe Claire could help her remember that. Or maybe Claire might inadvertently give her a clue how to heal without painting.

"Please, Mom!" Claire said, jumping up and down.

Sarah smiled indulgently. "Okay, love. We'll arrange a time."

"I'm going to paint," the little girl yelled, running around the yard with her arms out.

"Thank you," Sarah said, watching her daughter with love in her eyes. She faced Abby. "It hasn't been easy for her since we moved here, because her friends from school aren't close by and I've been so busy with work."

"What do you do?"

"Web design." Sarah gestured to the bed she was pruning. "I have a design I'm stuck on and gardening always helps me figure it out."

"The grounding." Abby nodded. She looked around the entire yard, taking it in with renewed appreciation. Evidence of Sarah's garden magic was everywhere. It made her fingers itch for some watercolors. "Your garden is beautiful."

"I've only been back a few weeks, but I've been trying. Wait a minute." She clipped a couple purple-blue hydrangea poofs and held them out. "A thanks for letting Claire come paint with you."

She took the proffered blooms. They were so cheery —Lynne would love them. "Thank you," she said sincerely.

"They say hydrangeas are a flower of mourning, or for 'persevering' love, but I've never believed that." Sarah touched the petals gently, her gaze longing. "As the story goes, a German doctor brought them back from Japan after he was kicked out of the country, and he named them after the woman he left behind. Because of that, I think their meaning is 'hope,' because you don't tend something so carefully unless you believe it's going to give back to you."

"You know a lot about flowers?" Abby asked.

She smiled. "My gran taught me. Like your rose bushes."

Abby looked to where Sarah pointed.

"Irish roses bloom every year with the hope to attract love," she explained. "It's the eternal hope of the Irish, that as long as the wild roses bloom, love is possible."

Abby looked at the neglected rose bush. There still wasn't a bloom in sight. She thought about that past life scene she saw with Finn and hugged herself. "I'm doomed, aren't I?"

Sarah laughed, not hearing the grain of truth in

Abby's grim joke. "They just need some attention. And, barring that, there are always miracles."

She thought about Finn and flushed.

Knowing she was running late, she gave the hydrangeas to Lynne to put in water and hurried to the pub. She'd walked for about ten minutes when Finn's SUV pulled up next to her. He lowered the window and said, "Get in."

She felt a tingle of anticipation when she opened the door. "I understand it's customary to offer candy."

He gave her a flat look as he waited for her to buckle up and then roared down the lane. His car hugged the road nicely, and she found herself relaxing into the ride.

She didn't say anything until they passed the turn that went to Hairy's. "I thought we were going to the pub?"

"We were, but then I decided I wanted to talk to you, and what I have to say requires privacy." He kept his eyes on the road, his jaw determined.

That sounded ominous. She worried the edge of her wrist brace, wondering what he could want to say to her. That he couldn't help Lynne? That no one could? What else could it be to warrant such bleakness?

He didn't say anything more until he pulled off the road onto a small patch of dirt. "We're here."

She wasn't sure where "here" was. High, uncut grass, a crumbling stone wall... Thank God she hadn't worn the heels.

"Let's walk," he said after they got out. He put his hand on her back to direct her to a path she hadn't seen.

As she let him guide her, she realized that she trusted

him—implicitly. Of course, from the moment she'd read about him online she'd felt she could trust him with Lynne—that was a no-brainer—but it hadn't occurred to her to trust him with *her*.

It rendered her momentarily mute.

"My twin sister killed herself after the doctors told her she was going to be paralyzed the rest of her life."

Her heart clutched. "You had a sister?"

He nodded. "She died when we were eighteen. I watched her go from a bright young woman excited to start life to a withered girl with nothing to live for."

She gripped his arm, knowing exactly how anguished he had felt. "That's why you became a surgeon. That's why you became the Miracle Worker."

He stopped in the middle of the path, the tall grass swaying around them, her hand still on his arm. He towered over her, eclipsing the sunlight, his expression as stark and grayed as the shadows he cast. "What happened three weeks ago in Dublin reminded me of Fiona, my sister. He'd fallen into the same sort of depression that she had and had taken the same way out. That's why I took a sabbatical. The hospital encouraged it to let the press die down, but I took it because I can't do surgery. Because every time I see a patient, I'd remember finding Fiona, I'd see Jaime Walsh again, and my hands start to shake." He held them out to her.

Her heart broke seeing them tremble. She heard that voice from the scene of his past life whisper *my fault* again, and she shivered. She took one of them in her good hand.

"Do you understand what I'm saying?" He looked at her

like he was willing her to understand. "Even if I can get myself back to a calm state, there's Lynne's emotional fitness. The road to recovery isn't easy. It requires mental fortitude. Lynne shows signs of depression, and I don't know that she'll be able to stand up to more treatment, much less more disappointment. It's been weighing on my mind. I can't chance that I'm pushing her to a breaking point."

"Not getting treatment will guarantee that she's depressed, though." She was tempted to reach up and brush her fingers over his third eye to ease the stress there. She knew in the pit of her stomach that the key here was that past life scene. Something in that time had gone wrong that had caused her death and that of their child's, and he carried the blame of that forward. He needed to reclaim his power there.

Maybe, if she got her wrist healed well enough to hold a brush, she could paint herself out of the picture. That'd fix it.

Her heart clutched at the thought of editing herself out of his life. She shook her head, not sure how she could care so much for someone she'd just met. But if it meant Lynne would be okay again, and so would he...

She felt his hand in her hair, and she looked up from her dark thoughts.

His hand tightened, drawing her head back a bit more. The grief was gone, replaced by a longing that made her breathless. Was he going to kiss her? Her lips parted on a silent exhale, and a sharp zap of desire shot through her body.

Though *zap* hardly qualified to describe what went

through her body. It'd been a long time since she'd had sex with anyone—a *really* long time—and what shot through her felt like a mini-orgasm. If him just tugging on her hair was that good, what would a kiss feel like?

She didn't have long to wonder.

He lowered his mouth so it hovered a breath away from hers. He touched his nose to hers. When she tilted her head to find his lips, he kept his mouth just out of reach. She protested with a soft gasp.

"Since I'm considering being Lynne's physician, I'm not certain this is a good idea," he said softly.

She felt his words caress her skin, and she moaned. "What?"

"This." He pulled her body closer so she could feel his excitement between them.

Lynne was right: *hung.* She pressed herself closer, just to make sure. "It feels like a pretty good idea."

"Doesn't it?" His hand swept down her back, and then he took a step back.

She shivered, not from the air for a change but from unrequited need. She took a few breaths and smoothing her hair, tried to gather herself.

Finn took a few steps back and forth as if he were trying to walk it off. Finally, he raked his hair back and faced her. "That was—"

"Unexpected," she finished for him.

"No." He frowned. "I knew once I had my hands on you I wouldn't want to let go. But I hadn't accounted for this in my life right now."

Who had? She nodded because she understood.

Without another word, she turned and led the way back to the car.

The drive back to her cottage was silent, but not uncomfortable—except for the desperate tingling in her girly parts. He pulled up to the house, not turning the car off, and faced her.

She waited for him to say something—to do something.

"I got this for you." He reached into the back seat and grabbed a small bag. Opening it, he held out a tube. "This is arnica for the bruising on your wrist. Use it according to the directions. You should notice a difference right away."

Blinking in surprise, she took the tube, holding it to her chest.

He took out another item. It was some sort of bandage.

"Use this instead of that brace. It just slips on." He showed her on himself before handing it to her. "It'll isolate better but still promote circulation."

She touched the material. It felt cool and silky thin, but still strong. "I haven't seen anything like this."

"That's because I worked with the engineering department at my university to design it."

"You happened to have one lying around?" she asked, blown away.

"Something like that." He sat back. "Lynne's doctors in New York faxed her records to my office. I should have them in a couple days. I ordered a different brace and some other things sent from Dublin for her too, but that'll be a few days as well."

She stared at him helplessly. "Really?"

"Don't make me into a hero, Abby," he said, his voice low and hoarse. "I'm just doing what anyone would."

She didn't think so, but she knew she wouldn't be able to convince him of that, so she pressed a kiss to his lips before she got out of his car, hoping to leave a promise of hope along with the pink of her lip color, all to remind him of her.

18

Finn's mom set a full breakfast in front of him, eyeing his mug. "Put that aside and eat."

His dad grinned, but he hid his mirth by pretending to focus on his breakfast the moment his wife turned toward him.

"Don't think I don't know what you're about, Conall Fionnlagh," she warned, her hands on her hips.

"Of course not, love," his dad said in false meekness.

She swatted Conall's shoulder and then soothed her hand over it lovingly.

It reminded Finn of the way Abby had soothed him when he'd told her about Fiona, as if she was willing to heal his hurt with her heart.

Heal his hurt with her heart. He frowned at the fanciful thought that was so unlike him. But he was acting in all kinds of surprising ways, like thinking about Lynne's case.

Like kissing Abby.

But it was more than that—he'd almost laid her down

in the field and taken her. He hadn't had that sort of urge since secondary. After Fiona died and he'd gotten over the grief, he'd been focused on becoming a doctor, so while he had women in university and after, his career had always been more important. He was no monk, but he never submitted to physical whims like he'd felt yesterday.

It'd shocked him to feel it. He didn't know how he felt about it.

"What are you going to get up to today, Carrick?" his mom asked, setting her plate on the table and sitting down.

"Maybe you can come help me in the fields," his dad said in that hopeful tone he'd had since Finn had come home.

He set his fork down, steepling his hands. "I know you've both been worried about me. I'm sorry I caused that."

His parents blinked at him like they were trying to figure out a way to deny it.

"I'm fine. I'm going to be fine." He didn't know how, but he was going to make sure of it. For the first time since Jaime's death, he felt like there was light at the end of the tunnel. "So you both need to step back."

His mother frowned. "Carrick—"

"Molly." His dad put his hand on her arm. "Our son is a grown man. He knows his own mind because we reared him that way. Let him be."

Finn knew his mom wanted to say something, but she and his dad exchanged one of their looks and she just nodded.

His phone buzzed with a text. His mom had a strict no phones at the table rule, which she amended when he was on call, but since he was on sabbatical, he was happy to cede to her rule.

After breakfast, he went to his room, checking his phone on the way.

He'd expected it to be Dermot who texted him. Instead, it was Lynne.

I got your number from Dermot. I wonder if I could ask a favor. I know it's presumptuous since we just met, but I need help putting together some things. If you're free.

Dermot gave Lynne his number? When had Dermot met Lynne?

As far as Lynne was concerned, he didn't need to think about it.

I can be over in half an hour.

She texted back immediately.

Super! Thanks. :)

Curious, oddly looking forward to seeing Lynne again, grateful for something to occupy his hands, he took care of his ablutions and went to find his mom.

She was in her "office," a converted bedroom where she did the paperwork for the farm. She looked up, concern lining her brow when she saw him.

"I'm going to help a friend," he said, leaning in the doorway. "I don't know when I'll be back."

"Dermot?"

He shook his head. "A new friend."

That maternal light that terrified him lit in her eyes. "That woman you met."

"Also no." He arched his brow, daring her to take this interrogation further.

"I know you're baiting me, my boy." She narrowed her eyes. "It's not going to work."

"You sure?"

She shook her finger at him. "I have other ways, if that's how you want to play it."

"Now I'm scared." He dropped a kiss on forehead and went to the Sea View Cottage.

The closer he got, the more anticipatory he felt—to help Lynne, because he genuinely liked her and didn't like to see anyone suffer, but also to see Abby. Since he dropped her off yesterday, he'd barely thought of anything else, which was saying something given how much he'd had on his mind before.

Lynne answered the door when he knocked.

"Hi!" Smiling brightly, she eased her wheelchair back enough to let him in. "I'm so happy you could do this. I tried to set Abby's studio up myself, but I couldn't understand the instructions. They might as well have been written in Chinese."

"I don't understand Chinese either," he said, taking off his jacket and draping it on a chair.

"It shouldn't be hard." She wheeled herself to the edge of the living room and looked around.

Where the house had been tidy before, it was like a wood factory had exploded in the center of the room. There were pieces of varying lengths haphazardly lying around. "What is all this?"

"Pieces of easels. I think. I hope." Lynne's brow furrowed, her overwhelm obvious.

"How are you getting around the room?"

She grinned ruefully. "Not very well."

"At least Abby didn't offer to clean this up." He began rolling up his sleeves. This looked like it might take a while.

"Well, I waited to open the boxes until she went out on errands." She shrugged, her hands held out. "If she knew I wanted to do this, she'd have insisted on helping. And since today for the first time in months her wrist actually felt better, I didn't want her overtaxing it."

"Her wrist is better?" A warm feeling filled his chest.

Lynne nodded. "Thank you for that."

Bent over to move some of the wood to make room, he asked, "Where did all this come from?"

"Her agent sent it. She probably hasn't shown you her work, has she? You know she's a famous, world-renowned artist, right?"

Abby hadn't told him she was a successful artist. That'd make her wrist being out of commission even more distressing, yet she was focused on Lynne.

"What are you doing?" Lynne called from halfway down the hall. "Come with me, Finn."

He knew that tone from his mom, therefore he knew better than to disobey. He followed her out of the living room, down a hall to a room on the right. The door was partially closed, so he reached above Lynne to push it open so she could maneuver in.

"This is Abby's room?" he asked, though he knew it was. He could smell her in here. The bed was made, but not perfectly, with its throw pillows on a chair to the side. There was a bit of makeup on the dresser, not nearly as much as some of the women he'd known. She had a few items of clothing on a chair too. Stepping closer, he realized it was what she'd worn yesterday.

Remembering her in them and then seeing them on the chair did something to him below the belt.

"On that wall," she said, pointing imperiously. "She did that painting for her mother when she was six."

He turned to look. On the wall there was a fairly large canvas in an elaborate gold frame. It was a passionate flurry of blue strokes, making up a man from what looked like the seventeenth century based on his clothing. The only things that stood out were his eyes, an intense sort of turquoise, and the white of the scarf around his neck. And the rose he held. The rose looked like it was just picked.

"Six," he repeated, shaking his head in awe. At six, he'd just played pirates with Niall and Dermot.

He'd been around art a lot since he'd become so successful. It seemed like there was always some sort of charity soiree to attend, another gallery opening, in addition to Dermot collecting art and dragging him to various auctions when his schedule permitted.

This defied description.

It was breathtaking.

It made him believe in something beyond the tangible.

"The eyes are oddly alive, aren't they?" he murmured, admiring the painting.

Lynne laughed, a delighted tinkle. "You have no idea."

"I must confess that when you said she was a famous artist, I thought you were exaggerating." He'd never heard of her, but that was little wonder because he didn't pay that much attention to art beyond the events, but he wondered if Dermot knew of her.

"I couldn't exaggerate about Abby's art. It's magnificent." She looked up at him, concern drawing her features tight. "Do you see why it's so important for her wrist to heal? I would have had to stop dancing professionally eventually, but Abby could paint until the end. I know what it's like not to be able to do what you feel called to do. I don't want her to have to give it up. She has to paint. It's how she heals people. You can't just shut down gifts. Bad things happen when you shut down your gifts."

He wondered if somehow she was talking to him, the similarities were so great. Finn looked back and forth between her and the painting, remembering how Abby thought her painting was responsible for the accident. "You really believe that she heals people with her artwork?"

"Yes." Lynne turned herself around awkwardly and wheeled out of the room. He glanced at the painting one more time and then followed her out.

When she reached the living room, she hauled herself out of her wheelchair. The resolve on her face was both painful and admirable. The doctor in him knew how important it was to encourage independence, but he didn't want her to traumatize her injury, so he gently helped lower her to the ground, her leg with the brace straight out in front of her.

She reached under a pile of wood and pulled out some papers, brandishing them at him. "I can't make out any of this. I even looked it up online."

"Let's take a look." He knelt on the floor next to her and took the pages.

She frowned at all the pieces around them. "It's turning out to be more complicated than the space shuttle."

"I thought you said you didn't want her to overtax her hand," he said, righting the schema so it faced the correct direction. Painting wouldn't be in her best interest at the moment.

"Claire, the little girl next door, is coming over to paint. I thought I'd help put things together so Abby wouldn't strain herself any more than she has." Lynne looked up, baleful. "It's my fault she's hurt."

"That's what she says about you."

Lynne shook her head. "She's not seeing reason."

If you could call believing that a painting could heal you "reason."

"Okay." He eyed the instructions and nodded. It was fairly straightforward, except for the fact that all of the pieces seemed to be intermingled with other things on the floor. "What are the other pieces of wood for?"

"A second easel."

He nodded. "Let's organize our workspace, and then we'll get this done."

Lynne wilted in relief. "Thank you for being competent."

"I'll just say 'you're welcome' as that appeared to be a compliment," he said, handing her a packet of screws to hold on to. "While I'm working, tell me how you know Dermot."

"I haven't met him. We've just texted a few times."

Finn looked up from his work, his brow raised.

Curiously, Lynne's cheeks flushed. "You like Abby. He's your best friend. He introduced us to you. It seemed like I should say thank you, at least. It's not like he's going to start a romance with someone who can't walk."

If she thought that, she didn't know Dermot. Finn didn't say anything though, instead resuming where he left off with the instructions. They worked quietly and easily together as he finally put everything to rights enough to get his bearings around the design. It wasn't difficult once he had all the parts lined up in the correct order that he needed them, much like surgery.

He reached for the first piece to the puzzle.

"Finn?"

"Yes." He stopped and gave her his full attention.

"You care for Abby a great deal." Her gaze was direct and surprisingly all-seeing.

"I can't abide anyone hurting," he replied as agnostically as he could.

"Duh." Lynne rolled her eyes. "But how you feel about Abby is different than how you feel about me."

He nodded. He couldn't dispute that.

"Which is why I just want to tell you that the women in her ancestral line don't do love."

"What does that mean?"

Lynne shrugged. "Some would call it unlucky in love. I think it's more than that, like a curse that gets passed down generation to generation. They never end up with the men they love. Not Abby's mom, not her grandmother, and no one before her. And no one has ever inspired Abby to want to heal it." Lynne leveled him a look. "So you're going to have to convince her that it's worth it, that you're worth the risk."

"We're getting ahead of ourselves, aren't we?" he asked as blandly as he could, trying to hide his suddenly shaking hands.

"Are we?" she asked, her gaze clear and focused in a way he hadn't seen since he'd met her.

His skin broke out in goose bumps. He was grateful his long sleeves covered it up. At the same time something in him balked and wanted to call shite. He didn't believe in curses or the like.

She handed him a screwdriver. "Abby doesn't believe in soulmates, so it's going to take some doing in order to convince her you're hers."

"Convince her of what?" he asked, confused.

"That you and she were meant to be together," Lynne said matter-of-factly.

He carefully began putting together the first pieces of the easel, taking his time to think. Because he liked Lynne, he was honest with her. "I don't believe in that sort of thing either."

"What? That people have premonitions or soulmates?" she asked with a wry smile.

"Yes. Both."

"I grew up in New Orleans," she said, shifting to scratch her thigh under the brace.

The brace he sent for should arrive tomorrow. It'd be more comfortable and lighter than what she had. He couldn't believe a doctor in this day and age would give someone that monstrosity she had strapped on her leg.

"Even the nuns in the orphanage believed in ghosts and psychic phenomena," she continued.

"That seems logical though." At her questioning look, he finished his thought. "They already believe in one illogical thing: God. It stands to reason that if you can believe in that, the rest is inevitable."

"What an interesting point." She mulled it over for a bit. "You don't believe in anything? Sixth sense? Intuition? You've never seen something you can't explain, or have just known something?"

"That's not some sort of psychic phenomena. That's extrapolation based on knowledge."

"Hmm," was all she said. She handed him the next piece that he pointed to. "Abby comes from a family known in Louisiana for their gifts. Her mother and generations back have been wisewomen, with varying sorts of talents."

He knew from the history of medicine that women healers had been branded as witches and such in order to diminish their power. Men became gods when they had power over life, and no man wanted to cede that to a woman.

"I always envied Abby that," Lynne said wistfully. "That she had access to this entire amazing world."

"You couldn't?"

"Nope. I wanted to be psychic so bad." She smiled ruefully.

"Why are you telling me this?"

"Because you're her soulmate."

She said it like it was a known fact, and despite his disbelief in the arcane, part of him wanted to embrace the idea. "You can't know that," he said, wanting the dismiss the idea but not able to.

"Before I'd have agreed with you, but the fall changed something. Now I just know." The corner of her mouth lifted sadly. "Abby is special, and the man who deserves her has got to know that. He's got to see all her facets and appreciate them all, encourage all of them. Even the parts he doesn't understand yet."

He thought about another man kissing Abby, and he wanted to take the faceless man apart with his bare hands. Talk about illogical. "I thought you said I was her soulmate," he said as dispassionately as he could.

"You are, for the moment, until you make a different choice." Lynne got a faraway look. "I used to think you only had one soulmate, but I see things differently now. There's the best option at any given time, and depending on your choices they shift, for better or worse."

He nodded. Having the guy you lived with virtually push you down a flight of stairs would make you reconsider how you viewed love.

She touched his wrist. "I like you. You're kind and smart, and you listen. And I saw the way you look at

Abby. Plus, you don't mind me being a pest." She gestured to the easel, which was starting to take shape.

"What are you saying?" he asked, feeling like he was missing something.

She leaned in. "Don't fuck this up."

He smiled despite himself. He wanted to help her, also despite himself. Tomorrow he'd call his office and check to see where her records were. "I hope you never meet my mother. You two together would strike terror in the hearts of men."

Lynne sat back and handed him the piece he pointed at. "I have a feeling I'm going to love her."

19

Abby returned home from a walk, expecting to find Lynne in the living room reading. She didn't expect to find the living room turned into an art studio.

The room was completely transformed. The stretcher bars were unpacked and piled neatly, organized by length, along a wall. The heavy-duty easel was set up and ready to go near a window that overlooked the Atlantic, and a smaller one was angled out from the opposing wall. There was a table between the two, she thought from Lynne's room, with all the tubes of paint, brushes, and palette knives neatly lined up.

It was exactly how she'd arrange everything if she'd done it herself. How did Lynne do this?

Then she heard Lynne's laughter from the kitchen. She hung her scarf by the door and went to see what was going on.

She stopped short a second time, in the threshold to the kitchen. The scene she encountered was even more discombobulating than the makeshift studio in the other room. Lynne sat on the counter, her right leg propped in front of her on a pillow, her left leg set on a chair, munching on a stick of celery, as Finn chopped garlic. They both looked up when she walked in.

"There you are," Lynne said, grinning. "Finn's making dinner for us."

"Pasta," he added, not taking his eyes off Abby. "With my special sauce."

"Special sauce?" Abby blinked, feeling like she'd stepped inside the best dream ever: a hot man in the kitchen cooking, hair mussed, his large body beautiful in a T-shirt and jeans. The only way the scene could have been better was if he was offering himself as her dinner.

"Finn came over to help me rearrange the furniture," Lynne said, pulling Abby out of her sexual reverie. Her friend leaned over to squeeze Finn's bicep. "He's a *braw lad*."

"That's Scottish, darling," he said to her, still holding Abby's gaze.

"Still applies," Lynne said with a shrug. "Then he *begged* me to make dinner for us. He was so desperate to do it, I didn't have the heart to tell him no. My only regret is that I didn't have an appropriately frilly apron to offer him."

"Have you been drinking?" Abby asked incredulously. Seeing Lynne sitting on the counter enjoying herself filled her with such gratitude. He really was the Miracle Worker, and it took everything in her not to go over and throw her arms around him.

"We were waiting to open the wine when you got

here." Lynne nudged Finn with her left foot. "*Garçon, por favor.* While you do that, I'll set the table."

Stunned, Abby watched Lynne pull out dishes from the cabinet. As if they'd been doing this all their lives, Finn silently took them from her and set them to the side before he lifted her carefully off the counter and helped her ease onto the wheelchair. Then he took out silverware from the drawer, piled it on the plates, and set them all in Lynne's lap.

Lynne rolled toward her. "Excuse me," she said sweetly, as though this was an everyday occurrence.

Abby silently got out of her way. Then she lifted her astonished gaze back to Finn.

"She called me for help," he said.

"And you accomplished *that*"—she waved her hand in Lynne's general direction—"without the aid of serious meds?"

His lips quirked. "Maybe I am a miracle worker."

"Maybe you're more than that." Before he could complete the thought, she launched herself at him and pressed her mouth to his with joy rather than finesse.

She wouldn't have been surprised if he pushed her away—she'd thrown herself at him, after all, and he'd made it clear he didn't think they should go there. But this moment needed to be celebrated, and a kiss seemed like the perfect way.

Only instead of detangling from her, he wrapped his hand in her hair and pulled her closer, taking control of the kiss, taking it from enthusiastic to smoldering.

All thoughts fled her mind—the studio setup, Lynne, everything. The only thing in her consciousness was the warmth of his lips, the subtle flick of his tongue, and the feel of his growing interest against her belly. She pressed herself against him, unable to stop herself, not wanting to.

His hand tightened in her hair. She guessed he didn't want to stop either.

But then a loud clink of silverware from the other room jarred her, and she broke the kiss, breathing hard. "Thank you," she whispered, her voice husky.

"Don't thank me yet. Your easel may fall to a heap of kindling."

"You did that?" She should have realized. One: Lynne's leg. Two: Lynne had never been able to read instructions to save her life.

"Like I said, Lynne asked for help. I like her."

"She likes you too."

"She thinks I'm your soulmate."

Abby winced and tried to step back. "She obviously needs psychiatric help in addition to physical therapy."

Finn held her in place, not letting her retreat. "She believes what she believes, and she's unapologetic about it. I admire that."

"I smell something burning," Lynne called from the dining room. "Can you guys stop canoodling long enough to make sure our dinner doesn't go up in flames?"

What went up in flames was Abby's face. "Jesus."

Finn just chuckled, slowly letting her go. "Don't worry, Lynne," he called, his gaze hot on Abby. "I won't let anyone go hungry."

"*Jesus,*" Abby said again, fanning herself. Then she scurried out of the kitchen before *she* burned up herself.

She stayed out of the kitchen until dinner was ready. She was going to help Finn bring in the steaming food, but he insisted on doing it himself.

"That smells delicious," Lynne said, heading to the table. "Finn, did you open the wine?"

"I feel like I'm in *The Twilight Zone*," Abby said, following Lynne.

Finn pulled out a chair for her. "It's more like an Oscar Wilde play," he said, waiting for her to sit down.

Lynne laughed, and the happy sound drove out everything else. Lynne loaded her plate with more food than she'd eaten in a week and then held her wine glass out for Finn to fill it up. "Finn, has Abby told you about the time she thought the courtyard at the orphanage needed some color, so she painted rainbows all over the place, not knowing rainbows represented the LGBT community, and Sister Mary Henry thought she was making a statement about some of the nuns?"

Abby groaned. "I got so busted. I couldn't sit for days after the paddling."

Finn smiled, passing Abby the pasta. "And that didn't stifle your career?"

"No, but I didn't think graffiti art was for me."

"What made you decide to become a doctor?" Lynne asked.

"My sister Fiona, actually."

"Is she older or younger than you?" Lynne asked, forking a mouthful of pasta into her mouth.

Abby opened her mouth to cut this conversation off, but Finn waved her off as he poured wine for her.

"She was my twin." He met Lynne's gaze without

flinching. "She had an accident, and the prognosis wasn't good, and she decided she didn't want to live."

Lynne gasped, putting her hand on his. "I'm so sorry. I shouldn't have brought it up."

"We don't shy away from talking about Fiona," Finn said to Lynne. "In fact, I think talking about it was one of the reasons my parents became even closer after it happened. Most marriages don't withstand the loss of a child, no matter how old they are."

"I'd like to meet your parents," Lynne said.

Abby almost dropped her fork. Then she turned to Finn. "Are you sure you didn't drug her while I was gone?"

Lynne laughed. "You're so funny, Abby. I'm just high on love. I have my best friend and my new friend here, and there's good food, and wine, and you're going to paint again. What can be better?"

Lynne dancing.

Kissing Finn again.

More *canoodling*, as Lynne called it.

Biting her lip, she caught Finn watching her. She felt her face start to flush, and his brow raised in curiosity.

"This is excellent," Lynne declared, waving her fork between them. "You guys already have nonverbal communication."

"Don't listen to her," Abby said to him.

Finn shrugged. "She's already said I'm your soulmate. I'm not sure she could say anything to surprise me more than that."

Lynne lifted her wine glass. "I'll wait to tell you you're going to have triplets for a couple weeks."

Putting a hand over her eyes, Abby groaned.

"Don't worry, Abby. I also told him you talk to ghosts, and he's still here, so he's got that going for him," Lynne said as her phone signaled a text. Setting down her fork, she lifted the phone, which was facedown next to her. "It's just Dermot." Lynne set the phone aside again and turned her brilliant smile on Finn.

For a moment, Lynne didn't look like herself, like something passed over her. But Abby couldn't sense a spirit or anything. When she looked again, Lynne looked like herself. Abby frowned. Weird. It was the second time she'd noticed it.

"So tell me about your parents," Lynne asked Finn.

When they finished, she cleaned up and made tea, and they sat in the living room talking about random things, like normal people. Finn entertained Lynne with stories about his mom and dad and the farm. Abby could have kissed him all over again for the way he'd brought Lynne back to life.

Not that kissing him was a hardship. *At all.*

She felt Bro Paul materialize behind her. "Imagine having that for the rest of your life," her guide said. "The kissing. This companionship. It, too, can be yours, if you stop being so hardheaded."

I'm not hardheaded, she told him mentally.

"Yeah, right." He snorted. "If your head were any harder, you could cut diamonds."

I know what you're doing. She sipped her tea, trying not to think about happily ever after with Finn. She'd never thought about happily ever after before. It'd never been in her consciousness. When she envisioned the future, it always involved her painting. Alone.

"Because happily ever after has been driven out of your line," he replied to her thought, frowning. "You weren't born with it."

Maybe she didn't need it. Painting had always made her feel fulfilled.

Bro Paul smacked his hand against his forehead. "Everyone needs love, kid. Without love, the human species would die. And you don't have painting right now. We're trying to broaden your scope here. Work with me."

Go away.

"Make me."

Lynne glanced over, rubbing her ear, a faint frown between her brows. She continued to listen to Finn, but every so often her gaze would search the spot where Bro Paul stood as if straining to see him.

Abby blinked in surprise. *Can she sense you?*

"Yeah. Isn't that amazing? Our baby is growing up." He burped and patted his belly.

Abby rolled her eyes.

"Don't underestimate her, kid. She's got a lot going for her." His big hand patted Abby's shoulder, almost causing her to fall off her chair, and then he vanished.

"Are you all right, Abby?" Finn asked her.

"Fine." She shot Lynne a look when she chuckled.

Finn set his teacup down and stood. "I should head home. Lynne, thank you for today. You saved me from my mother's clutches."

Lynne laughed, holding her arms out for a hug. "If you need to be saved again, just text me."

"Deal." He hugged her, gently but with a lot of warmth.

Then he straightened and turned to her. "Abigail."

"Well," Lynne said brightly, tucking her phone next to her hip and wheeling herself out of the room. "I think I'll go to my room. Good night, guys. Don't worry, I won't be listening at the door or anything. Be as loud as you want."

Standing, Abby took the pillow from her chair and threw it at Lynne's back.

Her friend just laughed as she rolled out of the room.

Abby turned to Finn and found him closer than she realized.

He brushed the back of his fingers down her cheek. "We need to talk, you know."

"We already talked yesterday."

"We have more to discuss." His fingers trailed down her neck and back to the nape of her neck. "About us."

"There's an us?" she asked cautiously.

"I don't know, but I feel like we're going to find out." He lowered his mouth to hers.

It should have been a soft kiss—that's what it started as—but something caught and suddenly they were pressed against each other, and there were hands and tongues and a whole lot of heat. She didn't know which one of them pulled away first, though she was pretty sure it wasn't her.

"Good night, Abby," he said, his voice so full of the promise of sex that she wanted to lead him by the hand down the hallway to her room.

Instead, she let him drop one more kiss on her lips before he went home.

20

Dermot had spent his entire youth being a victim to other people's vices.

Not anymore. Now he always got what he wanted. He made sure of it. In business and in pleasure. Sometimes he just had to work harder at it.

This was one of those times.

Leg tapping on the wood floors, he sat in the leather seat in his office at the Tullaghan house, like the lord of the manor. He listened to the meeting on the other end of the line impatiently, glancing at the time. Eleven at night in Ireland, three in the afternoon in California, and the meeting didn't feel like it was going to wrap up anytime soon. The idiots from the company he'd acquired in San Francisco hadn't realized yet that he'd bought the right to have exactly what he wanted from them. Because, there, he was also the lord and master.

But they'd realize it by the end of the call, unless they wanted to look for new positions.

They'd been confused when he'd informed them that

he'd patch into the meeting via phone from Tullaghan. Dermot knew it wasn't like him. He was known for being hands-on and present. Even his assistant couldn't hold back expressing surprise that he'd decided to stay in Tullaghan for the time being.

When he'd left, he'd vowed to only return when his mother died to bury her. He'd wanted to make sure she was dead and gone.

When he'd bought this house, it'd been in part to erase what he'd been as a child, to show the man he'd become.

Who'd have imagined that he'd be eager to stay here?

There were two reasons: Abigail and Madelynne.

They both called to him in different ways, but he was surprised to find himself drawn more to Madelynne. Not in the way he imagined a siren's call was: alluring and tempting, drawing him closer to ruin. No, Madelynne's soul was pure and good—like an angel with a secret blessing that was all for him.

He'd looked her up. She'd been a premier dancer in New York, with accolades all over the world. He'd watched clip after clip of her on stage. To call her performances breathtaking was an understatement.

She herself was more than breathtaking. He'd never seen a more beautiful woman, and he'd seen plenty. He bet that her pictures online didn't do her justice. She had a breadth of passion about her that a camera wouldn't be able to capture fully.

He'd also read that she'd had an accident six months ago. He'd heard about the American woman in a wheelchair. He knew that had to be her.

That might have caused some men to pause, but Dermot didn't see how a wheelchair made any difference. Fiona would have been in a wheelchair too. That didn't change who the person was within, or how that beauty was projected without. Certainly not a woman like Madelynne Broussard.

Just like that, the soul craving began to beat at him. His heart sped up, and heat suffused his body. Sweat beaded on his upper lip. He swiped at it, getting up to open a window. He felt the sweat pool under his arms, and he plucked his shirt away from his skin.

It happened this way more and more these days.

At first when he'd take a piece of someone's soul, he'd go for months without the compulsion for another one— long enough to think that he was over the craving and wouldn't need any more.

Each time he was wrong, and inevitably he'd be guided to the next soul eventually.

He hated the way it held sway over him. He was the one who chose when he took a soul piece; he was the one in power.

Though every day that passed made him feel more out of control.

He *hated* that.

Standing, he interrupted whoever was talking on the other end of the line. "We've spent enough time on this topic. David," he said to one of his VPs, "if you'll take over."

He disconnected from the call and began to pace, raking his hair back. If he took a piece of Madelynne's soul, this would all fade away.

He stopped abruptly. For how long would it stop? A week? A few days? He wasn't going to do that; she was nowhere near death and he wasn't a killer.

He thought of Abigail and how that ghost said she was his redemption. Maybe he should get together with her—as long as Finn was there as an extra check. Though Niall was there that first time with Fiona, and that hadn't made any difference.

His phone sounded with a text. He picked it up and saw it was Madelynne.

His heart immediately calmed, and he felt like he could breathe, as if she'd given him a soul piece already.

I got your text earlier. I missed talking to you too.

Her second text came on the heels of the first one:

How was playing master of the universe today?

He felt the first real smile he'd had since the last time they'd exchanged texts and quickly replied.

Exhausting.

Her return text was immediate.

Poor thing. Meetings that bad, huh? What do you need?

Dropping down on his couch, he undid a couple buttons on his shirt and thought about a response. He went with:

What can you offer me?

She came back with:

Well, we have leftover spaghetti...

He grinned. That was what he loved about their conversations: the unexpected. Bright and engaging and fascinating, Lynne surprised him at every turn.

He was also surprised that when he communicated with her, the hunger for another soul diminished. He'd barely thought about Abigail's soul since—not like that, in any case. He'd been examining that, and he couldn't come up with a reason that she'd affect him that way yet.

He tapped back his reply.

I love spaghetti.

Her response came a moment later.

I'd courier some over to you if it wasn't so late.

He debated telling her he could come over, but he hesitated. If she were here, alone with him, would he be able to control himself?

He wasn't certain.

He never hesitated.

Before he could figure out what to say, she sent him another message.

Anyway, I just wanted to say good night and that I hope your
meetings went well. TTYL <3

He sat there and stared at that last text for a long time.

Then the lovely peace from talking with Madelynne faded, and he had to pace. His heart pounded as the thoughts of Madelynne's soul started to dominate his mind anew, compounded by a thirst for Abigail's too.

Maybe he'd ask Finn about her, find out more about the woman. He didn't want to ask Madelynne; he didn't want her to think he was interested in her friend.

Not caring about the hour, Dermot texted Finn.

You good?

Oddly, Finn texted back immediately.

Getting there. Saw Abigail.

Sweat broke out on his brow. Wiping it, Dermot quickly tapped a reply.

Did you decide to help her?

Finn took longer to reply, as if he were pondering his answer. Then he sent:

Of course. I'm not a monster.

He leaned back against the backrest. Finn had such a propensity to help people, but Dermot knew helping

Abigail had nothing to do with duty or responsibility. Finn liked Abigail.

Finn sent another text before Dermot could reply:

Lynne said you gave her my number.

He stilled, surprised by the change of topic.

Shouldn't I have?

Finn's reply was immediate:

Just surprised. You like her?

Dermot wasn't prepared for that question, so he deflected. He was excellent at deflecting.

Do you like Abigail? Or is she just a case?

The response was so slow in coming that Dermot thought Finn had signed off. But then Finn said:

Abby's more than a case.

Abby.

Finn liked her, and Finn didn't like anyone. Dermot smiled, happy for his friend. He was also happy for himself, because if Finn was seeing Abigail, it gave Dermot time and opportunity to get to know what made her special.

If Finn was helping her, she'd stay here longer, and so would Madelynne.

Dermot paused at the unfamiliar feeling thinking about Lynne caused. It made his heart slow down again. He breathed slowly, deeply, exploring the strange sensations thinking about her caused.

Eventually, he texted Finn back.

What is it Molly always said? That you should follow your heart?

Finn was true to his character.

The women I've gone out with have said I don't have one.

Dermot grinned.

Then maybe it's time for a transplant.

He thought of Madelynne's soul again, so indomitable and bright.

His mobile dinged with a text from Finn.

Planning on coming back to Tullaghan soon?

Dermot replied:

Still here. Get together this week?

Not waiting for a reply, he tossed his mobile aside and leaned back, his arms over his head. He imagined getting together with Madelynne too. He touched his chest, surprised to feel the throb of the soul piece he'd taken from the family man surge to life. He hadn't felt it all day, and appreciation for the gift swept over him, as well as the warm emotion emanating from the soul piece itself.

Soon he wouldn't be able to feel it at all.

The thought left him empty and bereft.

21

Abby stood in front of the easel Finn had set up. She kept thinking about what Bro Paul had said about her painting with her left hand, but each time she went to pick up a brush, she got in her own head.

That's what helpers are for, she heard him chime in.

Helpers. She glanced out the window at the cottage next door. Before she could overanalyze it, she went over there.

Sarah answered looking harried, with her hair not as pulled together as the other times, but her smile was bright and friendly. "Abigail, this is a nice surprise."

"I wanted to see if Claire could come paint today." Before Sarah started to stress, she said, "I have everything already, so she won't need to bring supplies. Truthfully, it'd be a favor to me. I miss painting." She held up her wrist. "I haven't been able to pick up a brush in months, so it'd be a grace to engage in what I love in a different way."

Sarah's expression softened even more. "In that case, I'll send her over in a little bit."

"Perfect." She smiled and waved, her heart feeling light.

When she went back inside, Bro Paul was waiting for her again.

"Good job, you," Paul said, sprawled on Abby's chair, one leg over the side. "That is a special little girl. Her mom, though, she's chosen a hard path. But maybe that'll change, eh? That's the great thing about life. You can decide at any point not to do it the hard way. The question is, are *you* going to go for an easier path?"

Her heart sped up. "As opposed to?"

"One of suffering." He nodded at her wrist.

She hugged her wrist to herself. "I didn't get hurt deliberately."

"No, but you're using it to teach yourself this lesson." He eyed her. "You figure out yet what the lesson is?"

"Obviously not, if my wrist isn't better."

"Rocks for brains," he muttered, shaking his head. He stood up and stretched, his robes hiking up to show his hairy ankles. "Have fun with Claire." As he faded out, he said, "Try loosening up a little, do something outside the box. It's all going to be fine."

"Right," she murmured.

She heard the creak of Lynne's wheelchair coming down the hall. Abby smiled, grateful her best friend was there with her.

But her smile faded when she saw Lynne. The yellow-gray cast was settled over her again, and her features looked pinched.

"I'm okay," Lynne said listlessly as she rolled past Abby to the kitchen. "I just had a hard night."

"Is your leg bothering you?" she asked, following her.

"When isn't it bothering me?" Lynne asked with a bite. Then, sighing, she looked over her shoulder. "I didn't mean to snap. I didn't sleep well. I had bad dreams and I couldn't get comfortable."

But she'd been so happy the night before, with Finn there. What had happened? Abby had even heard Lynne humming from her room later—she couldn't remember the last time she'd heard Lynne sing.

At a loss, Abby said, "I'll make you brunch, and then we can go for a walk. Some fresh air will be good for you."

"I just want some tea," Lynne mumbled, awkwardly stretching sideways for the kettle.

"Let me do that." Abby stepped in and took over.

Lynne sat there quietly, watching her make the tea. For some reason, this made Abby feel guilty too, though she wasn't sure why. When she finished, adding a lot of honey, just the way Lynne liked it, Lynne accepted the cup with a subdued "Thank you" and carefully rolled backwards out of the kitchen, the cup secured between her legs.

"Where are you going?" Abby asked.

"To lie down."

Abby watched her go back down the hall, the closing of her bedroom door a quiet but definitive sound. She started to go after her when a knock sounded on the front door. It was light, a child's hand, so it had to be Claire.

With one last look at Lynne's closed door, she went to let the little girl in.

Claire was practically vibrating in place. "My mom said I could come paint," she said, bouncing up and down.

"Come in and we'll get you set up."

"I wonder what I'll paint," Claire said as Abby dressed her in a smock over her clothes.

Buttoning the shirt, Abby glanced down at her. "What do you like to draw?"

Claire blinked like she didn't comprehend the question. "I don't know. I just draw what they show me."

"They?" Abby asked.

"The angels. Like Brother Paul." Claire adjusted the front of the painting shirt so it fell straight.

Abby frowned. "Do they show you a lot of things?"

"Oh yes. Some of it I don't need to draw though."

"How do you know?"

Claire looked at her like the question did not compute. "They tell me."

If only everyone listened to their guides that diligently, Abby heard Bro Paul say.

Rolling her eyes, she led Claire to the table where oil paints were laid out and gestured to them. "Before we start painting, we pick our colors and set them up on a palette. Want to pick your colors?"

"I like blue." Her little brow furrowed with the seriousness of the choice. She picked a few shades of blue and titanium white.

Abby picked tubes of hansa yellow and naphthol red for her as well. "Sometimes we mix colors to get other colors, so we'll put a little of these in just in case."

Claire didn't look convinced, but she went along with

it. "What colors are you picking?"

She felt a pang of longing, the paralysis of uncertainty, and the need to be perfect. Then she stifled it all with a smile. "I hurt my hand so I'm just going to watch you."

"Is your other hand hurt too?" Claire pointed to her left hand.

"No."

"Why can't you draw with that one?"

Apparently, Bro Paul had already gotten to the little girl. She heard him laughing from far away. *This is what you wanted, kid. Listen to your helper.*

Abby took a deep breath and tried to release the tightness in her chest. "You're right. I'll paint with my other hand."

They prepped both palettes and Abby led Claire to the smaller easel, which she adjusted to the girl's height.

Kneeling next to her, Abby handed her a brush. "A painting is more than just a picture. It's a way to talk with colors to another person. A painting tells a story, or it has a message that it tells the person who's looking at it. It can make the person feel love or anger or sad or safe. It can make the other person feel good."

"I know." Claire nodded solemnly. Without another word she dragged her brush through the phthalo blue on her palette and began painting with the fervor and freedom of Chagall.

Abby watched, admiring the fearlessness, and then picked up her own brush.

It felt awkward in her left hand. She had to tell herself to calm down a bunch of times, to just feel the colors and let go of doing it "right." Her lines were messy, her technique clumsy, but the smell of the oil from her paint wrapped her in happiness and she fell in.

"You painted a house," she heard some time later.

Blinking, she came out of the creative stupor she always fell into and looked at her canvas. It was a large Irish house set on a hill, with a tree that had a swing dangling from a thick branch. Surrounding it were a profusion of roses blooming, full and abundant.

For some reason, it brought to mind the cottage in the past life scene with Finn, except that this house was modern and so much larger. Plus, all the roses were in bloom.

"I like it," the little girl declared. "What story is your house saying?"

"I don't know, actually." Abby frowned at the painting. What could a house that was devoid of people say?

Claire studied it with the seriousness of a Soho art critic. "I think it's saying you want to live there."

"You do?"

"Yes, because it's beautiful and big, and inside there's something good." Claire frowned at it. "But it's missing the people."

She couldn't draw the people, because they were Finn and her, and she wasn't going to chance drawing herself into another painting and hurting Finn.

Holding her paintbrush out, Claire came over to Abby's easel. Before Abby could stop her, Claire dabbed her brush in Abby's palette and touched the canvas.

Abby gasped, first taken aback at having her painting messed up.

That's a matter of opinion, Bro Paul chimed in. *You aren't doing this for money. You're doing this for Finn.*

She swallowed down the initial reaction, trying not to give rise to panic as she watched Claire add people to the foreground. She held her injured wrist to her chest, trying not to imagine the worst. Maybe Claire adding the figures wouldn't do anything.

But then she saw the blue bands around Claire grow, weaving around the painting. She gasped at the purity of the light blue and the delicate way it danced with every intentional brushstroke Claire added.

Abby looked back at the painting to see what Claire had drawn. She recognized the tall, broad man with bright-blue eyes as Finn. The woman holding his hand with dark hair flying all over the place was her. They smiled at each other.

Claire tipped her head and studied it. Dredging the brush in the paint, she quickly added another figure: a little girl with dark curly hair, also holding the man's hand.

"There," Claire said, setting the paintbrush down in a jar. "It's done now."

The figures, though rudimentary, looked like they belonged there. The painting should have looked mishmashed and odd, but instead it had an honest, innocent feel that was lovely. Abby could feel the healing of her part entwined with what Claire added, creating a harmonious blend.

"Do you like it?" Claire asked hopefully.

"I love it," she said truthfully. "We need to sign it."

Claire's eyes got big. "Okay."

Abby signed her name and then gave the fineliner to Claire to add hers. The little girl added her name in childlike block letters on the other side of the canvas.

"When are you going to give it to him?" Claire asked.

It shouldn't have surprised her that Claire knew, but it did. "I'll text him later." Because she needed space to process, she asked, "What did you paint?"

"It's for you." Claire went back over to her easel and gingerly took the painting down, holding it out to her. "I think it's Lynne."

Abby took it, freezing when she saw it. It was definitely Lynne—the woman Claire had drawn had a black stone around her neck and long blond hair, just like the other drawing Claire had done. This time, there was a man in a suit looming over her. He had his hand out and in it there was a pink triangle.

Abby looked at Lynne's figure again. The brace was on her leg and her hand was on her heart with what looked like blood oozing from between her fingers.

The first thing Abby did after Claire went home was hide the little girl's painting in her closet, taking care to stow it away safely so the wet paint wouldn't get smudged. You couldn't destroy someone else's art, but she also wasn't going to let Lynne see what Claire had painted. Certainly not before Abby understood it.

The second thing she did was text Finn. Healing him meant he could start getting Lynne physically stronger again. She sent him a brief message:

I have something for you.

He replied almost instantly.

I believe that should be my line. I'll text when I'm on my way.

Abby emerged from her room to find Lynne in the living room. "You better?" she asked her friend, going over and kissing the top of her head.

"Something feels off, and my ear is tinny." Lynne rubbed her ear, but her focus remained on whatever she was reading online.

Bro Paul, is Lynne's ear okay? she asked, trying not to worry.

She's going through the change, he replied. He chuckled. *A frequency change, to be able to hear her guides now that she's open to it. Don't worry, she's fine.*

Easier said than done. Sometimes it felt like she'd worried about Lynne all her life. She cleared her throat. "What are you reading?"

"Reading an article on Rosserk Friary."

"You're really fascinated by that place."

"It's got a fascinating history."

She went behind Lynne and looked over her shoulder at the phone. The open webpage had pictures of the remains of the friary. It was lovely against the green hills and blue water, but to her it didn't feel any different than other historical sites in Ireland. "What's the draw to this particular spot?"

Lynne shrugged, swiping the page. "It was once

magnificent, but now it's broken down. Like me. Why wouldn't I find it fascinating? I identify with it."

Abby swallowed thickly, grateful that she was standing behind Lynne so she couldn't see her face. It broke her heart. She put her hand on Lynne's shoulder. She wasn't going to let Lynne wither away.

Finn texted her again.

See you in 5.

Her heart flipped at seeing him; her stomach flopped at the thought of the painting not working.

"Is that Finn?" Lynne asked.

"He's coming over." She swallowed. "I collaborated on a painting with Claire for him."

Lynne froze, her eyes huge. "Abby, shouldn't you have said something?"

"I'm worried." She exhaled. "I'm worried it might not work, and I'm worried it might work like the last painting."

They were both silent, remembering that day in Manhattan.

"Can I see it?" Lynne asked softly.

"It's over here." She led the way to the easel and stood waiting for Lynne to join her.

With Lynne by her side, she felt calmer about looking at it. Folding her arms, Abby eyed it from the other place, from her inner eye where she saw the overlay of that past life and the healing Finn needed. It had a pulsing energy she could see, waiting to return to him.

"Wow," Lynne said. "I can feel its power."

Abby turned to look at her. "It's crazy, isn't it? The whole thing is so primitive, but somehow it's all pulled together. My lines are awful, and the house is wonky. Add Claire's stick figures…"

"And you have magic." Lynne took her hand, squeezing it. "One of the most beautiful collaborations I've ever seen. You're going to paint with Claire again, right? Until your wrist heals enough?"

"Yes." Already she was thinking of another paint date so she could do a healing for Lynne, to help get her to an easier place for Finn to help her heal all the way.

"Finn's going to love it," Lynne declared. "I'll get out of your way when he arrives. I'll go somewhere. Just put a pair of panties on the doorknob if you need me to stay gone for a while."

"You don't need to go away."

Lynne looked at her with an arched brow. "Well, I'm not going to stay and watch him express his gratitude, although I bet that man in action is a thing of beauty."

Good Lord, Abby hoped she got to find that out.

Finn arrived a couple minutes later. Abby answered the door, feeling schoolgirl-like excitement. She tried to remember the last time she'd felt eagerness like this and she came up short. Seeing him, her heart filled with light. She glanced down at her chest, almost expecting to see bright pink bursting forth from her body.

His gaze traveled all over her. Then he lifted his hand, using his thumb to rub her cheek gently. Such a tiny touch, but it caused a hum of pleasure all over.

"Paint," he explained, his voice low.

"I had a playdate. I used my left hand," she assured him.

He took her hurt wrist and examined it. "Feels better."

She smiled. "Come in."

Lynne rolled away from the dining table. "Hi, Finn."

Abby watched him assess Lynne, seeing how he frowned in concern. He went over to her and dropped a kiss on the top of her head. "How are you, darling?"

"Not as good as Abby is going to be." Her lips quirked a little as she wheeled herself toward the front door, her phone on her thigh.

"Where are you going?" Abby asked.

"A stroll," she said, grim determination written all over her face. "Remember what I said about the panties."

Abby wanted to call her back, but Lynne hadn't initiated going out on her own since the accident. Torn, she watched her best friend struggle in her low-tech wheelchair, down the uneven walkway to the sidewalk. She closed the door and turned to find Finn right there.

"She's in more pain today," he said with a frown. "Her color is off and she's very down."

"She didn't sleep well," she said, lifting her hands, at a loss.

Then he speared his fingers into her hair at the base of her head. "Lynne's medical records finally arrived today," he said, massaging her nape. "I haven't had a chance to look at them in depth, but I promise I will."

"Thank you," she murmured, closing her eyes at the delicious feeling of his fingers.

"I have to be honest, I expected her to be in better spirits today," he said candidly. "It's concerning that she's dipped so low compared to how she was yesterday. Extreme ups and downs don't reassure me."

Abby looked at him. "Don't decide yet. Look at the whole, and then decide."

He stared at her for a long time before nodding. "All right." Then he asked, "So what's this about panties?"

"You don't want to know."

"On the contrary, I believe I do."

She flushed. "Do you want to know what I have for you or not?"

His lips quirked. "I should have known it was too good to be true, to think that's what we were talking about."

"We can have that discussion later. First, this." She took his hand and led him to her easel.

His focus tunneled directly to the painting the moment he saw it. He stepped closer, his brow furrowed. She watched him taking in every detail, section by section, in a methodical sweep of the whole scene.

"Claire, the little girl next door, helped me." She cleared her throat. "It's not my normal work, but I had to try, and—"

"Abby?"

She blinked. "Yes."

"Let me look at it."

"Okay." Okay. She took a deep breath.

Then she shifted her attention to his field—the energy surrounding him. The darkness at the edges undulated and then began to slither away. His field began to clear, his soul visibly lightening with every breath he took. She exhaled, relieved that it was helping rather than doing damage. She gave his field a push with her mind, visualizing cutting the remaining tendrils of darkness and watching them wither away.

Then that soul piece that he'd lost in the life flew back into his chest. She watched it merge into his heart with a burst of bright green, pulsing with life.

"I'm touched," Finn said, still studying the painting. "It's really for me?"

"It's a moment from a former life you had, redone to correct what had gone wrong."

He frowned. "This is you with me."

She nodded, her throat thick with emotion.

He looked at it closer. "What is this correcting?"

"That you were responsible for circumstances outside your control. That you were a bad doctor."

Gaze narrowed, he faced her. "You believe this is going to help clear my head."

She shrugged. It already had, but she couldn't force him to accept that. If he wanted to, he could hold on to the pain of his patient's death, but at least that was from his own choice and not because of something energetic holding him back.

"I don't believe in things like this," he said.

"Yet you perform miracles in surgery all the time. How is this any different?"

"Surgery is driven by science."

"And this isn't?" She tipped her head. "One time, I saw a program where they showed two tissues taken from two different hearts. They were the smallest pieces of muscle, and they continued to beat with the rhythm of the heart they were taken from, even sitting in a Petri dish. But when they put them in the same dish and touched the two together, they began to beat as one. *That's* magic."

He studied her in a silence that extended for a long time.

She didn't break his gaze. She didn't say anything more, knowing she couldn't convince him. She just let him search her.

"I've never met anyone like you," he said softly, brushing her hair away from her face.

"Crazy?" she said with a quirk of her mouth.

"Passionate." His gaze fell to her lips, and his thumb traced a trail from there to her cheek. "Thank you."

She frowned. "For being passionate?"

"For the painting. For what it means to you. For wanting to help me." He lowered his lips to hers and brushed them gently, once, twice...

And then his fingers tightened in her hair and he deepened the contact. She lifted her arms around his neck and drew him closer. She gasped, feeling his hardness already pressing into her belly, and she rubbed herself against it, wishing their clothes would burn away.

"I haven't been able to stop thinking about you since I met you at Hairy's," he confessed, tugging her head back enough to trail his lips down her neck. "I haven't been able to stop thinking about kissing you again since that day in the kitchen."

She started to reply but his teeth nipped her and instead a moan escaped from her mouth. She gripped him tighter, feeling her legs turn to jelly as he soothed the bite with his tongue.

He began to walk her backwards, his embrace solidly

holding her up as he guided her down the hall, kissing her the whole time. Guiding her into her bedroom, he kicked the door closed with his foot.

"How'd you know my room?" she asked as he walked her backwards until the bed hit behind her legs.

Gently he lowered her onto it, following her as she scooted back. "Lynne showed me your first painting."

She paused, lifting her head. "Really?"

He nodded. "It's incredible, but you don't need me to tell you that."

She dangled her head over the edge of the bed to look at it. "It's the only thing of my mom's that I have."

He nuzzled her exposed neck, blanketing her with his body. Moaning, she refocused her attention completely on him.

His fingers tangled in her hair again. "How long?" he asked, his eyes a blaze of blue.

She lifted her head enough to meet his mouth with hers. "What?" she asked against his lips.

"At Hairy's you said it'd been a long time," he said in between kisses. "How long?"

"Over two years." She snaked her hands under his shirt, shivering at the muscular feel of his back. "Does it matter? I'm clean."

"I was asking because I want to make it good for you," he murmured, pushing her shirt up.

"Oh." Her head fell back as his hand touched her over her bra. "I don't think that's going to be a problem."

"Just so you know, I'm clean too. And I have condoms." He grinned ruefully as he tossed her shirt aside. "I decided to err on the hopeful side."

"Do they have Boy Scouts in Ireland?" she murmured, grateful he'd thought ahead, grateful he was considerate.

"I—" He leaned back, frowning. "What's this?"

She had no idea what he was talking about for a second. Then she realized he was touching the amethyst. She took it out. "What?" she said, trying to joke. "You've never got it on with a woman with a rock in her bra?"

He looked at the rock for a long moment, his thoughts inscrutable. Then he took it from her hand, carefully set it on the bedside table, and resumed kissing her.

She wrapped her hand in his shirt and pulled him back down to meet her gaze. "Get me naked."

His lips quirked but she felt his hardness pulse against her thigh. "That was direct."

"I believe in asking for what I want." She tugged up on his shirt. "Just so we're clear, I want you naked too."

He sat up and yanked his shirt off with one hand. "A clear line of communication is important."

"You make me wish I did nudes." She ran her hands over his torso. He was a work of art—muscles and smooth skin and just enough hair to add to the overly manliness of him. "Are doctors supposed to be this built?"

"I don't make a habit of examining my colleagues." He made quick work of her clothes, tossing them all on the floor, and then pulled her up to sitting. He dropped a kiss on her shoulder as his fingertips traced over her curves reverently. "Christ, you're lovely."

Before she could say anything, he drew her onto his lap to straddle his waist, flush against him.

She wiggled herself against him until he was nestled

right where she wanted him. She moaned, letting her head fall back into his hand, which had reclaimed its gentle grip on her hair. She felt his lips close on her nipple, and she moaned again, louder.

He licked, nibbled, and then licked some more until she was writhing in his lap. His left hand trailed down her back to her hip, and he urged her tighter against him.

The feeling of him pressing between her legs made her gasp, pure pleasure shooting all through her body. She rocked against him, panting.

"Look at me."

She opened her eyes at his low command and met his gaze. He watched her intently, and she could feel all of him focused on her. She could feel her heart opening to his, ribbons of reds and pinks and golds reaching for him.

Suddenly, something unlocked, and their heart energies connected and entwined, a pastel rainbow wrapping around them both. She gasped again, enchanted by the sparkly colors, feeling every one of them in a way she never had before.

He may not be able to see it, but she knew he felt it too—she could see it in the way his eyes widened, the way his hands gripped her closer. The way he relaxed into their physical connection, like they had until the end of time to explore each other.

It turned her on even more. It made her want to sink on top of him and keep him inside her forever.

Still looking at her, he took her mouth in a deep kiss that she felt down to her soul. "Now, Abby," he said against her lips. "Come for me now."

He pressed himself against her in just the right spot

and she felt that heart connection swell around them and she went off like a skyrocket. She cried out, muffled by his kisses, rubbing against him. And then his hand slipped between her legs, caressing her, and she climaxed again.

He eased onto his back, taking her with him so she was draped on his chest, her legs still around his hips. He kissed her like he was starving for her, like he never wanted to stop.

She didn't want to stop either. She felt him hard, resting against her, and she wanted more. "Again, but this time I want you inside me," she said, running her hands down his body.

He arched up on a hiss as her hands closed on him. Then he groaned. "Christ, Abby."

She sat up so she could see him. He was beautiful—thick and long and perfect. She squeezed him and ran her hands up and down his length, watching the wetness at the tip spread. "Now I really wish I painted nudes."

"*Christ.*" Reaching over his head, he scrambled for something on the floor, muttering until his hand closed on his jeans. He wrestled his wallet free from the pocket. "I bought these condoms after the last time we kissed."

God, she loved a forward-thinking man. "Bold."

"Hopeful," he said again, tearing the wrapper open with his teeth and then covering himself. Without any ado, he gripped her hips and settled her on top of him.

She inched her way down, moaning at the delicious feeling of him.

His right hand held her hair again, wrapping it around his wrist. His left hand trailed up her body to close over her breast.

She arched back into the feeling, rocking on top of him. "Promise me we'll do this again."

"And again." He kissed the swell of her other breast. "And again," he vowed as he licked over her nipple.

"*Finn.*" She cried out, feeling another orgasm rising.

He thrust his hips up, and her climax hit her stronger than the ones before, rolling over her in wave after wave of bliss. She gripped him, moaning, riding it out.

"Abby, yes." His hands tightened on her and he stiffened. She felt him get harder inside her, and then he worked himself faster until he came on a long groan.

It set her off again. He brought her against his chest, claiming her mouth again and again, until she was a limp heap on his chest. Without moving her, he got rid of the condom and continued stroking her hair and soothing her with soft kisses.

She put her hand over his heart, feeling the beat of it, seeing the soft gradients of pinks undulating around them. If her heart were next to it long enough, would it beat to the same rhythm?

"That wasn't bad," she said, trying to distract herself from mushy feelings she wasn't ready for.

He just continued to touch her softly. "Maybe if we try again it'll be better for you."

Again? She perked up at the thought. She'd almost expected him to go back home. She looked up at him, going warm at the mischievous look in his eyes. "I don't know that you have it in you," she teased.

"No, you'll have it in you." He rolled her over so he was on top, and the colors began to swirl all over again.

22

Finn woke up the next morning feeling...

Horny, he realized. He hadn't spent the night, instead having dinner with Abby and Lynne and then coming home despite wanting to stay. If he had spent the night, he knew the incessant desire wouldn't be any less.

He tried to remember the last time he'd had sex with a woman and immediately wanted more.

Never, actually.

In fact, he couldn't remember the last time he'd wanted to wake up with someone, to have her in his bed, in his arms, because he wanted to feel her warmth and explore her softness.

Never as well.

He stretched in his bed, looking across the room to the dresser, on top of which he'd placed both the painting and the copy of Lynne's medical file. He waited for his hands to begin to shake, thinking about helping Lynne, but they didn't. Abby would probably say it was because of her charming painting, but he knew physical intimacy had great benefits.

Whistling, he rolled out of bed and went to the en suite. It wasn't until he'd shaved half his face that he realized he was humming. Frowning, he looked at himself in the mirror, looking for signs of the distress that had been his constant companion the past few weeks.

He was still a little pale and he needed a shave bad, but he looked much improved, he realized with surprise. He still felt something unresolved from Jaime's death, but the heaviness of it all was less. He didn't feel depression closing in on him.

He knew the lighter feeling had to do with Abby: how he felt when he was with her, the heightened sense of everything, the need to touch her. How light he felt. How he felt settled and calm, like he was where he was supposed to be.

Abby, not her painting.

Would this feeling of ease fade? Or would it last? He felt...

He paused buttoning his shirt, surprised to find himself feeling hopeful.

He'd planned on going over there to talk to Lynne and examine her leg, but he realized he needed to see Abby just as much. He wanted to feel her again, and he saw no reason to hold himself back. He'd go there now.

His mom was at the sink when he strolled into the kitchen. She blinked at him in feigned surprise. "Isn't it himself, up before noon?" Suddenly frowning, she turned the water off and faced him, arms crossed. "Something's different about you. What happened?"

"I'll tell you later. I'm going out for a bit."

"It's the woman," Molly said with an entirely too satisfied look. "Invite her to dinner."

"Mother—"

"Don't 'mother' me. I'll put starch in your underwear."

He dropped a kiss on her forehead. "Dad is a lucky man."

"A smooth talker, just like your father." Shaking her head, she returned to washing the dishes.

He drove to Abby's as fast as possible.

When he knocked on the door, Lynne answered it. She didn't appear surprised to see him, instead removing the earbuds in her ears and greeting him with a wan smile. "Finn, you're just in time to share a morning coffee with me. Come in."

She shifted her wheelchair back to give him space to step inside. He kissed her cheek and closed the door. He gave her his no-nonsense doctor's look. "I'm going to take a look at your leg, but first I need Abby."

"I know you do," Lynne said, turning the wheelchair around and heading to the kitchen. "That's what I've been saying."

"I mean, I need to see her now."

"She's still in her room. I think you know where that is." Lynne gave him a cheeky look over her shoulder. "Don't worry, I'll put my earbuds back in."

He gave her a flat look, which made her chuckle, and headed down the hallway.

At her door, he knocked softly. When he got no response, he cracked it open.

Abby was still asleep, her duvet covering only her lower back and backside. Her legs stretched bare, tanned and smooth and lovely, on the white bedclothes. Her arms were tucked under her pillow, and her profile was turned toward him.

He stepped inside, kicking off his shoes, and padded to her. Sitting on the edge of her bed, he brushed her hair from her face, unable to stop himself from lingering on her skin—it was the softest he'd ever felt. All he wanted to do was take off his clothes and climb in next to her.

She stirred, mumbling his name. Then she gasped and popped up on her hands, blinking at him. "Finn!"

"I came to examine Lynne's leg."

"Then what are you doing in my room?"

"Examining you first." He pressed his mouth to hers.

She groaned and dropped her head back on the pillow. There was no struggle, no games, no protests. She just lay back, taking him in her arms, and gave herself over to him.

"I like you naked," he said, feeling her warm body against his, running his hands all over her.

"I like you naked too, which makes me wonder why you still have clothes on." She yanked at his shirt.

He stood up and undressed, liking the way she lay there, her arms stretched over her head and her body bare for him, watching him with hunger in her eyes. He took out the condoms he'd brought and slid back over her.

She hummed. "Oh good, you restocked."

"The first thing I did when I got home yesterday." He took her hair in his hand—Christ, he loved her hair—

and ran his other hand down her body, slipping his fingers between her legs.

She arched up, gasping.

"Lynne's in the other room," he warned as he kissed her.

She writhed under his hands. "Oh my God, was I loud yesterday?"

He loved every sound she'd made. "I believe she encouraged this. In any case, she put her earbuds in."

Abby lifted her head, her eyes wide. "She's listening to music?"

"I imagine so." He frowned at the sudden rush of emotion that flooded Abby's eyes. He pushed her hair back, cupping her face. "What's wrong, Abby?"

"She hasn't listened to music since the accident." She held his face, looking at him in wonder. "How could I not fall in love with you?"

He blinked in surprise. Love? But then she kissed him with a fervor that left him as breathless as her words had.

In the end, they didn't have to worry about being too loud because they never stopping kissing. Each time she came, he tasted her pleasure and knew his palate would never tire of it.

He washed up in her bathroom and got dressed while she took a turn in there. He walked back and forth in her room, her words echoing in his head. *Love.* Did she think she was in love with him?

In the past, he'd had a couple women say they loved him, but he hadn't believed them. They loved his status or his career—they didn't see him beyond a well-received doctor. Certainly none of them would have stuck with him through the media maelstrom of the past month.

But he wanted to believe Abby. He wanted it very much. Just the thought of being with her every day filled him with an excitement that he hadn't felt since he'd planned that world tour when he was eighteen.

She came out wearing a long robe of some sort of dark-red slinky material that hugged her body in a way that made him forget everything except how he wanted her all over again.

He walked to her and took her in his arms, nuzzling the hollow of her throat. He slipped his fingers inside the edge of the robe, running them down to brush over her nipples, more and more defined under the clingy fabric.

She groaned and went soft in his arms. "I thought you wanted to take a look at Lynne."

"She told me to go to your room."

"Of course she did. She thinks we're soulmates. She's going to encourage any kind of patty-fingers that leads to that outcome."

But did Abby believe they were soulmates? He wanted to ask her, but he told himself that was silly. Since when did he think about things like that?

Unaware of his thoughts, Abby reluctantly drew away from him. She took his hand and led him to the door. "She better have at least made coffee."

Lynne was in the kitchen at the ingenious station Abby had probably set up for her to give her some independence despite the wheelchair. Looking up when they walked in, she took out her earbuds and held out a cup to Abby.

"What are you listening to?" Abby asked, accepting the coffee with a hesitant smile. Finn knew her well enough now to know that her voice was husky with emotion.

"Nine Inch Nails." Lynne turned to him. "Would you like some, Finn?"

Abby snorted as she blew on the hot beverage. "He already got some."

Lynne grinned as she poured another cup. "Sugar? Cream?"

"He had that too," Abby said.

He arched his brow at her. "But I could use more sugar," he said to Lynne.

Smirking, Lynne doctored it and handed it to him. As he took a testing sip, she regarded him, her head tipped. Then she nodded at Abby. "His heart is so much lighter. But then love is the greatest healer of all, isn't it?"

Love again. He studied Abby, his heart beating hard. His dad talked about falling in love with Molly the moment he laid eyes—and hands—on her. Finn had always thought that was part of what his mom called "his father's glib tongue." He'd never actually believed that happened to people.

But he couldn't deny what he felt for Abby was foreign and strong. He'd known her, for what—a week? A little longer? After he'd met her, he immediately wanted to see her again. After their first kiss, he'd plotted how to kiss her next, if he wanted it slow and teasing or fast and hard most. He'd left yesterday and since then all he wanted to do was take her to his bed and keep her there until she couldn't move, until her voice was hoarse from screaming his name.

It was not normal.

Looking at Abby, he tried to analyze his feelings as he sipped the coffee, but all he felt was satiation and the desire to hold her hand.

He set his coffee cup down and knelt in front of Lynne. "I'd like to take a look at your leg, if that's okay with you."

For a second he thought Lynne was going to refuse, but then she nodded. He brusquely took her lap blanket and handed it to Abby. Lynne wore a long flowing skirt, so he folded it up by her knees, smoothing it down to preserve her modesty.

The brace was archaic, like the wheelchair was. He'd never worked with the doctor who'd treated Lynne in New York, but he'd heard of him by reputation. He should have done better than this.

Unfastening the Velcro, he set the contraption aside and looked at her leg overall. The incisions were still livid, and there was more discoloration through her leg than he would have expected at this point. The swelling was pronounced where the brace stopped, all the fluid collecting where there was no compression. He compared it to her other leg and estimated that there was twenty, twenty-five percent atrophy. Too high.

Abby sidled over and leaned against the counter close to them. "Finn, what are you doing today?"

He glanced at her, aware she was trying to distract Lynne, who'd gone stiff. "I have a few work things I want to take care of." He hadn't looked at Lynne's X-rays yet, and he wanted to put in a personal call to her doctor to discuss the case.

Lynne cleared her throat. "You guys should have dinner tonight."

They both looked at her.

She smiled weakly. "So you can tell your grandkids that you went on an actual date without lying."

"I don't need to go on a date," Abby murmured.

Something about that softly spoken statement made him want to give it to her all the more. He refastened Lynne's brace, pulled down her dress, and stood. "Are you busy later?"

She pursed her lips. "Finn—"

"Go out with me. I'll pick you up early and we can go for a walk before dinner." He dropped a kiss on her mouth to stop her protests. Taking the blanket from her hands, he tucked it gently around Lynne's legs.

"I wonder if that's a euphemism for 'get it on outside' in Irish," Lynne said as she watched him with eyes that held both hope and fear.

Abby shot her friend a look before she turned to him and solemnly said, "I'd like that."

He kissed her again before turning to Lynne. "I need you to elevate your leg as much as possible. Can you do that for me?"

"Yes," Lynne said softly.

"I haven't finished my due diligence, but I have some ideas to make you more comfortable." He dropped a kiss on Lynne's head. "Thank you for the coffee and the amusing commentary."

"You're welcome." Lynne looked at him with her

solemn eyes still clouded with discomfort and lethargy. "Thank you for making my best friend glow like that."

"You're welcome," he said gruffly, leading Abby out of the kitchen by the hand. At the front door, he said quietly in her ear so it wouldn't carry, "She's going to PT?"

Abby nodded.

"The atrophy and the swelling concern me, as well as her disposition," he said frankly. "I still need to look at her X-rays and I have a call in to her doctor in Manhattan."

"Is it bad?" she asked in a whisper.

"Yes, but we'll see what we can do." He took her wrist and looked at it. "How are you?"

Abby smiled ruefully. "After this morning, I feel no pain."

She had on the brace that he'd given her, and he could smell the arnica cream. Good. It always surprised him how many patients didn't follow instructions when they were in their best interest. Her hand and fingers looked minorly improved from what he could see around the brace. He lifted her hand and placed a soft kiss on her knuckles. "I'll pick you up at five."

She got up on her toes and pressed a kiss to his lips. "I can't wait."

Strangely, he couldn't either.

23

Abby didn't know what to do with herself while she waited for five o'clock to happen, so she decided to paint.

If only she could figure out what to paint. She'd been trying to channel what Lynne needed in order to heal fully, but it wasn't coming to her. She didn't know why—usually she could focus her intention and the scene she needed was right there.

A few years ago, Abby had met an author who often took up residence in the French Quarter as she was writing her next book. One time, Abby had sat with her for a coffee, and while the woman nervously drank her spiked chicory, she'd told Abby that she'd written over forty books but each time she faced a blank white page she was struck with terror.

Abby hadn't understood then, but now as she stared at the canvas in front of her, she had an inkling of what that woman was talking about.

"Just start to paint," Lynne said from where she was reading by the window. "You'll know what to do."

Yeah, right.

Lynne rolled her eyes. "You're so grumpy. You shouldn't be grumpy, Abby. You got laid, and it was good, if the muffled screams were any indication."

She felt her face flush so deep that it likely rivaled alizarin crimson. "Jesus, Lynne."

"Just start painting what's in your heart," she said, putting her earbuds in.

Abby tried not to stare at her, but Lynne hadn't listened to music at all in the past six months. It felt like a sign that things were getting better.

Feeling a burst of warm gratitude for Finn—which felt an awful lot like horniness, truth be told—she picked up the first color that caught her eye—Opaline Green—and began to spread it on the canvas awkwardly with her left hand.

As she moved the paint, she remembered the way Finn had looked in her eyes that morning, like he couldn't imagine seeing anything better, and she remembered what Bro Paul had said to her: *The women in your line don't find happily ever after, do they?*

She'd never thought about happily ever after, really. She thought about her mom and her grandmother, wondering what their lives would have looked like without this curse. Then she pictured her own daughter that Claire had drawn.

A longing sang through her heart, a bittersweet tune that had no ending.

She'd never imagined having a child.

But there the little girl was, the vision as real as Lynne sitting in the room with her: bright and sunny, with long dark curly hair and expressive violet-blue eyes. She seemed to look at Abby with knowledge beyond her years, even though she was only about six from the look of her. She arched her brow, daring Abby to choose a different future for her, and for all the daughters to come in the future.

She dared Abby to choose love.

And then the vision came: that moment in a past life when the happily ever after had been deleted from her maternal line. She saw it all—her ancestor who had long flowing hair like hers, the man who'd broken her heart, and the curse she'd put on her baby daughter, and every daughter to come after that—a curse meant to protect the hearts of those who came from her.

What's the source of the wound? she heard Bro Paul ask.

The woman's heart.

Abby turned her gaze and saw the woman's spirit suddenly standing in front of her. Like that spirit she'd seen in the hospital the day she'd met Dermot Farrell, there was a large soul piece that was missing right in the area where that woman's heart was.

A literal broken heart.

She felt a moment of compassion for her ancestor, understanding why she'd done what she'd done, even if it wasn't the best course of action. She wondered what it'd take to fill that missing soul piece in.

The scene came to her gently: the woman, with the man who she'd loved next to her, both holding the baby. Not caring about perfection or technique, Abby outlined in their forms quickly. It looked abstract given she wasn't used to using her left hand, but she decided to go with it. It was the intent that counted, right?

You got that right, sister, Bro Paul sounded in.

She did the best she could do, weaving her own magic into the canvas. When she got to a place where she thought it was done, she stepped back.

Her ancestor stepped up next to her.

As Abby faced her, she realized that they were surrounded by a circle of ghostly women. It wasn't until she saw her mother and her grandmother that she realized it was all the women in their line. Each one had an empty space over their heart, all identical.

Abby looked down, not surprised to see that she had one too. How had she never noticed?

That first ancestor held her hand out, and the missing piece of her soul, the part of her that she'd given away, flew into it. She took it and pressed it to her heart, and the emptiness filled.

Suddenly, the soul pieces for the rest of the women flew back, each one being whole before Abby's eyes.

And then it was her turn.

When it flew back to her, she gasped. She put her hands over it, feeling the fullness and warmth. Finn, she thought, wishing he was here.

Her mother stepped forward and touched her head, her eyes full of emotion. Abby heard her voice in her head: *Thank you, baby.*

With that, all the spirits faded away.

A bit shell-shocked, she set her brush down and turned to find Lynne gaping at her.

"What the hell was that?" her friend asked with huge eyes.

———

"You saw that?" Abby asked for what seemed like the tenth time.

"Yes," Lynne replied, also for the tenth time. This time she added an eye roll to it.

How was that possible? Bro Paul said Lynne was coming into her own, but this was amazing. "All of it? My mother and everything?"

"Well, I never met your mom, so I didn't recognize her or anyone." Lynne pursed her lips. "And I didn't hear them or see much more than outlines, but, yeah, the room was full of spirits for a second."

Abby crossed her arms, studying her friend. Some of the gray surrounding her gave way to pink, and her eyes looked a little brighter. Most importantly, she looked like herself. "How long have you been able to see spirits?"

"I started to see things right before the accident. I think maybe it was when you gave me the painting, but I can't quite remember." Lynne frowned, her gaze distant. "You know how I always said I wanted to be psychic? Do you think it can just happen?"

"Bro Paul seemed to think so. He said that you were finally ready to hear again."

"Abby, I know things now, without any doubt. Like I knew your soulmate was here." She took Abby's hand. "Don't be mad at me."

Shaking her head, Abby knelt in front of her. "What would I be mad at you for?"

"Because I saw Kevin attacking me, but I didn't believe it. I didn't want to believe it." She swallowed audibly. "I saw all of it in a vision the day before, but I thought I was being fanciful. So it's not your fault this happened, it's mine. I could have done something to change it if I'd trusted myself. I could have kept him from hurting you."

Abby opened her mouth to say something, but she didn't know what to say. She remembered what Bro Paul said about her not trusting her gifts—it seemed to be an epidemic.

Lynne speared her with an unflinching look. "I know I could have changed it, so don't say that I don't know that. I'm not going to ever mistrust myself again."

"Okay." She rubbed a hand up and down Lynne's arm, trying to soothe her. "Okay."

Her best friend didn't say anything for a long time. "Dancers have a shelf life. I was going to have to figure out what to do with myself once I got too old anyway. It's just happened sooner than I thought. I was just avoiding it." She looked Abby in the eye, her gaze the clear gold-green that it'd been before for the first time in six months. "You know the part that makes me most angry, though?"

"What?"

"That he was the one who chose for me." Her voice shook with anger and sorrow. "That I let him take my choice about when I'd retire away from me. I *let* him do that. I should have stood up to him instead of trying to fix it. Instead, I thought if I tried harder, if I asked you to fix me, that he'd love me and stay. And I let you get caught up in it." She took Abby's face in her hands. "I'm so sorry."

"Listen to her," Paul said, materializing behind Lynne.

Abby looked up. *I still feel like my painting was a catalyst.*

"Yeah, but it was her choice on how it went down." He shrugged. "We could debate this all day, but it doesn't change the current facts, and it doesn't help anyone move on."

Lynne frowned and looked over her shoulder. "Is something behind me?"

"Just Bro Paul." Given what Lynne said she'd seen earlier, Abby shouldn't have been surprised, but she was. "You can see him?"

Twisting to look over her shoulder, she shook her head. "Kind of. A vague outline. I smell something too. Like beer."

"I always knew she had potential." Bro Paul moved in front of Lynne and waved his arms, his Franciscan robes flapping. "Hey, Lynne!" he yelled. "How you doin', kid!"

Lynne recoiled, rubbing her ear. "What *was* that?"

"Leave her alone," Abby told him.

"This is so weird," Lynne said. "I always wanted to be psychic, but I never thought it'd happen. It feels like I'm suddenly just open. Is my soul the same?"

Abby let her vision go soft-focus. She knew Lynne's soul inside and out because she'd been next to it for over twenty-eight years. It was duller than usual because she'd been infirm for so long and her spirits dimmed, but the light was still there.

Then she saw two things she never had before: the faintest blue band, right around her waist, and a section near her heart that was missing, just like Abby's had been before she healed the women of her line.

Abby had never looked at the women of Lynne's line. Lynne had been orphaned when she was six and couldn't remember very much of her mother, much less the people she came from. Not that Lynne liked to talk about her mother anyway.

Now, Abby looked deeper, going on a gut feeling.

"That's what I'm talking about," Bro Paul said from the sidelines.

She ignored him, focused on following the thread back in time from generation to generation of the women in Lynne's family.

Then she saw it.

It was a woman, back centuries. She had a little of Lynne's look about her: long blond hair and light eyes. While Lynne's eyes looked kindhearted, this woman's were creepy—a color so pale that it looked leached of all emotion.

Abby observed scene after scene: the woman having sex with a burly man, the woman watching the man marry another woman, the woman alone on a cliff screaming in anger, the woman very pregnant, alone.

And then the woman with a baby basket next to her, making some sort of potion as she chanted, sprinkling it on the child. Not all the words were audible, but Abby got enough to know that the woman was cursing the women to never forget how much a man could hurt them.

Similar to what her ancestor had done, actually, though to her it seemed like the potential for destruction was greater.

"Is everything okay?" Lynne asked, her voice wavering. "It's worrisome when you get that far-off look in your eyes."

"I think I see something that needs to be addressed, from your family line."

"Finally!" Paul exulted. A stein of beer materialized in his hand. "This a cause for celebration!"

"What is?" Abby asked, looking over her shoulder at him.

"You'll see soon enough." He toasted them.

She shook her head. "I want to know now." But he'd already disappeared.

"He's gone," Lynne said. "Why did I smell beer?"

"In his Franciscan lives, he always elected to be the brewer." She checked the time. "Finn's going to be here soon, but I can tell him we'll go out another time."

Lynne frowned. "Why would you do that?"

She gestured with her left hand. "To paint a scene to fix this."

"That's crazy. Go out. Have fun. Get freaky." Lynne made a shooing motion. "This has waited this long. It can wait another few days."

Abby hesitated. "You sure?"

"Yeah." Lynne leaned in, her gaze earnest. "But I need to tell you that you stink of paint."

Abby choked out a laugh.

"Go take a quick shower." Lynne patted her ass. "Knowing how Finn feels about you, he'll be here early. I'll clean your brushes."

Abby stopped short. "You hate to clean brushes."

"Yeah, but I like Finn." Lynne shrugged. "It works out in the end."

She bent down to kiss her on top of her head. "Thank you."

"Wear something nice," Lynne yelled as Abby entered her room. "Not jeans."

Her jeans *were* nice. Mumbling to herself, she stripped out of her clothes and stepped into the shower. In quick order, she cleaned up, got dressed—hopefully Lynne would approve of the red off-the-shoulder top and the gold pants—and swiped on a bit of mascara and lipstick. She put her favorite earrings on—she hadn't worn them in months—and got boots that had enough of a heel for her to feel sexy but comfortable enough to wear on a walk.

Five minutes to spare. She fluffed her hair one last time and went into the living room.

Lynne was sitting by the window, talking to Finn who had pulled what was usually Abby's chair closer to the wheelchair. They had their heads bent, their conversation intense.

Abby took a moment to enjoy their obvious amity, her heart warm. If she were ever going to be with someone, he'd have to love Lynne like she did, wouldn't he?

Smiling, she sauntered into the living room.

They both looked up at the clack of her boots on the wood floor. Finn stood up slowly, rubbing his palms on his gray wool pants. He wore a dark-blue shirt that deepened his eyes, open at the collar and the sleeves rolled up. Who knew forearms could be so sexy?

He came over to her, his arms wrapping around her, one hand in the ends of her hair. "You look lovely," he said for her ears only, placing the softest kiss on her lips. "Different somehow though."

In the little while since she called the soul piece back for her ancestral line, she felt different. It'd stand to reason it affected her—she had a whole heart for the first time in her life. She had a momentary pang, wondering how her mother's life could have been different if someone had healed the line heart sooner, but that wasn't to dwell on now. "How do I look?"

"Light. Glowing, with a new confidence in your eyes." He ran the backs of his fingers down her cheek. "Even more radiant than before."

Her smile turned into a gasp when he tugged her hair, just enough to remind her of that morning. "That's not going to be conducive to an evening out."

"Just giving us both something to look forward to." Taking her hand, he turned to Lynne. "You're going to be okay tonight?"

Lynne gave a dismissive wave. "I have male strippers scheduled to arrive in half an hour, so you guys should leave now."

Finn laughed. "Darling, if you hired strippers here, I hope you like old hairy men with sagging—"

"Please, Finn." Lynne held up her hand, turning her face away. "Don't poo-poo my fun."

Abby went to her and kissed her cheek. "Text me if you need something?"

"I won't, but yes, Mom, I'll text." Lynne gripped her hand and looked her deep in the eyes. "Be happy," she whispered.

Abby nodded. She waited for Finn to say his goodbyes and then took his hand as they left the house.

As they reached his sleek SUV, he beeped his car unlocked, but instead of opening the door for her, he pinned her against the car with his body. His mouth hovered over hers. "I'm torn," he said.

She glanced at his mouth. When was he going to kiss her? "Is that a confession?"

He shook his head. "It's a dilemma. I like your lipstick, but I want to kiss you. Do I wait, to preserve it, and drive myself crazy? Or do I say fuck it and muss your lipstick?"

"Both options have merit," she said, rubbing herself against him.

"I see you're just trouble." He reached around her and opened the car door.

"I don't think I've ever anticipated an evening this much," she said as she got in. She waited until he closed her door and got in his side before continuing. "I don't even think my first gallery showing felt this exciting."

"Tell me about that," he said as he started the car and pulled away from the curb.

She shrugged. "It was in New York, with a lot of important people that I didn't care about. I had two paintings showing, both done with general thoughts of healing, for prosperity and love. I was nervous, and then I was bored because I realized that the people coming to see my work weren't any different than I was." She pursed her lips, looking out the side window. "Where are we going?"

"My favorite place." Without taking his eyes off the road, he said, "I looked at the X-rays and surgical notes."

Abby felt her entire body tense. "And?"

"I think I can help her." He glanced at her again. "That's not saying she'll be able to dance professionally again—that'll depend on her—but I think there's a good chance we can get her more mobile."

"And?" she asked, feeling like there was more.

"Her mental state concerns me, but I think with extra attention and care we can make sure she stays stable."

Tears flooded her eyes, and she had to swallow the thick gratitude that rose in her throat before she could say, "Thank you."

He shook his head. "Don't thank me yet. It's a long road ahead."

Didn't matter. She couldn't wait to tell Lynne. The next ten minutes gave her time to pull herself together. She mostly had her emotions under control again by the time he pulled over onto a patch of dirt. "We're here," he said.

She got out and looked around.

He walked around the car and took her hand. "It'll be worth it, I promise. And we won't walk too far or in anything too rough."

She didn't think she'd ever gone out with a guy who'd cared about her comfort while walking. That was enough for her to fall even more in love with him.

They walked hand in hand in silence down a narrow

path. He walked slowly, making sure she had sure footing rather than forging ahead.

"Do you hear that?" Abby asked after a few minutes.

"What?"

"The sound of peace." She inhaled the hope. "I can breathe here."

He squeezed her hand.

They crested a hill and then the Atlantic came into view. She gasped. "Look at all the blues."

"Magnificent, isn't it?" He led her further on the path, occasionally holding briar vines out of her way. They were almost to the cliff when something made her turn her head to the left.

There was a house there—a large cottage with blue shutters. It was surrounded by red roses, with a purply blue hydrangea in front for a kick of color. It was the wrong angle, but it looked exactly like the cottage she'd painted with Claire.

"It's for sale," Finn said.

She frowned at him. "What?"

"That house." He nodded at it. "It's been for sale for quite a long time."

"What's wrong with it?" she asked.

"The price." He smiled sardonically. "And it's rather modern inside. I've always liked it, though. I like the remoteness."

She bit her lip to keep from pointing out that it looked like the house she'd painted. She thought about how Claire had painted them outside it, holding hands just like they were now, and wondered if it was a sign.

Duh, she heard Paul say from far away.

"It looks like the house you painted," Finn said. "I realized it as I was getting ready to come pick you up. I can't believe I didn't see it before. I wanted to show it to you."

"I really like it," she said softly, trying not to think about the little girl she'd seen.

He pulled her into his arms and nuzzled the side of her neck. "I want to sleep with you tonight and wake up with you in the morning," he murmured in her ear. "If we were in Dublin, I'd take you to my house."

"But we're here," she said, burrowing into him.

He nodded. "Come have dinner with my parents tomorrow. You and Lynne. My mom will be a pain in the ass, but I can promise you she'll love you, and she'll feel compelled to use all her mothering on Lynne. It'll be win-win."

Abby laughed. "That's brilliant."

"I think so."

She could feel his smile against her neck. She rubbed her head against his face. "And tonight?"

"We'll try to be really quiet in your room, and we'll fail miserably. I'm hoping you don't mind if I have coffee in the morning with you and Lynne."

She pulled his arms tighter around her, hugging them to her. "I don't. Not at all."

24

Dermot shifted on his meditation pillow, trying to settle, but the rush of the family man's soul had faded, and it was becoming increasingly difficult to not go after another one. He tried to still his mind like the Buddhist monk who'd shared meditation techniques with him had taught him, but something in him kept urging him to return to the hospital to look for the next soul.

He tempered that need by reminding himself of the day of Fiona's accident. Thinking about that day was never comfortable. He knew it was because of him that Fiona killed herself.

He hadn't meant for that to happen.

He hadn't meant for any of this to happen.

That day, he'd gone home from school to change into a nicer shirt—he'd only had one that he wore on the rare occasions Molly Fionnlagh made him go to church. That day, he'd wanted to change his shirt because Fiona had agreed to walk to Drowes Bridge with him.

Inhaling deeply, Dermot closed his eyes. Every time he thought of that day, it was like it repeated all over again in real time. He remembered the euphoria he'd felt walking home, knowing Fiona was going out with him; he could still smell the sour smell of beer when he stepped inside his house; he could still see the hateful look his mother gave him after he'd walked out of his room with the fresh shirt. And he could feel the stickiness of the warm beer she'd thrown on him, for no reason other than she was a mean drunk.

Breathe, he told himself, feeling the press of anger on his lungs. His mother was long gone now and no more significant than the spider he'd killed in his bedroom the other night.

Fiona was also gone, but that still upset him.

He'd been furious when he'd stormed out of the house. He'd put his other shirt back on, but he could still smell the beer. He didn't have time to do anything about it—he was already late to meet Fiona.

When he'd arrived at the place where they said they'd meet, Fiona was there. So was Niall, leaning too close to her.

Dermot's hands clenched, seeing it over again.

Everything backed up on him—his mean mother, the feeling that he had nothing to offer Fiona like Niall did, the fear of losing her—and he lost control. He went over and punched Niall, who'd punched him back. He could still hear Fiona screaming at them both to stop it.

And then he'd looked at her, all the rage swirling in his chest. He thought about all their plans, how they talked about going to uni together and conquering the business world. He remembered kissing her and planning to live with her in Dublin. And he'd thought, *Mine.*

Out of nowhere a car came careening around the curve. He and Niall jumped out of the way. Fiona didn't.

He remembered her scream and the startled look on her face as she got hit. He could see the large shard that rended from her chest—a deep rose color—floating toward him, and the feel of it when he reached out and took it.

He hadn't known it was possible for that to even happen.

He'd gone on instinct, leaning over Fiona, holding her hand, waiting for the ambulance, that piece gripped in his other hand until he was alone when he realized he needed to do something with it. So when some instinct told him to push it into his own chest, he did.

And he was overcome with the most pure sensation of love he'd ever felt in his entire life. It felt like anything was possible, that he could *be* someone.

The next day he'd found out that Fiona was paralyzed from the accident, and he knew without a doubt that the piece that flew from her was key. He'd wondered if he could give it back, but he couldn't figure out a way.

Eventually he read enough esoteric books to know that it was a soul piece, but he couldn't find any reference on how to return a soul piece to someone. Then it didn't matter because she committed suicide and was gone.

So he looked on it as a gift—the last gift she'd given him. He'd had to, or he would have followed her for the guilt. To honor her, he contributed to charities she would have liked and donated to hospitals to help people stay alive and whole.

But sometimes they were on the verge of dying anyway. Taking a piece of their soul ensured that they lived on in him. He learned from them. He didn't want to do it, but he couldn't stop it, so he made sure that he deserved it with the good he did.

He relaxed his fists, rubbing his palms on his knees, trying to relax. He would not think of the hospital. He would not think about souls.

He would think about Madelynne.

Over the course of their stream of texts, he'd discovered that Madelynne had grown up in an orphanage with Abigail, and that dance had been her way out. He admitted how much they had in common was part of the attraction—like recognized like, after all. But he especially admired her wit and humor, which had to have been hard to cultivate when it appeared that her career might be at an end.

She always made him smile.

Taking his mobile out of his pocket, he texted her.

Distract me.

Her reply was instant.

There's a kraken outside my window.

He surprised himself with a laugh.

Is it hungry?

She said:

Krakens are always hungry. Their hunger comes from deep within, a dark place that they've forgotten exists. There's only one thing that'll appease a kraken and stop them from doing destruction.

He froze, reading her reply several times before he could formulate a response.

There was only one thing to say:

What's that one thing?

Her text was immediate:

Love of course.

25

"I'm so excited to meet his mom and dad," Lynne said.

Amused, Abby looked up from where she sat on the floor organizing her paints. She was hoping to invite Claire over tomorrow to paint with her again and wanted things in order.

"What do you think they're like?" If Lynne could have paced in her wheelchair, she would have. As it was, she rolled back and forth in the living room, the floor creaking with every rotation of the wheels.

"Probably down-to-earth and no-nonsense like Finn," Abby said.

"Oh my God, then I'm sure to love them," Lynne exclaimed.

Abby was so grateful Finn had invited them over for dinner. He'd already had such a profound impact on her best friend, and he hadn't even started treatment.

He'd had a profound impact on her too. A delicious shiver rolled over her body thinking of the way he'd kissed her after their date last night. An hour of slow, endless kisses, one after another until she was a puddle in his arms.

She sighed. She could have kissed him all night. But he'd brought her back home, where he proceeded to rock her world.

"How do you think it'll be, Abby?" Lynne rolled to where Abby sat on the floor. "I never knew my father, and I can barely remember what it was like to have a mother."

She eyed her best friend. "You know, it won't do you any good if you come out of your skin before we go there. You should go for a walk."

Lynne snorted. "It'd be more of a roll for me. How is it you're not coming out of your skin? You're meeting your beloved's parents. Shouldn't you be a wreck?"

"I feel calm, actually." She thought about the house he'd shown her and felt hope. They hadn't talked about her gifts and his skepticism but taking her to the house had to be a good sign. "Plus, I'm happy that he thinks he can help you dance again."

"And he's going to spend the night shagging you silly again," Lynne said with a saucy smirk.

Abby looked at her friend. "Are you happy he's going to help you?"

Lynne's humor faded into a wide-eyed look of fear. "I'm thrilled," she whispered, "but I'm terrified too. Abby, I kind of like Dermot. I want to dance again, but I also want to be well enough to be with someone like him."

"What do you mean 'someone like him'?" Abby frowned. "Any man would be lucky to have you."

Lynne smiled sadly. "Abby, no one wants someone who's going to be a burden."

"You're not a burden," she insisted.

"Says the woman who's been taking care of me all my life."

"Exactly. So I would know."

The corner of Lynne's lips quirked up.

"How does Dermot feel?" Abby asked.

Lynne worried the corner of her scarf. "We're just text pals, Abby. He, of course, must know that I'm in a wheelchair."

"That's only temporary." It was true, though—the invisible man couldn't hide in Tullaghan. And if someone in Tullaghan hadn't mentioned it, Finn would have.

"He hasn't asked to meet up or anything," Lynne said with a frown.

"Maybe he's just busy," she offered, trying to buffer Lynne. She'd have to ask Finn about Dermot. Lynne hadn't had the best taste in men to date. The last thing they needed was another Kevin-type situation.

"Maybe." Lynne looked away. "When we were kids, we never talked about growing and getting married the way little girls are supposed to."

"Because who could have thought of happily ever after with Sister Mary Catherine breathing down her neck?" Abby tried to joke.

Lynne faced her, giving her a knowing look. "Or with a curse passed down in her family from generation to generation."

Abby grinned ruefully. "There's that."

"Do you believe in soulmates now?" Lynne asked earnestly.

Her friend wanted a real answer, so she paused to

think about it. Clearing her line had changed things, but so had meeting Finn. But did that mean she believed in soulmates?

She pursed her lips. "I want to believe," she finally said.

Lynne nodded. "So do I."

26

F inn looked at the dishes his mom put in his hands. "These are Grandmother's plates."

"The fine china, yes." She put her hands on her hips, narrowing her eyes at him. "What are you looking at me like that for, Carrick Fionnlagh?"

"I'm wondering if you want me to polish the silver and the doorknobs."

"When was the last time you brought a girl home to meet us?" she demanded.

He thought about it. "Mary Bridget Kelly when I was eleven."

"Precisely. So I'll fuss as much as I want for this momentous occasion." She shooed him with her hands. "Set the table in the dining room."

He arched his brow but knew better than to comment.

He was folding the napkins the way his mom had shown him—he knew she was going to redo them when he wasn't looking—when his phone signaled a text. He pulled it out of his pocket and looked at it, hoping it was Abby.

It was Dermot.

Drinks tonight?

Finn was planning on going home with Abby after dinner. Again. And for as many nights as she'd let him.

Dinner with Abby tonight. Talk tomorrow.

Dermot replied:

Lucky. Tomorrow it is.

Finn frowned, feeling something amiss. He sent a follow-up.

Everything okay?

Dermot took longer than usual to reply.

Busy with work. Have fun with Abigail.

"Is the coast clear?" his dad said, popping his head around the corner.

"Mostly." Putting his mobile away, Finn grinned at him. "She's fussing."

"And isn't that her right, as your mother?" Conall leaned against the doorway. "You look calm."

"I'm more than calm. I'm"—he searched for the word, surprised when it came to him—"happy."

His dad's expression softened. "This is the one, then?"

Finn thought about how he felt taking Abby to the house, about the peace as he held her while she slept. He thought about kissing her, and how he couldn't imagine a world where he didn't have the privilege of her lips every day. And he said, "Dad, I can't remember what it was like before I met her, and I'm not sure I want to."

His dad teared up. Sniffing his nose, he clapped a hand on Finn's shoulder, coughing to cover up the emotion. "Well, then." Striding to a cabinet in the corner, he pulled out two small glasses and a bottle of poitín. He gave Finn a warning look as he poured them small amounts of the clear liquor in the glasses. "Don't tell Molly."

"I value my life too," he said, accepting the glass from his dad.

"And your bollocks." His dad raised his glass. "To your woman. May all your ups and downs be between the sheets. Sláinte."

"Sláinte." He downed the poitín, surprised by how smooth and round it was. "I was expecting something more like turpentine," he admitted to his dad.

"That's from Robbie Ferguson. The recipe is passed down from his great-grandfather. 'Tis good, it is."

"Finn, stop drinking with your father and come wash the lettuce for me," his mom called from the kitchen.

He and his dad looked at each other in sympathy.

"Conall, go wash up," Molly yelled. "The girls will be here shortly, and you still smell like your cows."

"Good Lord, woman," his dad bellowed. "I'm the man of the house!"

"Only until I send you to sleep in the barn," she replied.

Conall shook his head ruefully. Then he grinned at Finn. "I love that woman."

His mom kept him occupied right up until the moment Abby and Lynne were due to arrive. At first he wondered if she was doing it for him, but he quickly realized she was the one who was nervous.

When the car pulled into the gravel drive in front of the house, Molly looked up from turning out her freshly made soda bread onto a cooling rack. "That's her." She quickly brushed her hands off on her apron and untied it. Crumpling it in one hand, she patted her hair with the other. "How do I look, Carrick?"

"Like a goddess." He kissed her temple. "Don't worry, Mom."

She harrumphed. "Easy for you to say. It's always the mother-in-law that's hated."

"Then I promise I'll never marry her," he said blandly.

She hit him with her apron. "Get on with you."

Grinning, he kissed her again and went to meet Abby and Lynne. Stepping out of the house, he walked to the passenger side of the car to help Lynne out. Abby looked up at him as she closed the boot, stars in her eyes. "Lynne wanted to use her crutches tonight," she explained, wonder in her tone, coming around the car with them.

"And why wouldn't she?" He took a moment to kiss Abby, softly so he wouldn't muss her lipstick. The barely-there kisses were oddly erotic. Then he turned to Lynne, who was shifting her leg out of the car carefully, and kissed her cheek. "There's freedom in movement, isn't there, darling?"

"There's something," Lynne said with a self-deprecating smile.

"Come on." He helped her ease out of the seat and made sure she was secure against the car before taking the crutches from Abby and offering them to Lynne. "You ready to try this out?"

"I hate the crutches," she murmured, tucking them under her arms.

He didn't blame her. He knew what an effort it was to walk with crutches. "Then we have incentive to get you walking without them fast, don't we? And your new brace should be here tomorrow."

Lynne stopped and looked at him. "You got me a new brace?"

"And a few other things. I apologize that it's taken so long." The brace had gone missing in the post, and the herbalist, his mom's friend, had been out of town visiting her new grandchild so he'd had to wait to fill the order he wanted for Lynne.

Lynne blinked back tears, her hands tight on the crutches. "Thank you, Finn," she whispered.

He brushed her face. "Come now. My mother will accuse me of making a guest cry, and then I'll never hear the end of it."

She huffed a laugh like he'd hoped. Slowly, she pivoted toward the house, moving slowly on the gravel drive.

He stayed close behind her to make sure she didn't lose her balance. It also gave him an opportunity to observe how she moved. He shook his head. Her leg wasn't capable of bearing weight. Her doctors should have encouraged her back to weight-bearing as soon as it'd been possible.

Abby suddenly exclaimed, "Is that a horse?"

Finn looked over to his mom's horse, which had come around the house to see what was going on. "Dark Chocolate is less a horse and more my mom's pet."

"Your mom has a pet horse?" Lynne shook her head. "And here I thought I couldn't love her more."

"Can I touch him?" Abby asked.

"Sure." He watched Abby ease over to see the horse. She was wearing dark-red pants and tall boots, with a soft-looking white sweater that made him want to stroke her curves. Though, truthfully, she could be wearing cardboard and he'd want to stroke her curves.

Lynne paused a moment to breathe before resuming their walk to join Abby. "If she could see how you look at her, she wouldn't doubt the future so much."

"What does she doubt?" he asked, still looking at Abby. He only saw a confident woman, not one who'd question anything.

"She doubts if you could truly love her. *Her*, not the idea of her. The whole of her." Lynne stopped again and looked up at him with fathomless eyes. "The spiritual side of her as well as the earthly."

He frowned. "I'm not a spiritual person."

"I disagree. Your spirituality is just different than the common person's. But so is hers."

The horse trotted over to them right away. "He thinks everyone will give him treats," Finn said when the horse nudged his pocket. He stepped in to divert the horse so he wouldn't push Lynne off-balance.

Leaning heavily on her crutches, Lynne held out one hand for the horse to sniff her before touching his face. "You're a pretty boy. Of course you'd want to be spoiled."

Abby looked over her shoulder and snorted.

Lynne stiffened, and then she glanced behind her too just as Dark Chocolate shied back, shaking his head.

Finn gripped Lynne to keep her steady. "What is it?"

"I just heard—" Lynne shook her head.

Abby faced her friend, looking astonished. "You heard him again?"

Lynne smiled, albeit a wobbly one. "Yeah. Crazy, huh?"

"What?" Finn asked again.

Lynne just said, "Abby's guide. Let's go in. Your mom's probably waiting."

Probably waiting impatiently, but Lynne's words about Abby's spirituality ran through his head and he found he wanted to understand. What guide? He looked around and saw nothing.

As Lynne began her slow journey to the front door, Finn took Abby's hand. "What was that?"

"Nothing." She tugged his arm. "Come introduce me to your parents."

He held her there. "Explain it to me, Abby."

She looked him in the eye, measuring. She nodded with a sigh. "Everyone has guides to help them. Some people are just aware of theirs. That's all it is."

"So, like a ghost?" he asked as neutrally as he could.

"I'd call him a spirit, but yeah." She tipped her head. "Is this really the time for this conversation?"

Finn shook his head, his frown deepening. "Abby, assuming you're actually talking to someone, what if they tell you the wrong thing or mislead you?"

"A guide would never do that. It goes against Divine law. If a guide did that, he'd be out. And, ultimately, the decision is mine. It's no different than someone I trust advising me. You can counsel your patients on what to do, but they have to decide what's right for them, right?"

"You believe this." He stared at her. "What did he advise when you did the painting for Lynne?"

He wished he hadn't asked the moment her eyes clouded over. "He didn't, because I didn't ask him."

She turned and followed Lynne toward the house.

Shite. He hurried after her, feeling like a heel. He reached out for her, pulling her to a stop. "I'm sorry," he said softly. "I just want to understand."

Abby studied him for a long silent moment. Nodding, she pressed a soft kiss to his lips and tried to smile. He kept her hand as they walked to the house where his mom was waiting in the threshold.

Lynne reached the front door a couple steps ahead of them, slightly out of breath.

His mom's gaze went between Abby and Lynne, and then she unerringly focused on Abby. "You must be Abigail. I'm Molly Fionnlagh."

Abby looked startled when his mom grabbed her in a hug.

Lynne laughed.

Molly didn't let Abby go, keeping an arm around her waist. Probably so Abby couldn't run away, Finn figured. His mom turned to Lynne and smiled. "And you're the sister."

"Adopted sister," Lynne said, "but yes."

"A sister is a sister, blood or otherwise." Still holding Abby, she reached to hug Lynne too, gently though, careful not to pull her off-balance. It was Lynne's turn to look startled.

Then Molly, sniffing back tears if Finn wasn't mistaken, gruffly said, "Into the kitchen, the lot of you. Conall!" she yelled. "We have guests."

Once his mom had dragged Abby into the kitchen, Lynne whispered to Finn, "This is what it's like to have a mother?"

He nodded. "Unfortunately."

"I want one." She looked around in wonder. "You are *so* lucky."

"I'm sure I can arrange to give you Molly, if you're that desperate."

"I would take her in a heartbeat." Lynne pursed her lips in thought. "Abby will be her daughter-in-law when you marry, but maybe she'll just adopt me. Unless you have a brother?" She looked at him hopefully.

"She thinks of Dermot as a son," he said, going on instinct.

Lynne brightened. "Really?"

He pulled out a chair for her and she gratefully sank into it. He pulled another chair closer, setting the back cushion on the seat before helping Lynne lift her leg to prop it up. "Though why you'd be interested in him is beyond me. He uses more hair products than any woman I've ever met."

"He's sweet."

"More of that and I'll wonder if you don't need a psychiatrist rather than an orthopedist," he teased.

Lynne laughed.

Abby glanced up from where Molly had her cornered, checking on Lynne with a soft expression in her eyes, before returning her full attention to his mother. He wondered if he should save her or let her experience the totality of Molly Fionnlagh.

"And now who wants a glass of our finest?" his dad said in his normal bellow, blustering into the room, carrying a bottle of wine in each hand.

Lynne held her hand up. "I do!"

His dad staggered to a stop in front of her. "Aren't you a lovely one?" His dad set the bottles on the table and took Lynne's hand in both of his. "Conall Fionnlagh. And you must be from heaven?"

Finn rolled his eyes at his dad's so-called charm.

Lynne laughed. "Sister Mary Catherine would have disagreed."

"Dad," he admonished with a lift of his brow.

Conall waved him away, still holding Lynne's hand. "Open the bottle, boy." He leaned in and whispered conspiratorially loud. "And rescue your woman from your mother before she runs away screaming."

"I heard that, Conall Fionnlagh," Molly called from the other side of the kitchen.

His dad winked at Lynne. "Now tell me about you. Are you liking your stay in Ireland?"

Shaking his head, Finn took the wine bottles and set them next to Abby, where she was leaning against a counter and listening to his mother, who appeared to be talking a mile a minute. He opened a drawer for the wine opener and made quick work of the cork before sliding a hand around Abby's waist. "Mother, isn't the point of inviting Abby to dinner to get to know her?"

"And what do you think I'm doing?" Molly put her hands on her hips and glared at him. "Make yourself useful and pour the wine, Carrick."

Abby raised her brow at him as he did what his mother said.

Handing her a glass, he leaned in and softly said for just her ears, "It's going to be a long dinner."

Smiling, Abby took a sip from her glass. He was conscious of her watching him distribute the other glasses to everyone, taking the last one for himself. When he was done, Abby turned to his mother and said in a sweet voice, "Molly, do you mind if Finn shows me the house?"

"Please." She waved them off. "Just not the laundry, Carrick. I haven't tidied in there."

He set his wine glass next to hers and grabbed the reprieve, taking her hand and leading her down the hall.

"Where are we going?" she asked, trying to look into the other rooms.

"My bedroom, where I can properly apologize for earlier." He pulled her inside and closed the door, wrapping her in his arms.

He felt the tension melt from her body, and he knew it was going to be okay.

"Isn't it against the rules to bring a girl to your room?" she asked, slipping her arm around his waist as she looked around.

He wrapped his hands in the ends of her hair and lowered his mouth to nuzzle her neck. "Don't tell on me."

"Maybe you can give me incentive not to." She arched her neck, offering herself to him. "There isn't much of your youth in here, is there?"

"Not anymore." He'd thrown away most of the reminders after Fiona had died, but he didn't want to introduce a sad subject after his earlier gaffe. He wanted to focus on the good tonight.

"Too bad. I was looking forward to seeing if you had NSYNC posters," she replied.

Chuckling, he inhaled her scent, a spicy and mysterious fragrance, and groaned. "I've missed you today, Abby."

She sighed, melting against him some more. "It's rather surprising, isn't it?"

"Are you still okay with me spending the night with you?"

"Won't your mother mind?" she asked.

"She practically packed my bag," he said with a dry laugh.

Abby chuckled, and he felt it against his skin. He pulled her closer. "I need to let you go, or else you'll be naked and dinner will be late, which Mom would never forgive."

Laughing again, Abby pulled his head down for a light kiss. She wiped her lipstick off his lips with her thumb and said, "If you're a good boy the rest of the night, I'll give you a treat later."

He looked down at his erection. "That isn't the way to get me presentable."

Smiling in her sexy way, she ran her hand up his length. He put his hand on hers and pressed it there before taking it away.

She arched her brow and sashayed out of the room. He groaned and tried to think of things that would douse his ardor—sutures usually worked—but the only thing he could think of was licking into Abby's mouth as he pressed into her body.

He adjusted himself. It was going to be a long dinner.

Dinner was wonderful. Abby sat back in the glow of the lively conversation around her, sipping her tea, enjoying every single thing about it.

The only moment that had given her pause was outside, when Finn had questioned her about Bro Paul.

But she put that aside. For now. At some point, it needed to be addressed, because being a healer was as much a part of her as it was a part of him. She couldn't be with someone who didn't respect that. Even if she loved him.

And Abby definitely loved Finn.

She'd felt she had before she'd deleted the curse on her family line, but now that she could feel with her full heart, there was no question: she loved him body and soul.

Just because she'd corrected the family curse didn't mean that a happily ever after was guaranteed. She knew better than that. Two people were involved here. Finn could choose differently in the end. Or she could decide that him not believing in her, because that's what doubting her gifts came down to, wasn't enough.

Tonight, though, she was going to bask in the warmth and conversation and connection. She felt deliciously full and happy, and she was grateful to Finn for it.

And then there was Lynne.

She'd been animated in the way she used to be. She'd laughed and eaten and joked with Conall. She'd let Molly mother her and tell her which men in town to stay away from. Abby hadn't seen her best friend look so happy since even before the accident.

Abby was grateful to Molly and Conall for that. Finn was so lucky he had such wonderful parents. She tried not to imagine what it'd be like if they were hers too, but she couldn't help herself.

It'd be wonderful.

As if sensing her thoughts, Finn took her hand under the table.

She glanced at him. She'd promised him a treat when they got home. Little did he know that the treat was her body.

His eyelids lowered, going sexy and slumberous.

Okay—maybe he knew already.

When it was time to go, Finn helped Lynne into the car and then came around to the driver's side, leaning down into the open door. "I'll follow you home."

The word *home* caught on her heart. She nodded, not

trusting herself to speak because of the surprising burst of emotion hearing him say that little word caused. She pictured that house with the roses.

He kissed her, lingering on her lips as if to remind her of her earlier promise. He ran his knuckles down her cheek and then shut the car door.

"You know how you can get a contact high from someone smoking pot?" Lynne snapped her seat belt secure. "I think I just got a contact orgasm."

Abby shot her a quelling look as she turned the car on.

"I loved his parents," Lynne declared. "*Loved* them. Conall was so charming, and Molly was just like I'd always imagined a mom should be. Finn is so lucky. You're lucky too. You scored on the in-law front, and for that, I say thank you."

"Let's just focus on the present and getting you back up and running."

"That's not what Finn is going to think about tonight." Lynne snorted. "He has it bad for you. He'd tie you to his bed and keep you there forever if he were a less civilized man. A blind person could see that. Even Molly saw it."

Abby groaned.

"Don't worry. Molly looked like she wanted to hand him rope so he'd get it done." Lynne laughed when Abby groaned again.

They arrived at the cottage quickly, Finn pulling into the driveway behind them. He came around and helped Lynne out of the car. Handing her the crutches, he discreetly escorted her inside.

They'd left the wheelchair by the front door, and

Lynne eased into it with a relieved sigh. She smiled up at them, tired, as she handed Finn the crutches. "Well, kids, I'm off, and then you can get off too."

"Jesus, Lynne." Abby shook her head, her face burning.

Grinning, Finn just leaned down and kissed Lynne's cheek. "Good night, darling."

Winking at him, Lynne rolled down the hallway. When her door shut, Finn turned to her. "She fancies Dermot, doesn't she?"

"Yes." Glancing at Lynne's closed door, Abby worried her lip.

"Is that bad?" he asked with a frown.

"She hasn't picked very good men." She shrugged apologetically. "I know he's your friend, but I have to ask if he's a jerk."

"Dermot is many things, but I've never known him to be anything less that honorable with a woman. He dated Fiona, you know."

That was somehow reassuring. Still, she thought about the strangeness of his soul and couldn't help but think something was off.

Smiling, unaware of her doubts, Finn held his hand out.

None of that was for now, she realized. Now was for her and Finn. Abby took his palm and led him to her room.

Inside, she sat on her bed as he closed the door. She began to pull her boots off, feeling him watch her as he unbuttoned his shirt. As they slowly got undressed, she was aware of the intimacy of it, like this was what they did. She was aware of him, of how natural it was to have him stripping there. With each article of clothing that he shed, the anticipation grew—the need to touch him and feel his skin against hers.

She shimmied out of her panties and dropped them on the floor on top of her other discarded clothing. Lifting the comforter, she scooted under it, holding it open for him in invitation.

He eased in, gliding on top of her. She wrapped her legs around his waist as he nestled between her thighs.

He held her face and began to nibble at her lips, his other hand teasing her nipple hard. "My parents loved you both," he said between the kisses.

"The feeling was mutual. I miss my mom, but until tonight I didn't know that I missed my dad too. I never knew who he was."

Finn stopped kissing her and really looked at her. "You don't talk about it."

She shrugged. "What am I going to do? Whine about being a poor little orphan? It was what it was."

He rolled onto his back and pulled her into him so her head rested on his shoulder. "How old were you when your mom died?"

"Eight. Brain aneurysm." She smiled sadly. "My mom was very beautiful and very talented. People used to come from all around to have her read their cards. They swore by her sight, but she was always careful to tell them they needed to rely on their own judgment. She had rules, like she wouldn't see anyone again for six months after she'd done a reading for them."

"You don't do that."

She tried to parse how he felt about that, but all she felt was his curiosity. "Cards were never my thing. But she also didn't heal people, not like I do. My grandmother was known for poultices that could cure anything, but I only knew her by reputation. I saw her ghost a couple times when I was little, but that was all." She hadn't seen her mother's ghost ever. When she'd first gone to the orphanage, she used to call to her mom and wait for her to show up, but she hadn't seen her mom until the day she'd cleared the curse. Abby wasn't sure why. She wasn't sure thinking about it would be useful—it just made her feel sad.

She cleared her throat. "Lynne came to the orphanage after me. She was six. Her mom had just died, and she was so confused and scared. I remember seeing her and understanding, because I felt the same. In fact, every night until then I prayed that they'd send me a sister. When I saw Lynne, I knew she was the one they'd sent. So I went to her and took her hand and told her that I was happy the angels sent her to me."

Finn kissed her temple. "She loves you."

"I love her too." She rolled on top of him. "My mama used to say love heals the world."

"My mom used to tell us that if we didn't wash behind our ears, we'd grow cabbages there," Finn said self-deprecatingly.

Abby laughed.

He brushed her hair back from her face. "She didn't scare you away. You must like me."

She felt the curve of his smile and couldn't help

returning it as she arched into his touch, silently asking for more. "You're not bad."

He looked at her, suddenly serious. "About Lynne."

Abby groaned. "She was mostly kidding about the stuff earlier."

"About her leg."

Abby stilled, her heart suddenly beating even faster than it had been.

He eased up just a little and gazed at her solemnly, connected to her still. "I told her earlier that her new brace will arrive tomorrow, in theory. I have some herbs I want her to take and maybe soak in. I didn't tell her that I talked to her doctor, not that it was helpful." He pressed a quick kiss to her lips before he continued. "I'm going to do whatever I can to help her, Abby. I just want you to know that. We'll keep her upbeat like she was tonight and make sure she has everything she needs."

When she looked at him, she knew she must have her heart in her eyes. "*Thank you,*" she whispered.

"I've grown to care about her too." He flashed a wry smile. "We'll get her up and running in no time."

"I love you," she said, tucking her head under his chin and squeezing him to her.

He gathered her closer and rolled them both over, so he was on top of her again. Her legs wrapped around his waist because it was natural, and she wound her arms around his neck.

His hand wound into her hair, the way he liked to do. He angled her head up, staring into her eyes. His gaze was that beautiful cerulean that she'd always loved, deep and mysterious, an ocean that she wanted to dive into.

"I love you, Abby," he said softly, kissing her. "I didn't know I could possibly feel for anyone the way I feel for you."

Like all the magic in the world was possible, she thought. Though she didn't say it out loud, because Finn didn't believe in magic.

That made her sad for a moment, but then he began to kiss her in earnest, and the colors of his love wound around her—all the shades of red and green, blending with her own feelings—and she let herself get lost in that beauty.

27

A bby woke up feeling filled with hope.

It was partly because she woke up with her wrist feeling remarkably better. She'd been using the brace Finn had given her, and she'd put the arnica on her wrist and hand every night since he'd given it to her. She hadn't thought they'd help, but she'd promised to use them.

She wiggled her fingers. She couldn't believe how improved they were. They felt less like sausages and the green of the bruise seemed like it'd faded by a couple shades.

But, mostly, she owed her ebullience to Finn. She'd woken up with him all around her, tucked securely in his arms, feeling his skin against hers. It made her realize how much she'd undervalued feeling home. She hadn't had that since her mother had been alive. She wouldn't have even called her place in New Orleans *home*, per se. It was more her sanctuary.

She stretched in her bed, where she'd stayed after

he'd left earlier. She felt buoyant. If she were a color, she would have been opera pink. Bouncing out of bed, she went into her bathroom.

Tying the sash on her robe, she came out and got dressed. Then she called Bro Paul.

He appeared in front of her, studying her carefully. "Love looks good on you, kid. You realize what you did there, right?"

"I healed that moment in the past where my ancestor cursed future generations to avoid being hurt by a man."

"You called back that piece of her soul, her broken heart." He gave her a thumbs-up. "And have you looked at yourself lately?"

She looked down at her body. "In what way?"

"Your soul. Your heart feels more full, doesn't it? Because in calling back her soul piece, you called back pieces of your soul that had been missing." Hands on his hips, he grinned like a proud papa. "Healing in one fell swoop. Way to go, Abs."

"I didn't know you could heal spirits."

"A soul is a soul, alive or not." He shrugged. "It's no different. In painting the edited versions of the past, you eliminated the root cause of what plagued a person and gave them the soul pieces they lost in that past moment. It was a profoundly beautiful way of healing, but you didn't need to paint it. You just need to see it, understand it, and know what to call back. In this case, it was someone in another time, and the waves of it carried forth all the way to the present."

She thought about all those years and all those paintings, including the one she'd done for her mom, that hung in her bedroom now. "I didn't put together specifically that I was calling soul pieces back."

He nodded. "And imagine how powerful your work will be now that you know and can do it consciously."

She took a deep breath. "So what happened that day with Lynne's painting? If my painting cleared an obstacle and called back a soul piece, I don't understand how it went wrong."

Bro Paul got down on her level. "What did you do differently in the painting?"

"I was in it." She shook her head, at a loss. "But the person I'd been in that lifetime was in the scene I saw. I edited it so I defended her this time, which I didn't do that last time."

"Maybe you weren't supposed to defend her." Bro Paul shrugged. "Maybe the point was that she was supposed to stand up for herself."

Abby reared back. "Well, shit."

His laugh was booming. "Isn't this fun? What an adventure, eh?"

"That's one way of putting it." She thought about it. "So I painted the wrong solution."

"I don't know that I'd call it wrong," Bro Paul said, scratching his chin. "That's a judgment. You painted what you painted to call back a soul piece for her, and she reacted how she did, and so did that asshole. They could have chosen differently. Taking responsibility for someone else's actions is saying you have control over them, which is its own hubris, isn't it?"

"I guess so." She frowned. "Can I heal Lynne's leg?"

"You can't heal someone who doesn't want to heal. Finn's right on that one."

"Are you saying Lynne doesn't want to get better?" she asked in disbelief. "She said she wants to."

"She said she wants to because of Dermot," he pointed out.

Abby bit her lip, thinking about this. "So you're saying she wants it more for him than herself, so that's not really wanting it?"

He nodded. "That's what I'm saying."

"I'm missing something here," she said, looking at him for confirmation. "I'm not putting it together."

"You're close though."

It hit her suddenly. "Does it have to do with the women in Lynne's line? They've been cursed too, but with something different."

"Bingo!" He put his finger to his nose and then pointed it at her.

"I haven't seen how to correct it yet."

He shrugged. "Then it's probably not time, or Lynne isn't ready for it to be healed."

Abby wrinkled her nose. "I hate that."

Bro Paul laughed. "Tell me about it, kid. You know how frustrating it is, standing here waiting for people to choose to be happy so I can do my job?"

"I'm choosing happy." She went up to him and kissed his cheek. Looking him in the eye, she said a heartfelt, "*Thank you.* I'm sorry I was upset with you for so long."

"I figured you'd get your head out of your ass eventually." He patted her shoulder. "Your man's coming back, so you should get out there. Oh, and, kid?"

"Yeah?"

"You're on the right path, Abigail Angevine." He gestured to the window. "The path to love. And isn't it grand, because love is the most important thing."

She went over to look at what he indicated. Outside on the rose bush, there were a bunch of tiny buds that showed the promise of red blooms about to burst.

"External confirmation of internal growth. Good job, kid." He patted her again. "Keep it up," he said as he faded out.

She didn't have much time to marvel over the roses before she heard Finn's car pull up in front of the house. Feeling buoyant, she went to let him in.

He carried a large bag in one hand. Stepping inside, he leaned in to kiss her, lingering on her lips. She felt his lips and the way they seemed to connect all the way to her heart, which felt different. Full. Almost overflowing.

"You're going to distract me," he murmured, kissing his way down her neck.

"I'm just standing here."

"That doesn't seem to make any difference." Smiling, he brushed her hair back. "Where's Lynne? I have presents for her."

"Lynne!" Abby yelled.

Finn arched his brow at her. "I could have done that."

"Next time." She touched his chest. "You want something to drink?"

"I want to take you to your room and sip from you," he said in a low voice. "But I'm going to appease my desire for you by examining your wrist."

She blinked. "You don't have to. It's fine. It's better than fine, actually."

He didn't listen to her, taking her hand and turning it this way and that. He eased the brace off it and inspected the bruising and her mobility. "It's improved."

"I know. Thank you." She kissed him lightly.

Lynne's wheelchair creaked into the room. "I'd tell you to get a room, but you have one down the hall," she said as she joined them.

"I have something for you," Finn said, running his hand down Abby's hair one more time before going to Lynne.

"Words every woman longs to hear from an attractive man," Lynne joked.

"And this is definitely sexy." Grinning, Finn opened the bag and pulled out the new brace. "Shall we try this on, darling?"

Lynne frowned but she nodded.

Abby went to perch on the chair close to them so she could watch.

Finn knelt on the floor and efficiently took the old brace off and put the new one on. It was much lighter than the old one, and even Abby could feel the difference in it when he strapped it on.

"It's not bulky," Lynne said, hinging her leg back and forth the slightest bit.

"That's the point." He took a small jar out of the bag. "Salve," he said, unscrewing the cap. "My mom's herbalist friend makes it. It has cistus in it. You put it on the incisions to help them heal."

Abby watched as he gently dabbed it on the still-livid cuts on Lynne's leg.

Then he took out a big baggie of herbs. "Comfrey. Add a large measure to hot water, like a tea bath for your feet, and soak them for as long as you can stand. Once this week, and then we'll reevaluate. You soak just your feet. Don't get the incision points wet."

"Yes, sir," Lynne said meekly.

He looked up at her. "We're going to make this better."

Abby hadn't thought she could love him more but apparently with Finn anything was possible.

28

F inn couldn't remember the last time he had a date that wasn't a charity event. And the only reason he took a date to charity galas was that he'd learned early in his career a date provided a certain amount of security against the women who used those events to prowl for prospects. He'd gotten the tip from a female colleague who always brought a fake date with her to ward off men looking to score. What was good for the goose, and so forth.

As he walked into Hairy's, he realized that he'd had more real dates this week with Abby than he'd had in the past ten years.

Not that they felt like dates. They just felt right. Spending time with her was as natural as holding a scalpel in his hand. And waking up with her every morning was a habit he wanted to adopt for the rest of his life.

How things changed in such a short period of time. That thought would have set him back two weeks ago, but now he couldn't imagine not spending a day with Abby. He remembered what his dad had said about grabbing love when it appeared and not letting it go. He planned to do exactly that. In fact, he felt a sort of primitive urge to make Abby his immediately.

He rolled his eyes. Next he'd drag her by her hair to his cave.

He strode to the bar, lifting a hand in greeting to Niall, who came out from the back room.

"If it isn't the doctor himself." Niall set a polished glass under a tap. "Pint?"

"Please." He pulled out a stool at the end of the bar and sat down.

Niall, with what he called his publican's sixth sense, studied him as he built the Guinness. "You meeting Abigail?"

Finn believed it was less a sixth sense and the obvious look of sexual satisfaction that was etched on his face. "Is it that obvious?"

Niall laughed. "What does Molly say?"

"My mother is threatening to start knitting baby booties." Finn gave him a baleful stare.

"She knits?"

"No. That's the scary part." He nodded his thanks as Niall set the beer in front of him. "I'm meeting Dermot first, though."

Niall's countenance changed completely. "Bah."

As if on cue, the door opened and Dermot walked in, smiling when he saw Finn. Finn noticed he ignored Niall.

"Finn." Dermot clapped a hand on his shoulder and

studied him as he sat down. "You look better. Abigail's influence, obviously."

"Is it that evident?"

"Yes." Dermot grinned. "As soon as I have a pint, we can toast your new happiness. No one deserves it more."

Maybe it was the new love feelings that made him sappy because Finn heard himself say, "You deserve it too. We all do."

"It seems past time, doesn't it?" Dermot said, though his tone said he didn't feel it was possible.

Finn frowned. He didn't sound like a man embroiled in a romance with a beautiful woman. Dermot couldn't still harbor feelings for Fiona, could he? Dermot had dated women, much like Finn had, but no one had lasted long-term either. Finn had never thought about it, and maybe it was just because he'd found Abby, but he wanted Dermot to find someone special too. If that was Lynne, all the better.

Niall suddenly placed a Guinness in front of Dermot with a heavy *thunk* and a scowl before stomping off to the other end of the bar.

Dermot chuckled without mirth. "And then some things are timeless."

"You two need to go to couples' counseling."

"Niall likes things the way they are." Dermot faced Finn and lifted his glass. "A toast to Abigail, for showing you the way to your heart."

Oddly, Finn thought about the painting Abby and little Claire had done. Each time he looked at it, perched on his dresser, he'd get a soft feeling in his chest. A few times, he even felt like he could feel a little girl's hand in his.

He'd never imagined having a daughter, and here he was longing to hold this one in his arms. He could see her, with Abby's curly hair and that same mysterious twinkle in her eyes, like she knew all the secrets of the Universe.

Jesus. He drank a healthy gulp of his beer. Next he'd write a letter to Santa Claus.

"Tell me more about her," Dermot said, unaware of Finn's flight of fancy.

"She's a famous artist." He'd Googled her. "You know I don't pay attention to things like that, but apparently she's world-renowned. Maybe you've heard of her? Abigail Angevine."

"Abigail *Angevine*?" Dermot set his glass down abruptly. "*Angevine*, who does the paintings that heal?"

Dermot would, of course, believe in that. Finn himself didn't know what to say about it so he didn't deny or confirm it. "You've heard of her then?"

"She's the darling of the art world, but more than that, her paintings are in high demand for their healing." Dermot gaped at him. "Abigail is *Angevine*?"

Finn nodded. He had no reason to feel proud of her, but he did. He knew how Dermot felt about art, and for him to be so impressed said something. "Even the painting she gave me, that she did with her nondominant hand and the help of the little girl next door, is charming. But I saw the first painting she did when she was six, and it's stunning."

Dermot played with his cuff absently. "I'd love to see

them. I admire her work, and it's rare to find it displayed given the private nature of the subjects. She only does commissions these days, you know."

"I didn't."

"She did a painting for you?" Dermot studied him with a curious searching gaze.

"Just a painting that the little girl next door contributed to. Charming, like I said." Finn smiled. "It's not Abby's usual style, but you're welcome to come by the farm and see it. Maybe tomorrow afternoon? Mom would love to catch up too."

"Yes, that'd be brilliant."

"Abby's meeting me here tonight," Finn said. "Stick around and talk to her."

"Can't tonight. Conference call with the West Coast. But give her my regards. See you tomorrow." Dermot dropped some money on the counter to cover their drinks, clapped a hand on his shoulder, and walked out.

Niall wandered over. "What were you talking about?"

"Abby."

Niall's expression flattened. "Don't trust him around Abigail, Finn."

"Dermot would never make a move on Abby. And besides, she's not leaving this"—he gestured to himself —"for Dermot."

Niall shook his head. "There's something not right about Dermot. He's hiding something, I can feel it. Keep Abigail away from him."

"Niall—"

"I don't trust him, Finn."

Finn stared at Niall. He'd known Niall since they were

kids. They played pirates together, talked about girls, and had been together during the worst of times. Niall wasn't given to fits of fancy, and he trusted Niall when it came to people. It was in the Ferguson blood. They'd been publicans for generations; Niall used to say that bred in a knowledge about people.

Niall leaned across the counter. "I like Abigail. A lot. She's not like others. You don't come across women so kind and smart every day. I'm telling you that you're lucky, and you need to guard her, because that man"—he pointed where Dermot had just walked out—"doesn't give a fuck about any of that. The only thing he cares about is his own gain, and if he thinks Abigail can forward that, he'll use her."

Finn nodded slowly, more because of the surprising vehemence than agreeing with Niall. Dermot may have been self-important on occasion, but he was hardly heartless. And what would Dermot have to gain from Abby? Dermot had everything. "I'll keep an eye on Abby."

"Good." Apparently satisfied, Niall stomped to the other end of the bar.

Finn had expected to spend more time with Dermot, so he ended up waiting a bit until Abby arrived.

He turned around the moment he felt her push open the door. The evening sun poured in around her, highlighting her dark hair in gold. She was smiling, and it lit her profile.

He'd tasted that smile. He wanted to taste it again.

What he didn't expect to see was Lynne coming in

with her. She rolled in as Abby held the door open for her, looking winded and overwhelmed.

He stood and waited for them to join him.

"Hey, Niall," Abby called out as she approached the bar, her gaze on Finn though. She stopped in front of him, her scarf twisting in her hands. "Hi."

He could see something was wrong. Going to her, he put his hand on her waist and brushed his lips against her cheek. "What's wrong?" he whispered.

She shook her head and angled it subtly to Lynne. "She's been on edge all day. She said she has a bad feeling. She insisted to come, which I was happy about, but she's been up and down all day."

"Did you use the herbs I left you?"

"Yes."

"Her mood could have to do with the herbs drawing toxins out. Don't worry. We'll cheer her up." He ran a soothing hand down Abby's hair and then leaned over to kiss Lynne's cheek. "Aren't you intrepid, darling?"

Lynne tried to smile, her hand clutching the black stone necklace she always wore. She looked around as if she was looking for something. Then she shuddered, as though shaking something off. "I'm crashing your date. I hope you don't mind."

"It can only help my reputation if I'm seen with two beautiful women. Besides, I had an idea I wanted to run by you." He studied her carefully. "You look like you snuck into the liquor cabinet and drank too much poitín last night. You all right?"

"I'm getting there." Taking a deep breath, she began to haul herself out of the wheelchair.

"What are you doing?" Abby asked, stepping forward to brace her friend.

"I want to sit at the bar," Lynne said, determination all over her face.

"Hold on, darling," Finn said, scooping her up in his arms. He nodded at the barstool and waited for Abby to pull it out before carrying Lynne over to it.

He waited until he was sure she was settled before he pulled out another barstool for her to prop her leg up. He took Abby's purse, set it on the seat, and then gently eased Lynne's leg onto it. "How's the new brace?"

"So much better." Lynne sighed, rubbing her thigh. "I hated that old thing."

"There you go." Bringing a seat around for Abby, he said, "From here, you can distract Niall so he stops flirting with Abby."

Lynne shimmied to get comfortable on the seat. "Niall is the bartender, right?"

"Right. But be warned, he fancies himself a ladies' man."

"Niall doesn't like me like that," Abby said, smiling her thanks at him as she sat.

Lynne rolled her eyes. "Abby doesn't think anyone notices her. She doesn't think she's beautiful."

Finn brushed Abby's hair from her shoulder, trailing his hand down her back. "I noticed her from the start."

"Because you know a good thing when you see it," Lynne said smartly. She drummed her fingers on the counter and looked around, visibly relaxing more with each moment.

Abby leaned in and whispered, "I don't know what was wrong. I had to bring her."

"It's good that you did." Finn kissed her softly.

"There's a back room for that sort of activity," Niall said, coming over with a couple glasses in his hands. He winked at Abby as he set the glasses down. "Abigail, the men of Tullaghan will be crushed when they find out you're with this one. A lot of hearts will be broken."

"That's why I brought Lynne," Abby shot back.

Niall clutched at his chest as he really looked at Lynne. "Oh now, a ray of sunshine in my humble bar."

Lynne smiled at him, her tenseness easing.

Putting his hand on Abby's thigh, Finn shook his head. "You think you can focus long enough to get these ladies a beverage?"

"I'll pour my heart into them," Niall promised, setting pint glasses under the tap.

After Niall set the beers in front of them and went to help another customer, Lynne turned to him and Abby, holding her glass up. "To the future."

"The future." His hand tightened on Abby's leg as he clinked his glass to theirs.

"So," Lynne said, nodding at his almost empty pint. "You been waiting for us long?"

"Dermot met me for a drink before," he said, signaling Niall for another pint.

"Dermot was here?" Lynne frowned, holding her necklace.

"You just missed him. If he knew you were coming, he'd probably have stayed."

Lynne glanced at the door before she turned back

around and picked up her beer. "Yeah, probably," she said in a flat tone.

Abby leaned in and said something that only Lynne could hear. Lynne shook her head, took a sip of her beer, and then forced a smile as Niall wandered back over and began to chat her up.

Abby looked at Finn helplessly. "I don't know what's the matter. She keeps saying she doesn't want him to see her until she's better, but then she acts like this."

"I'll talk to him." He squeezed her leg. She took a breath and murmured her thanks, easing next to him. But the rest of the evening was stilted and heavy with the weight of Lynne's withdrawal and Abby's worry.

29

Dermot paced in the living room of the Tullaghan house. He knew Abigail was special from the moment he saw her; he just hadn't realized how special.

She was Angevine. No wonder he'd been drawn to her.

He'd seen one of her works on exhibit in New York a few years back. It'd been a loan, as Angevine only did commissions, and then only sparingly.

He'd been drawn to the artwork immediately. From a technical perspective, the painting had been exquisite—an abstract mix of colors done with strong strokes. But what had captured his attention was the power it radiated. Standing in front of it made him feel the promise of the same rush he felt when he took a soul piece.

He'd immediately found the owner of the art gallery and requested a commission for himself. The owner had called him the next day and said that the artist wasn't at liberty to paint one for him at that time but could put him on a waitlist.

Dermot Farrell did not wait for anything. He'd toyed with finding the artist in person—Dermot was very convincing in person—but his interest had been diverted by other things.

And now she was here.

He looked at the walls of his house, where some of his art collection hung. None of it compared to what he remembered hers being. None of it evoked the same response within him.

In his mind, he heard one word: *redemption*.

He stopped pacing abruptly. She was the answer. If she painted for him, she could heal him of his craving for souls.

He began to sweat again. It'd gotten worse over the years, but it'd never been this bad. He could feel himself on the knife's edge of control.

He didn't want that. He prided himself for being able to keep a tight rein on his needs.

He couldn't wait until afternoon to see what she'd done for Finn—he had to go now. He could almost taste the promise of a cure.

He took out his mobile and texted Finn to say he was going stop by early. He waited, pacing, for Finn to answer, but ten minutes went by without a response so Dermot decided to just go.

When he arrived, Molly was at the kitchen table. He made sure his smile was in place and knocked lightly on the door before walking in. "I hear you've been missing me."

Grinning, Molly stood up and held her arms out for a hug. "Well, if it isn't himself, finally. When I texted you last week, you said you'd come visit sooner. And here I thought you'd forgotten all about us."

"Never." He went into her arms and felt a moment of peace. The family man's soul piece flared, and Dermot lowered his head to Molly's, feeling emotions he didn't quite understand rise in his chest. He inhaled her usual lavender scent, grateful for its sweetness and that it wasn't the acrid stench of body odor and beer.

When Molly finally let him go, she patted his shoulder. "Sit. I'll make you tea. Have you had breakfast?"

"Yes, thank you."

She glanced at him over her shoulder. "So you'll have scones if I make them."

"Yes, ma'am," he said with a smile. Molly's scones were the best.

She nodded and reached for her apron. "Conall is out in the cowshed. Did you see him?"

"Not yet. I came to see Finn."

"Carrick isn't home. Yet." Over the cannister of flour, Molly gave him a look that said a thousand words.

"Abigail. Of course." Dermot felt a strange longing flare in his chest. He rubbed the spot absently, thinking of Madelynne. "He's taken with her, isn't he?"

"Have you met her? She's absolutely lovely." Molly pointed a wooden spoon at him. "You'd do well to find a woman like that. Like maybe her friend Lynne."

"Tell me about Lynne," he said, wanting to hear about her from a trusted source. Inside, the longing expanded, like it was going to crush his lungs with its force.

"Ah, that's a lovely woman." Molly smiled softly. "Beautiful. Cultured. 'Tis a lucky man who wins her heart." She gave him a pointed look before continuing her mixing.

He wasn't worthy of her. All the money in the world, and he couldn't figure out how to stop the incessant hunger. He wouldn't put her at risk that way.

He decided to change the subject. "I came over because Finn was going to show me the painting Abigail did for him. Have you seen it?"

"It's so dear, it is, the way the Connelly girl's daughter helped with it." Molly stopped mixing and studied him. "You've heard of Abby before, have you?"

"I saw her work in an exhibit a few years ago."

"I loved her," Molly said, resuming her scone making. "And her friend. Both lovely women. You know Carrick has never brought home a woman before."

"He's very private, yes."

The kitchen door opened and Finn walked in, wearing what he had on yesterday. Dermot arched his brow in quiet ribbing.

Finn gave him a look that was the equivalent of *fuck off*. "Don't you have your own kitchen table?"

"Yes, but why would I sit there alone when I can sit here with Molly?" Dermot said, smiling at her. "I didn't expect you to still be out."

Molly winked at Dermot. "Some things are worth taking your time, aren't they, Carrick?"

"I like to do my best," he said, bending his head to drop a kiss on his mother's temple.

"Dermot and I were catching up. I'm making scones."

Watching, Dermot felt a frisson of warmth in his chest. When he was a child, he used to wonder why Finn had a mother like Molly and he had a drunk. To a young boy, it hardly seemed fair.

It occurred to him now that it didn't matter how he was born. He had family who cared about him here, and he had for a long time. What he felt had to be gratitude, he realized, and love. He put his hand over his heart, to hold on to it.

"I'm going to change my clothes," Finn said, heading to his room. He gestured with his head to Dermot to follow him.

He fell into step behind his old friend. He'd walked down this hall too many times to count, always in step with Finn.

"The painting is on the dresser," Finn said as he pulled his shirt from his pants and began unbuttoning it. "It's still wet so be mindful of touching it. And I feel like she'd want me to iterate that it's not what she normally does."

"I saw her wrist. I understand." Dermot waited until Finn went into the bathroom and closed the door before he took his first look at the painting.

The moment he saw it, something shifted inside him, leaving him feeling bereft. He examined it greedily, taking in the brush strokes and the flashes of light on the landscape. It wasn't what Angevine was known for, but there was a primitive brilliance to it still—avant-garde in its simplicity, like Matisse's line drawings.

Even the three childish figures in the foreground were

inspired somehow. He didn't know how it was that it worked as a whole, but it did.

The artistry of the painting wasn't its strength, though: it was the power behind it. He could feel the "other" in it, the hint of the supernatural that he'd felt in the other paintings that he'd seen from Angevine. He leaned closer to it, trying to feel it deeper, but he had the impression that because it wasn't for him, he wasn't going to get anything else out of it.

Would she paint for him?

He put his hand over his heart, wondering if this could be the answer to the corner he'd backed himself into. If she could heal him of this addiction—

"What do you think?"

He started, jumping back. Catching his breath, he schooled his face before turning around and facing Finn. "She's a master. It's clearly not her usual style, and there's the whimsical element the child added, but it has a brilliance that is compelling nonetheless."

"And she did it with her nondominant hand." Finn stood next to him, his arms crossed over his chest as he regarded the painting.

Dermot nodded. "I can imagine how that would have been not just daunting but distressing to someone who's a master at what she does."

"She claims that her paintings have healing woven into them."

His heart began to hammer. He cleared the need from his voice and said, "You don't believe in that sort of thing."

"No, but you do." Finn faced him. "What do you think?"

He kept his gaze on the painting, making sure not to show any of his desperate desire to own one of Abigail's pieces. "Was this painting done to heal you?"

"She said yes."

"And do you feel healed?" he asked, already knowing, because he'd felt the change in Finn the day before.

Finn rubbed his chest with the edge of his hand. "I feel something."

"Yes, you do, don't you?" he said absently, studying the canvas. He remembered the Finn of two weeks ago compared to the Finn today. Two weeks ago Finn had been in a place almost as dark as where he'd been when Fiona had died. Now, Finn was light and eager for life, excited about the possibilities and this woman who'd obviously captured his heart.

Dermot's excitement rose. If she could help Finn, someone who didn't believe anything arcane, what could she do for *him*?

"I love her," Finn said softly.

Dermot turned to look at his friend. It was all over his entire being, the emotion he had for this woman. Awe hushed Dermot's voice as he said, "You've been numb since after Fiona died, and now for the first time you've admitted that you love someone other than your parents. And still you doubt that Abigail healed you?"

"That's certainly a point," Finn replied.

Shaking his head, Dermot took one more look at the painting, reluctant to leave it. He had to convince her to help him. Dermot had a sense about people, and he had an unassailable feeling that money didn't motivate her. Plus, there was her injury and the evident difference in her painting; he imagined that any artist of her caliber would be reluctant to produce anything under such circumstances.

He was not going to use Finn to get to Abigail. That went against the code of their friendship.

Neither would he ask Madelynne to influence her friend.

He'd just have to figure out a way to appeal to Abigail himself.

30

F inn had taken Lynne to PT today. He told Lynne he wanted to watch her therapist to make sure that he was treating her right, but Abby knew he wanted to observe the course of her therapy to see what more could be done.

Though it'd only been a matter of days since Finn had started working with them, and Lynne was already improving. Her moods were more stable and uplifted, and the swelling in her leg seemed to be less. Even the incision points from the surgery appeared less livid than before.

If Abby hadn't loved him already, this would have sealed the deal.

Abby knew that Finn took Lynne to give her a break too. She'd luxuriated in a long bath that morning, Finn bringing her tea and sitting on the edge of her tub, just to be with her, before he took Lynne out.

She was dressed, refreshed, and quietly content when

she heard someone at the door. Recognizing Claire's knock, Abby smiled and went to open it.

Claire stood there, a hopeful look in her eyes. "My mom said I could come ask to paint today."

"That's a wonderful idea," she said, stepping aside to let Claire come in. "I've been wanting to ask you over for days."

The little girl skipped inside and turned around. "Is Brother Paul coming to visit today? I want to paint him a picture. What are you going to paint, Abby?"

Taking the smock she'd put over Claire's clothes the last time from where she draped it on the corner of the easel, she got the girl ready. "What do you think I should draw?"

"What do you want to say?" Claire asked very seriously.

She wanted to say that Lynne would be okay and that she'd dance again, but she wasn't sure what that looked like yet. "I'll have to think about it. You want to pick your colors?"

"Yes, please." Claire skipped to the table where Abby had the paints laid out and began pulling the tubes she wanted.

Once Abby got their palettes sorted, Claire began working on her painting with an abandon that Abby envied. She watched the little girl for a bit before she turned to her own blank canvas.

What did she want to say?

Bro Paul suddenly appeared next to her. "Out of the mouths of babes, right? How you doin', kid?"

"I don't know what I want to paint." She couldn't see

how to help Lynne yet, even though she'd been meditating on it.

"Maybe it's time to focus on yourself instead of other people," he suggested.

She turned her stare onto him.

He shrugged. "In case of emergency, aren't you supposed to put your oxygen mask on first before you help someone else?"

"You're right," she said after spending probably too much time thinking about it.

"Of course I'm right." He rolled his eyes. "Yo, Claire! You havin' fun?"

"I was going to paint you a donut, but then I had to paint this for Abby instead." She waved her brush around. "Don't look yet. I'm not done."

"That kid, I'm telling ya." Bro Paul shook his head. Then he returned his attention to Abby. "So, what's it going to be? You gonna do something, or are you gonna stand here like you really do have rocks for brains?"

She made a face at him.

He just laughed. "I love you too." He turned to Claire and put a fond hand on her head. "And I love you too."

"I love you, Brother Paul," Claire called after him as he disappeared.

Abby had a flash of her daughter saying the same thing, and it caught her up for a second. Then she set everything aside and focused on what she needed.

The vision came on like it always did, a past life that was in a time and place she didn't recognize. Someplace foreign—she could smell the faint hint of exotic spices in the air and the cacophony of people yelling in different languages.

Guards led a woman in chains toward a building made out of shiny stone. Instinctively, she knew it was where the sultan lived and that the woman was her. When they reached him, the guards pushed her to her knees, her forehead on the cold stone. She knew she was in trouble, that she'd done a healing that hadn't gone the way the sultan had wanted.

Another guard stepped forward, taking her hands and pressing them against the ground. Abby saw the flash of the scimitar, felt the terror of the woman she'd been, watched the cold hatred in the eyes of the sultan as the guard brought the blade down on her wrists.

Abby jerked out of the vision with a gasp. She hugged her healing wrist to her chest, trying to catch her breath.

She felt a tug on her shirt.

"Abby, I'm done now." Claire smiled at her, a streak of turquoise on her cheek. She held out the painting reverently. "This is for you."

Her head still swimming, Abby shook it to clear the vision and took the painting Claire offered, careful not to smudge the wet oil paint. "Thank you."

"I love it, and so does Brother Paul. Right, Brother Paul?" Claire looked behind Abby.

"Sure do," Bro Paul said, beaming at the girl. He came to stand next to Abby. "Do you love it, Abs?"

Abby looked down at it. It was her—Claire always drew her with her dark hair blowing all over the place. She was wearing a blue dress without shoes. Her left hand had a paintbrush that was floating out of it. Her right palm was faced out, a yellow nimbus glowing around it, expanding out to the edges of the canvas. It looked like healing hands, the magical touch that they said could heal anything.

"Well, Abs?" Bro Paul prodded her. "You love it too?"

Claire came over to cuddle closer to Bro Paul, who put his arms around her shoulders. "I didn't know how to show that her hands were magic, but they told me," the little girl said. "Did I do good?"

He squeezed her affectionately. "You did great, kid. Didn't she, Abs?"

"Yes," she said, her voice hoarse. Because she had to ask, she looked at Bro Paul. "What does this mean?"

Bro Paul looked her in the eyes. "How do you heal people?"

"By editing their past lives."

"Exactly." He pointed at her. "You think painting is the only way to do that?"

It had been to this point.

"Rocks for brains." He sighed. "It's been the only way because you haven't tried to do it any other way. Trauma from another time and all that."

She pointed to Claire's painting. "Are you saying I could heal with my hands?"

Pursing his lips, he rubbed his chin. "Well, you can't heal anyone unless they want to be healed, but yes, your healing isn't restricted to just painting. Hands, feet, whatever. Painting is just the vehicle you chose. If you'd have loved fishing, you would have found a way to heal people through that."

"Fishing?" She arched her brow.

"I had a charge once who put his healing in fresh trout and bread, because no one turns down food if they're offered it." He shrugged. "It worked for him."

"I'm not taking up fishing."

"Missing the point there, kid. Keep your eyes on the prize."

She didn't know what the prize was here, and she had no idea how to heal in any other way than through her paintings.

"I'd like the prize to be a donut," Claire declared.

Bro Paul laughed. "That's why I love you, kid. You got priorities."

31

Madelynne's text sat on his phone unanswered for a day.

I missed you last night at the pub.

Dermot sat at his desk in his home office, staring at it. He hadn't known Madelynne was going to be there, or else he would have been tempted to stay.

I missed you...

He missed her too. He hadn't missed anyone since Fiona.

He wanted to reply to her, but his control was tenuous. Even over text he could feel the pull to be closer to her, which he liked. What he didn't like was the predator inside him prowling, looking for a weak point in her soul.

He would not allow someone he cared for to get hurt.

He sat back in his chair, examining that statement,

trying it on. He hadn't even met her in person, but somehow, yes, he did care.

Which is why he tried not to text her again.

Instead, he researched everything he could find about Abigail Angevine.

There wasn't very much, but most of the articles touted her work as "transformative." A few called the healing aspect of her paintings "sensational" and "overexaggerated," but they still agreed that her artwork and technique were masterful.

He knew that Abigail could help him. She'd see how to get rid of the predator inside him that was getting harder and harder to leash. Then maybe he could approach Madelynne.

As if knowing he was thinking about her—though when wasn't he thinking about her?—Madelynne texted him again.

I guess you and your steed have gone for a ride. You don't need to avoid Finn or Abby. You don't need to worry about me making you uncomfortable. I understand that you wouldn't want to be with someone like me.

He blinked at that. He wasn't going to reply, but he couldn't help himself.

Someone perfect?

She answered instantly.

snort

Shaking his head, he sent:

If you think that being momentarily incapacitated makes you less than you are, you need a different kind of doctor than Finn.

Her reply took longer. He drummed his fingers on the table while he waited, sighing in relief when it finally arrived.

You think I'm momentarily incapacitated?

He frowned.

Don't you?

Her text caused the part of his heart that could feel to bleed:

I feel too beaten down to know.

It made him feel all sorts of emotions that he normally didn't feel in association to other people, but the strongest feeling that rose in him was the desire to take her in his arms and to hold her close.

He tried to think of a time when he'd held someone close. He couldn't even remember holding Fiona.

Madelynne texted him before he could reply.

I don't want to bring you down with me. You deserve better.

What was she talking about? *She* was better. That was why he was staying away from her. He sent:

I couldn't imagine anyone better than you.

He waited for an answer but it never came.

32

Finn left early the next morning, saying he needed to check with his office and let them know that he was going to end his sabbatical soon.

Abby got up with him, knowing her head was too full to go back to sleep after he left. So she made him a to-go cup of coffee and sent him off before fixing herself one and sitting near the window to think. Yesterday's painting session with Claire was haunting her.

Well, it was the vision that was haunting her. And the fact that maybe she could heal with her hands instead of just painting.

If she could figure out how to do it, she could maybe help Finn heal Lynne faster. She looked at her own wrist and tried to will it to heal, but nothing happened.

Well, that was a bust.

Lynne's bedroom door opened, and the wheelchair creaked down the hall.

Abby turned around, holding her breath. Lynne had yo-yoed up and down the past few days, complaining that something didn't feel right. Abby kept asking her if she meant her leg or something else. Yesterday morning Lynne snapped at her, saying if she knew she'd verbalize it. Lynne hadn't looked like herself again either, which Abby still didn't understand. Abby had no idea what to expect today.

Lynne rolled into the living room, stopping at the edge. "I want to apologize for my attitude yesterday. I don't want you to think I'm not grateful for everything you've done."

"I know," Abby replied softly.

"Is Finn here?" Lynne said as if reading her mind, looking around.

"He left a while ago."

"I'll apologize to him later. And I want to thank him, because my leg feels better today. I think the herbs are making a difference." Lynne continued on to the kitchen, coming back a few minutes later, her coffee wedged between her legs. "Also, I know I've been a mess the past few days. I decided this morning that I'm going to do better."

Abby's heart melted with compassion. "You don't have to do anything, Lynne."

Lynne's brow furrowed. "Yes, I do. Something is coming, and I can't figure out what it is, but regardless, I don't have to be bitchy all the time. That's not me."

She thought of how Lynne hadn't looked like herself and a chill went up Abby's spine.

"I'm also sorry if I was weird about Dermot," Lynne continued. "I've stopped that. He's too good for me anyway."

Abby sat up. "What do you mean? If anything, you're too good for him."

"For a billionaire who dates models and has everything he wants?" Lynne arched her brow.

"That's just stuff. It's not love. You deserve love." She took Lynne's hand. "You deserve someone better than the guys in the past, someone who'll love you."

"Abby, that's not going to happen," Lynne said in a soft, sad voice. "The only times I've ever felt loved besides with you is when I've been on stage, and that love is gone now."

"You'll dance again," Abby said with as much confidence as she could call up.

Lynne smiled, but there was skepticism laced in it.

She thought about pursuing it, but she believed the lynchpin was the family curse in Lynne's line. She needed to figure out why she was being blocked from clearing it.

In an obvious effort to change the subject, Lynne said, "So, you and Finn stayed up late last night, huh?"

"Again." Abby couldn't help the satisfied smile thinking about it caused.

"You're gloating," Lynne said good-naturedly. "The real question is how long do you think you'll be able to go on before you have to take a nap?"

Abby didn't last long, as it turned out. She chatted with Lynne for a little while, did some laundry, and then went to lie down just after noon. She had dark dreams, where she watched the people she loved die over and over and she couldn't do anything about it.

When she stumbled out of her bedroom hours later, Lynne was sitting at the window, staring out at the ocean. She had a cup next to her that looked like it had tea in it at one point. Without looking up, she asked, "Have a good nap?"

Abby grunted as she stumbled into the kitchen, rubbing her eyes, feeling like she'd been drugged. She probably shouldn't have slept that long. She made them both tea, taking a fresh cup in for Lynne.

"You never were a good napper," Lynne said, still watching out the window.

Abby gave her a look as she plopped onto a seat. She looked to see what had captured Lynne's attention: a surfer, lying on his board, waiting to catch a wave.

Lynne picked up the fresh teacup. "I guess if I'd been up night after night having wild jungle sex, I'd need a five-hour nap too."

"I thought you had earplugs," Abby said, feeling her cheeks blush.

"The walls in this place are solid stone. I barely heard anything," Lynne said with exaggerated innocence.

Her cheeks got warmer, and it wasn't because of the steam from her tea. "That's supposed to reassure me?"

Her best friend smirked. "It's definitely not going to stop you."

No, it wasn't. She held the warm cup in both her hands, letting the steam refresh her. Being with Finn was a revelation. In the past, on the rare occasions when she'd decided to get physical with someone, it'd always been good. It had never been like this, though. But she hadn't ever loved a man truly, she realized.

"Finn's coming over this evening, right?" Lynne asked.

She gave her friend a look. "Yes."

"Good." Lynne angled her wheelchair toward her. "What are we going to make for dinner? You two are going to need something filling for stamina. Maybe lots of carbs for endurance?"

Shaking her head, Abby focused on her tea.

33

Finn knocked on the door earlier than expected. Aside from recognizing the rhythm of his knock, Abby could feel him close, like her heart was attuned to him already.

"I'll get it," Lynne said, wheeling away from the table.

Abby stayed where she was, even though every cell in her body woke up and began to tingle in anticipation. She heard Lynne greet Finn. She heard his low response and the pause where she knew he'd kissed her hello. She heard mumbled conversation—Lynne apologizing?—and then his footsteps following Lynne's wheelchair.

"Abby just woke up from a nap, so she's crabby," Lynne declared.

"I woke up a while ago, and I'm just groggy," she murmured, goose bumps rising on her skin as Finn's hand touched her back.

"Maybe you can wake her up," Lynne said mischievously. "Can I get you something to drink?"

"Tea would be grand. Thank you," he said as he pulled out the chair next to Abby and sat down.

Abby turned to face him.

He touched her face with his fingertips. "You're crabby?"

"I'm groggy," she corrected.

His hand slipped down her neck and to her nape, where his fingers speared into her hair. She moaned softly at the feel of him massaging her head. He dropped a kiss on her mouth and then delved deeper until she was warm and pliant.

"Awake now?" he murmured against her lips.

"Ready to go back to bed," she corrected.

His mouth curved under hers, and then he chuckled.

"I'm coming back out," Lynne called in a singsong voice. "I hope everyone is dressed."

Abby rolled her eyes, but Finn just laughed, sitting back in his seat. He kept his hand in Abby's hair though.

Lynne had a tray spanning the arms of her wheelchair with a cheese plate, some grapes, tea, and wine. She rolled carefully into the dining room, keeping watch on it to make sure nothing toppled.

"Do you need help?" Abby asked, starting to get up.

"I'm good." Lynne carefully parked herself at the table and began to unload the tray. "I brought a pre-dinner cheese snack. And wine, because a girl can't live on tea alone. If only we had champagne."

"Are we celebrating something?" Abby asked.

"Life," Lynne replied. "And that you're finally getting laid on a regular basis."

She swatted at Lynne's arm.

Finn cleared his throat. "Actually, we do have reason to celebrate."

Abby and Lynne both stilled, looking at him in surprise.

He took Lynne's hand. "I had an idea to help you. It'd be a short surgery, minorly invasive, but I think I can improve your range of motion dramatically as well as correct some of the ligament damage. We'd need to increase therapy and be more proactive about keeping the swelling down, but I feel like it's a good option. You're responding nicely to the herbs and I'm happy with your therapist here. He's good."

Abby held her breath, her heart pounding.

Lynne swallowed audibly. "I'll walk again?"

"Yes." He gave her a level look. "If you work hard, I don't see why you wouldn't be able to dance, but I'm not qualified to make an assessment on what it'd take to perform."

She nodded, lowering her head, thinking about it.

Say yes, Abby willed her, but she knew the decision had to be Lynne's.

Finally, her best friend lifted her head with a hesitant smile. "Let's do it."

"Whoop!" Abby jumped up and grabbed her in a tight hug. Then she turned to Finn and gave him the same.

"I think you're getting lucky tonight," Lynne said to Finn.

"I'm lucky every night," he replied.

Lynne's smile grew. "Forget the tea. Wine, Finn? Now we have a real reason to celebrate."

"Indeed we do," he said. He glanced at Abby.

Her throat full of emotion, Abby silently helped Lynne unload the tray and arrange everything on the table.

"Want to do the honors?" Lynne asked, holding out the wine opener to Finn.

Finn accepted it and reached for the wine bottle. As he cut the wrapper from around the top of the bottle and began twisting the opener into the corkscrew, his phone signaled a text. He paused as if wondering if he should check it.

As a doctor he must be on call a lot of the time. Abby touched his arm. "Answer it."

"Sorry," he muttered, pulling it out. He tipped his head as he read it. "It's Dermot, wanting to meet for a drink."

Abby shot a glance at Lynne, who retracted.

Then Lynne tipped her head and said, "We have wine. Tell him to come here."

"No," Abby vetoed, shaking her head.

"Yes," Lynne insisted. "It's fine, Abby. There's nothing to worry about. It's not like we banged. I've ever even met him in person. There's no reason to be awkward."

Finn looked at Abby. It was Lynne's decision, and she was trying to be less protective, so she nodded. He quickly typed out a reply.

The answer came back immediately, and Finn tucked his phone away. "He's on his way."

Lynne searched for the pendant around her neck. She was the color of buttermilk that was on the edge of going bad. She reached for her glass of wine and took a bracing swig.

Abby touched Lynne's arm. "You want us to tell him not to come?"

Finn took Lynne's hand. "I can call him off."

"I'm good." Lynne shook her head, and Abby saw something strange around the edges of her eyes. "Let's have wine. Finn, how are your parents?"

Finn glanced at Abby but he answered Lynne, regaling them with a tale about his dad's cows getting loose and scaring a family from England who was out for a bike ride through Tullaghan.

By the time Dermot knocked on the door, Lynne was relaxed. At the knock, she froze for a second before she eased back in her wheelchair. She rearranged the scarf around her shoulders and smoothed her hair, almost coquettishly.

That wasn't like Lynne. Abby stared at her, trying to figure it out. But then Finn was back with his friend.

"Abby," Finn said, rejoining them. "You remember Dermot."

She turned around. Behind Finn, his friend Dermot followed, his gaze trained on her, his hand outstretched. He was still dressed in subdued elegance, just like the one time she'd met him, and he still had that strange rainbow spiral that she didn't understand circling his soul.

"Of course." She stood up and, after a moment of hesitation—the pandemic had really changed social etiquette—took his hand. "I hope this time you won't give me a lame pickup line like you did the first time."

His smile grew slowly, delighted. He held her injured hand with great care, cupping both his hands protectively around them. "Careful, or Finn will have my head. He's a jealous one."

"He is?" Abby glanced at Finn. "You are?"

He slipped his arm around her waist and drew her closer to him. "In this, yes."

Lynne sighed, a strange longing in her expression that didn't look like it belonged on her features.

Abby watched Dermot turn toward the sound and do a double take. He blinked at Lynne, unconsciously taking a step toward her—or so it seemed to Abby.

Then he took a deliberate step toward her best friend, his gaze entirely trained on her. "Madelynne," he said in his posh voice, holding his hand out. "Dermot Farrell, owner of unicorns."

Lynne's face lit with the most beautiful smile. "Madelynne Broussard," Lynne said, a rare hint of Creole coming out. "I hear one only takes one's unicorn out on Sundays."

"Today was special," Dermot said, sitting next to her, keeping her hand.

Abby looked at the two of them, trying to feel happy for Lynne. Dermot didn't seem like Kevin, or any of the other guys. But something was niggling her and she couldn't figure out what.

Finn sat next to her and put his hand on her leg. "What is it?" he asked under his breath.

She shook her head. She could articulate that Lynne didn't seem like herself. Maybe she'd ask Bro Paul later. It had to hinge on Lynne's family curse.

She felt pressure to fix it now. *Bro Paul?* she called out.

She's not ready for it to be cleared, kid, he replied in her head. *There's nothing you can do.*

She hated that.

As if sensing her frustration, Finn ran a soothing hand on her leg.

She flashed him a grateful smile. It'd be okay, she told herself. She'd make sure it worked out.

34

Yesterday, Dermot had meant to make inroads to talking to Abby about a commission, but he'd gotten ensnared by Madelynne and her loveliness. All thoughts of paintings and healing the thing in him that needed soul pieces flew from his mind.

He was going to do it today. Madelynne texted him to ask him to come visit her, saying that Abby would likely be there too. Dermot accepted the invitation immediately, canceling all his meetings for the afternoon to make sure he had the time he needed to secure a commission with Abigail.

He stood in his closet, looking at his clothing. Normally, he wasn't one to fuss but this afternoon was important. He needed to impress Abigail to help him.

Truthfully, he wanted to impress Madelynne as well.

She'd been more than he'd expected, but it'd been her eyes that had especially touched him. Something in them tugged at the hollow feeling in his chest. He felt an echo of the family man's soul piece, like a dying heartbeat, rise for a moment when he'd taken her hand.

It'd been the most exquisite emotion he'd ever felt. It'd left him gobsmacked.

Dermot surveyed his clothes, finally picking out a shirt. He selected this one for its soft texture. Maybe Lynne would like to touch it.

He hoped she did.

He buttoned it up, tucking it in his slacks. He paused, a hand on his heart, trying to feel a part of Fiona. She'd given him so much—without her he would never have advanced as he had, he'd never have done as much good. Without her, he'd probably still be living in that old stone shack his mother had died in.

Thinking about Madelynne, he felt warmth and anticipation—and hope. Fiona would have been happy he met Madelynne.

He closed his eyes and thought of Fiona. He saw her beautiful face and heard her bright laugh. He reached out to her, but like always he couldn't touch her. The fleeting scent of coconut teased him for a second before she drifted further and further away until, like always, he could no longer see her.

When he opened his eyes, he couldn't breathe for a moment, his chest felt so hollow.

Then he thought of Madelynne and the void filled a little.

He parked in front of their cottage and went up the walkway. She opened the door for him as soon as he knocked. He knew that she'd been waiting, as eager to see him as he'd been to see her.

Something about her looked different. Maybe her hair, which was in an elegant twist behind her head. She had the lightest dusting of makeup and wore a long dress that hugged her torso and fell full to the floor. Around her shoulders she had a scarf draped with the panache of a French woman. She wore diamond earrings and a thick bracelet encrusted with a few gemstones.

He'd expected that she'd be in the wheelchair, but she was propped on crutches. She looked awkward and uncomfortable, and something melted in him because he knew that she made the effort for him.

"Do I look so weird on these?" she asked. Her mouth lifted in a faint smile, but her eyes were serious, like she was concerned.

"You looked lovely last night, and you look even lovelier today." He stepped up to her, sliding his hands around her waist to steady her, and lowered his lips to hers. It was a hello, the slightest glancing kiss, but he felt his body begin to hum.

The predator in him wanted to pounce, so he quickly cut the kiss off, stepping back while he tried to push it back down.

Unaware, Madelynne hummed, listing toward him. "Come in before all of Tullaghan walks by to watch us."

He hesitated, suddenly not sure that was a good idea. "Is Abigail in as well?"

"She went to run errands. She'll be back soon." Madelynne limped inside on her crutches, moving slowly toward the dining room table. "I have refreshments, such as it is."

"I didn't come to be entertained," he said, moving to

the table to pull out a chair for her. "I came to see you." And to talk to Abigail.

Sitting on the seat, she studied him. He knew she was looking to see if he meant it. He knew she'd find no hint of dissembling, because he did.

He brought a chair close to her and sat down, taking her hand. "To be honest, I'm surprised by this. I never expected to find someone I was interested in out in the hinterlands of Tullaghan."

She tipped her head. "You don't like it here."

"There are a lot of bad memories," he said as diplomatically as he could.

"I understand bad memories." Her hand kneaded her thigh above where he could see the outline of her brace.

"What does Finn say about your leg?" he asked, taking her hand.

"He thinks he can correct the damage. That I might even be able to dance again, but I just can't see that." She made a face. "Does that make me a quitter, or just a realist?"

"It makes you neither, because if you wanted to dance, I think you'd do it." He made a mental note to tell Finn that he'd cover all the expenses. He stared into her pale-green eyes. He felt like he could lose himself in them.

"And you and reality?" she asked.

"Today my reality is quite wonderful, actually."

She leaned her elbow on the table, her chin in her hand. "What's your secret?"

"A delightful companion." He stretched out his hand

to brush her face with the back of his fingers. "Am I being forward?"

She smiled, this time genuinely. "I may want you to be more forward."

He smiled. "Then if I may, tell me about dancing."

She blinked in surprise, looking away, her expression distant and sad. He thought she wasn't going to answer, but then she said, "It's like flying. The beat begins, and it lifts you up higher and higher until you can touch the clouds."

He watched her, enthralled. As she spoke, her soul began to shine. It was akin to listening to Fiona talk about all her business ideas. He hadn't heard anyone discuss anything with such excitement and passion since then. "Tell me more," he encouraged.

"On stage, nothing exists except your own dreams and the hushed breathing of the audience." The sadness ran away from her face, leaving bliss. "Your heart and the music beat as one, and everyone follows you avidly, eager to go on the journey with you."

"You love it," he said, his attention rapt by the piece of her soul by her heart that started to grow larger and glow brighter, a beautiful soft rose color.

She closed her eyes, swaying to music only she could hear. "I love it. I love every moment of it, even the bleeding feet and sore muscles."

He couldn't take his eyes away from the beauty of the soul piece by her heart. He tried to turn his gaze away, but he couldn't. He shifted in the seat, trying to put space between him and it. "Is Abigail going to be home soon?" he asked.

"I love the movement and expression," Madelynne continued, oblivious. "I love the freedom and the strife. I love telling a story with my body. I love inspiring people to *feel*."

Without any warning, the soul piece began to tear from her soul.

The part of him that craved it rejoiced.

No. Dermot sat up, his heart beginning to pound. Sweat broke out on his upper lip as he tried to think of a way to stop it.

"There's only one thing about dance that's awful." She laughed under her breath, but it wasn't a happy sound. "Dancing is a finite career. You can only do it so long until your body can't handle it any longer. At thirty-four, I'm ancient in the dancing world."

He watched that piece around her heart like a hawk, willing it to reincorporate back into her soul. Maybe if he left nothing would happen. He stood up. "Madelynne, I need to—"

"What I had planned collided with reality in an unexpected way," she continued, unaware that he'd gotten up. "But while it lasted it was the most wonderful, amazing thing I'd ever experienced. I was blessed."

With that, the soul piece tore off and flew into his hand.

Lynne gasped, her hands going to her chest, her eyes wide and shocked. She looked at him like she'd never seen him before. Then she began to cough.

Dermot looked down at his palm, horrified to see the piece of her soul resting there.

Go back. Go back. He tried to get rid of it, to will it

back.

It stayed in his hand, taunting him with its purity and passion.

Lynne gaped at him, trying to breathe. "I don't know what's wrong," she rasped.

He watched the panic in her eyes. He saw the hole in her soul, a large black maw.

Then he felt the tingle that precipitated a new soul piece entering him.

It started at his core and spread through his body, like it always did. The other soul pieces shifted to make room for the new one. He felt the tease of the euphoria on the periphery and the beginning of an erection.

He stepped back, hitting his chair, which toppled with a loud clatter. He looked down at his hand. Instead of the longing and anticipation to infuse himself with this one, he felt dread and despair. He didn't want to take it from her—he wasn't trying to do it. He didn't want anything to happen to her.

He remembered Fiona and his chest gripped. Would Lynne die?

His mouth went dry, and he stumbled backwards.

"What...?" Lynne reached for him.

He took another step back. He could already see the vitality drain from her eyes. He'd watched the same thing happen with Fiona, until she was an empty husk with no desire to live.

Would that happen to Lynne?

Panic made him sweat more. He took another step back, and then another. The next he knew he was outside rushing down the walkway to his car.

35

Abby was arriving back at the cottage when she saw Dermot hurrying down the walkway. She blinked in surprise. Lynne hadn't said he was coming over. Maybe it was impromptu. Maybe they'd done a little canoodling of their own while she was away. Finn assured her Dermot was a good guy, so she was trying to warm up to him. Leaving her packages in the car, she got out to say hi.

Except Dermot was walking fast with his head lowered. Not the mannerisms of a man who'd gotten lucky.

He was going to run into her. Abby frowned and called out to him before they collided. "Dermot."

He stopped abruptly, looking up. His face was gray with upset and what looked like guilt. He edged around her, his hand fisted.

Frowning, she took a hesitant step toward him. "What's wrong? Is Lynne okay?"

He flinched, glancing down at his hand. He blanched

even more, if that was possible. "I have to go," he said, his voice harsh with emotion.

As he rushed past her, she caught a glimpse of his palm and something glowing a deep rose in it. Before she could ask him about it, he stopped and turned around. "I'm sorry," he whispered, his voice ragged. Then he practically ran to his car, got in, and tore off.

She turned to the cottage. *Lynne.*

The door was ajar. Abby hurried in, scenes from that day in New York with Kevin running in her head. She pictured Lynne lying at the bottom of the stairs and thanked Bro Paul that this place had none.

But that didn't mean that it couldn't be worse.

She halted abruptly on the threshold, seeing Lynne at the dining table. Abby wilted in relief.

But then she realized Lynne wasn't moving.

Her heart in her throat, she ran to her best friend. "*Lynne.*" She skipped to a stop and knelt in front of her chair, taking her hand. "Good Lord, Lynne. What happened?"

Lynne turned blank eyes toward her. "He left."

"Dermot? Did something happen with him?" Abby surveyed her best friend, touching her, trying to figure out what was wrong. It was like a part of her was gone.

Then she gasped as she saw the huge hole in the center of Lynne's soul.

She'd never seen anything like it. Usually a missing soul piece looked like a shard of glass, sometimes as big as a piece of pie, the edges smooth even where they were crooked. This looked like someone had reached into her and cut the piece out with the dullest knife they could find.

That hadn't been there before. There'd been the missing soul piece by her chest, the remnant of the family curse Abby hadn't been able to clear yet, but that was nothing like this. She held her hand out to Lynne's soul, feeling it out. The moment she touched the spot, she gagged, jerking her hand away.

She inched closer to her best friend. "Lynne, can you tell me what happened?"

"Dermot came to see me."

"And?"

"I like to talk with him. He listens. But then something happened and he left." Lynne shrugged, the slightest lifting of her shoulder. After a long pause, she asked in a deadpan voice, "He doesn't want me, does he?"

The room filled with heaviness, and something pressed on Abby's head. She looked around for a spirit, but she didn't see anything. She felt another wave of that sick feeling, like she was going to gag again.

Get it together. She swallowed back the nausea. She needed to focus in order to help Lynne. "I'm just going to put my hands out here, a little outside your body, okay?"

Lynne hummed noncommittally, like a pale shade of herself. She hadn't been this vacant even in the worst moments since the accident.

Panicked, Abby looked at the edges of Lynne's missing soul piece. Closing her eyes to better focus without the wound distracting her, she felt out the energy surrounding the hole in Lynne's soul. There were tendrils laced from that missing piece to Lynne's hurt leg, linking them together.

"He didn't mean to do it, Abby," Lynne said in a hushed voice.

Abby stilled. She looked up to find Lynne staring at her, though it was like someone else was looking out from Lynne's eyes.

"Dermot didn't mean to do it," Lynne whispered again.

36

Abby got off the floor and looked around for Lynne's phone. She finally found it in her room, under a discarded scarf. She typed in the code to unlock it and scrolled through her contact list until she found Dermot's number.

She called him, willing him to pick up the phone. She kept replaying him saying *I'm sorry.*

He wasn't picking up the phone.

She disconnected and tried calling again. Still nothing.

Tossing the phone aside in frustration, she went back into the living room. She didn't know what to do about Lynne—she just sat there staring at nothing except for moments of looking at Abby with stricken eyes. So she gently helped her to her room.

Lynne never made her bed, so Abby pushed the covers aside and helped Lynne on top. She propped Lynne's foot up on a couple pillows and made sure she was comfortable.

Abby brushed Lynne's hair back from her face. "Do you want your iPad?"

Lynne shook her head, turning it away and closing her eyes.

Biting her lip, Abby stared at her best friend. Because she didn't know what else to do, she took her amethyst out of her bra and tucked it under the pillow supporting Lynne's leg.

"Okay, think," she said to herself as she went back into the living room. Dermot looked upset, and he had something in his hand. Lynne's missing soul piece?

"Bro Paul," she yelled.

He was there instantly. "Jeez, kid. Not so loud."

"Did Dermot take a soul piece from Lynne?" she asked without preamble.

He screwed up his face. "That's not the right question. Ask me in a different way."

Hands on her hips, she thought about it and then asked, "Does Dermot have Lynne's soul piece?"

"Yes." Bro Paul gave her a thumbs-up.

She shook her head, confused. "But you're saying he didn't take it?"

"Semantics." He waggled his hand from right to left and back. "Can you really take something that's offered to you?"

Abby gasped. "Lynne *gave* him her soul piece?"

Bro Paul scratched his neck under his woolen robes. "It kind of goes back to that family curse of hers. The women in her line are doomed to be hurt by the men they want. It really sucks, actually. At least in your line, your great-great-great-great-great grandmother was interested in protecting you all. In Lynne's family, she wanted to punish the women for wanting love. That's just plain bitchy."

Abby blinked at all that. "So if Lynne wanted Dermot—"

"He'd end up hurting her," Bro Paul concluded. Then he held a finger up. "Unless he makes a different choice and breaks his part in the whole affair. That can happen too, but most people have a hard time breaking karma like that. They get pulled by the familiarity of the situation they're in and can't see a different path."

She thought back. "And it happened with Kevin too," she said with dawning comprehension. "Which is why the missing soul piece looked like it was linked to her leg."

"Lynne was fated to it," Bro Paul said neutrally. "The things families pass along, huh? She's a strong, determined woman, which is why she didn't die like her mother did."

"Jesus," Abby said in a low voice. She pushed her hair back as she thought. "Okay, so how do I get the soul piece back?"

He looked at her like she was crazy. "Maybe the same way you always get soul pieces back?"

"But—"

There was a knock on the door. Abby didn't recognize the energy of it—it was a man's hand but not Finn's. She looked at Bro Paul.

He shooed her toward it. "You'll want to answer."

When she opened it, she saw it was Dermot.

37

The first thing Abby noted about him was his grim expression and the lack of color in his face. She took in his soul, which seemed dimmed today except for that band of rainbow colors winding around it. Knowing what it was now made her look at it in a new light, like a horrible beauty that shouldn't exist.

"Hello, Abigail." His hands were shoved in his pockets, his shoulders hunched in a way she wouldn't have expected from a man with his status. In his eyes there was entreaty and contrition.

Without thought, she looked at the kaleidoscope in his soul again. There was a slice that stuck out from all the others. It was a dark-rose color, clear but with jagged edges—Lynne's soul piece.

Seeing where her attention was, he put his hand over it, rubbing it like he was trying to wipe it away. "I didn't mean to do it."

"Why did you do it?" she asked.

"I don't know how it happened." He shook his head,

his expression confused. "One moment I was listening to Madelynne. Her passion is beautiful, and I was pulled in immediately. Then it began to tear from her, and nothing I did stopped it. I fought it as hard as I could. I started to leave but it was too late." He put a hand over the soul piece, protruding out from the band wrapping around his soul.

"Good Lord," she said softly. Swallowing thickly, she nodded at all the colors in that band. "Those are all from other people?"

He slumped in himself. "They were dying. It just started happening. I tell myself that a part of them lives on in me, but the truth is I can't make it stop."

"Good Lord." Abby covered her mouth and stepped back. Horrified, she stared at all the pieces—there had to be close to a hundred, all nestled in together, filling in Dermot's soul.

Something began to press on Abby's forehead. She recognized it—the touch of a spirit trying to get her attention. It shouldn't have been in the house, so she figured it had to do with Dermot. She opened her senses to it cautiously because she couldn't tell if it was helping him or not.

It was the spirit she'd seen in the hospital, of the older man with the blazing emerald eyes and the hole in his chest. Now she recognized the hole as a missing soul piece. Most spirits didn't have that much emotion in them, and she was surprised by the fury that hadn't faded in the time since his death.

In her mind she heard an ethereal whisper: *I want mine back.*

She blinked in shock. When she reached out her mind to it, she saw the whole thing. This man, lying in the hospital bed. The man's family gathered around him, rallying him to get better. The man in moment where his soul piece had been ripped out of his chest and the startling pain of it. Dermot standing over him, sadness and regret in his gaze, a soul piece in his hand.

She looked at the kaleidoscope of soul pieces wrapped with Dermot's soul and saw that piece that he'd taken from the man.

"It started as an accident, you see," Dermot said, remorse in his voice. "With Fiona, the same way it happened with Madelynne. I couldn't stop it, and I couldn't figure out how to give it back. And then she killed herself, and it was too late."

She tried to imagine taking a part of someone's soul from them without their consent. Was that even possible? On some level, Fiona's soul had to have agreed to give it to him.

Bro Paul, she called silently.

"Kid?" Bro Paul materialized next to her.

Can someone take a part of someone's soul without permission? Just the thought of it was terrifying.

He scratched his chin. "Sometimes, but it's less common. Most of the time, the souls have a contract to help each other."

Is that what's going on here? she asked him mentally.

"That, and a whole lot of karma to break." He patted her back. "You got this, kid, but it's not all your responsibility. Lynne's got her part. Don't step in for her."

His unspoken words echoed in her head: *like she had with Kevin.*

"You've just got to stop babying her," he said gently. "She needs to stand on her own two feet."

Dermot frowned, looking around. "Do you hear that?"

Bro Paul nodded at Dermot. "He's got gifts. If only he'd chosen differently. But that's what happened when two cursed people like his parents come together. They create someone who causes destruction."

As if he could hear Bro Paul, Dermot echoed, "I couldn't help myself. But because I felt responsible for Fiona, I promised myself I wouldn't hurt anyone like that again. Abigail, if there had been a twelve-step program for this, I would have done it."

"What about Lynne?"

"I mean it when I said I tried to stop it. But I couldn't. This isn't how I wanted her." The anguish on his face was almost heartbreaking to see. "I came to ask you to help me. That was my aim all along. When I found out you were Angevine, I thought I could commission you to do a painting to cure me of this"—he swallowed—"illness."

She backed away. "You want me to heal you? After what you did to my best friend? My sister?"

"You're right. I'm sorry." He looked her in the eyes, the anguish the starkest pale blue she'd ever seen. "*I'm so sorry.*"

The torment in his tone took her aback. She put her hand to her throat, startled to find that she believed him.

The scene came over her suddenly: Dermot lying on the ground, his body turning to a husk as soul pieces flew out of him. He turned to Lynne, who watched with horror as he died, his mouth forming the words *Forgive me* though no sound escaped.

"I won't ask to see her, though I want to." His smile was sadly bitter. "I won't risk harming her more. But will you tell her I'm sorry and—"

He faltered. Looking away, he ran a hand through his hair. When he spoke again, his voice was colorless. "I'll make this right." He faced Abby, his gaze unfaltering. "I promise I'll make this right."

With that he walked back to his car. She watched as he sat there, staring at nothing. Finally, he slowly drove off, the purr of his engine as lifeless as the look in his eyes had been.

"Well." Bro Paul put his arm around her shoulders. "That gives you some things to think about, doesn't it?"

38

Right then Claire came running out of her house, waving a paper over her head. "Abby! I have something for you!"

Bro Paul lit up. "The answer to your prayers. I *love* it when that happens."

"I don't have time for this now," she said, crossing her arms. "Lynne needs me. I need to start painting the scene I just saw."

"Rocks for brains," he muttered, shaking his head. "Have you already forgotten how helpers show up when you need them most? The Universe is setting you up to succeed. Don't slap its hand away."

"Abby, I drew this for you. It's just what you need." Claire handed over the lined paper.

On it were three stick figures, all men. The one in the center was obviously Finn, with very blue eyes. He had his arms around the other two figures. One had a beer glass in his hand—Niall. The other wore a suit.

Dermot.

"They're friends," Claire said. "They're supposed to be together, like you and Lynne."

Abby frowned, thinking of the scene that she just saw where Dermot lay dying. "I don't know, Claire. It—"

"They're supposed to be together," she insisted, putting her fists on her little hips. She looked past Abby. "Right, Brother Paul?"

"I defer to your infinite wisdom, my lady." He made an elaborate bow to the girl.

Claire giggled.

"Claire, won't your mother wonder where you are?" Abby asked.

"She said I could come paint with you." She pursed her lips. "Brother Paul's friend said I should come paint with you too."

"Your friend?" Abby asked him.

He shrugged. "More like a colleague."

"I know what we're going to draw," Claire continued. "Do you have more blue? We need lots of blue."

"Helpers," Bro Paul said. He went over to Claire and held his hand down low. "You're a good listener, C."

She low-fived him. "But sometimes my mom says I have potatoes in my ears."

"Potatoes are delicious." He gave Abby a pointed look before looking at Claire. "You got this?"

"Oh yes." The little girl nodded solemnly.

"Good." He touched her head. "Call me if you need me," he said as he faded out.

"Maybe when I grow up I can do that too," Claire chattered, going inside and directly to where her shirt was hung to slip it on. "Do you think so, Abby? It must be nice to disappear sometimes."

Abby didn't know what to say about that, so she took a deep breath and focused on the situation at hand. "Come, let's pick our colors."

———

It turned out that they only needed yellow, red, and blue. Abby put plenty of paint on their shared palette—especially blue, at Claire's insistence—and then looked at the girl. "Who's starting this?"

"You." She waved her brush at the canvas. "You know what you need to do."

She really didn't. She wanted to debate that, but she couldn't debate a six-year-old. In that respect, it was clever that they'd picked Claire to help her.

"Close your eyes," Claire said.

Abby did as she said, expecting to see what she'd seen earlier when Dermot had come back. She jumped when she felt Claire's little hand touch her arm, but then she settled into it.

The vision came differently than usual, emerging from a fog. It took a few breaths for it to clear enough that Abby could see what it was.

Dermot, she realized. That strange rainbow band laced into his soul was pulsing. He looked at her imploringly, holding his arms out. In the center of that band of color was a jagged, rose-colored piece.

A small hand nudged her.

Opening her eyes, Abby looked down to find Claire holding out a brush. "Just start," the girl said.

So Abby did.

She outlined Dermot's form minus the mosaic of soul pieces. She sketched Lynne's form, full and healthy, in the same scene, her soul piece back with her.

She was so engrossed in what she was doing that she didn't realize the Claire was painting on the canvas alongside her. She drew in figures of dozens and dozens of people, indistinct, standing in the background, colored triangles flying all over the place. As Abby was putting the finishing touches on Lynne, Claire added one more figure in the foreground: a woman all done in blue, with curly dark hair around her head and her hands glowing with fire.

Me, Abby thought.

Because she was drawn in it and she didn't want anyone to get hurt, she checked the painting to make sure it was okay. The combination healing that she and Claire had intertwined in it was strong. She stepped back and took a breath.

"This is good," Claire said in her child's simplicity.

"Yes, it is." Abby leaned down and looked Claire in the eyes. "*Thank you.*"

Claire smiled. "I like to draw with you, and you listen to me. Some people don't think I hear Brother Paul and the others, but I think they're just jealous they can't hear them too."

"I bet that's it," Abby agreed.

Claire wiggled out of her smock and handed it to Abby. "My mom says you and Lynne should come to dinner. But after we come back, because we have to go to Dublin today. I think we should go to Niall's restaurant, and then I can pour beers for you, but my mom says we should have a girls' night just us instead. Do you want to have a girls' night? After we come back from Dublin?"

Abby walked her to the door. "I think that'd be brilliant."

"I'll tell my mom. Bye, Abby!" She skipped out the door.

Abby watched until Claire was back in her house before going back inside and calling Dermot.

39

Dermot sat in the dark of his office, his hand on his chest. He could feel Madelynne's soul piece in him.

It didn't feel euphoric like it normally did. He would have clawed it out and given it back to her if he could have.

He kept seeing the horror and anger on Abigail's face as she learned what he'd done. He didn't blame her. He was a monster.

But he was going to fix this. He'd already taken the logical steps to ensure that Madelynne was taken care of in the future. The only thing left was to make sure her soul was whole.

He had an idea for how to return it. When he'd started thinking about it, it was obviously simple.

What happened to souls when people died? They were released from their body.

If he died, his soul—and all the soul pieces he'd collected—would be released.

He didn't even think about what it meant to die, or if there was a heaven or not. It was ridiculous to think he even had a shot at heaven—the only heaven he'd had a glimpse into was Madelynne, and he'd fucked up that chance. Even if he managed to return her soul and live, there wasn't any way she'd consider being with him. He wouldn't have let her.

Dying would be a grace. Plus, Madelynne would be saved.

He hoped.

He felt a pang about what Finn and his parents would think. He hated the thought of causing them more hurt. They'd likely find out about Fiona and hate him anyway.

Dying was too good for him.

But it'd set everything right, so that was that.

Resolute, he stood up. It was time.

40

A bby called a dozen times, but Dermot wasn't answering his phone.

Because she had to try, she took the painting she and Claire had done to Lynne to see if it'd do anything.

It didn't. Lynne didn't even blink at it. The gaping hole was still in her chest, and she remained distantly vacant, a hollow shell of herself.

Abby placed the wet painting back on the easel and stalked in the living room, trying to decide what to do. She was wearing out the floor when Lynne shuffled out of her room on her crutches.

"Are you okay?" Abby rushed to her, her good hand out.

"Something's wrong." Lynne looked paler than ever, and her eyes didn't look right, but she was more present than she had been.

"Here." Abby pulled out the chair she usually sat on by the window. "Sit down."

"I don't want to sit down," she said in a monotone. "I want to find Dermot. Something's wrong."

Abby crossed her arms, not sure what to do. On one hand, she believed Dermot in that he didn't want to harm Lynne. On the other, it still happened. "Lynne—"

"He needs help, Abby." She looked her in the eye. "You can help him."

She glanced at the painting. The vision she'd had was gruesome. What if this painting led to that? "He's not answering his phone," Abby finally said.

"Finn can find him." Lynne shuffled to the chair and sat down. "Finn knows where he is."

Calling Finn was a good idea anyway. But he didn't answer his phone either, so she left him a message.

"I'll wait here," Lynne said, staring out the window sightlessly, her crutches still loosely in her hands. Abby dragged a chair to sit next to her, a hand on her arm.

They sat that way for twenty minutes, until Abby heard Finn's car pull up.

"Thank goodness." She hurried to open the door, waiting for him to come up the walkway.

"I didn't get your message till a bit ago," he said, kissing her briefly. He brushed a hand down her back. "I called you back, but when you didn't reply, I decided to come over."

The contact soothed her. She just barely resisted the urge to wilt against him. She'd been holding it together for so long, just her, in crisis after crisis, that to feel his support unmoored her. "Something happened with Lynne."

Before she could say anything more, he rushed inside

and knelt in front of her best friend. "Hello, darling," he said in a soft voice as he got down in front of her. "I don't normally make house calls, but I'm making an exception for my favorite girls. Can I take a look?"

Lynne nodded without looking at him.

He eased her leg off the wheelchair's footrest and lifted her skirt to look at it. His brow furrowed, and then he efficiently began undoing the new brace. "Her leg is really swollen again. What did she do today?"

"Dermot came over to see her," Abby said.

"Dermot?" Frowning, Finn set the brace aside and gently ran his hand down the swollen skin, the scar tissue from her surgery an angry red. "I mean, did she spend a lot of time on her crutches?"

"Not as far as I know." She took a deep breath. "I didn't call you over about her leg."

"You should have. It's terribly inflamed. I don't understand it. It was doing well this morning when I checked it." Finn lowered Lynne's skirt. "Let's get you to bed and ice this. What do you say, darling?"

"We need to find Dermot," Lynne said in a monotone. "He needs help."

Abby lifted her hands helplessly. "I've been trying to call him, and he won't answer. We need to find him."

Finn stood, his brow furrowed. "Why does Lynne think he needs help?"

"Something happened." Abby bit her lip, trying to think of what to say. In the end she just shrugged helplessly and blurted it out. "Dermot took a piece of Lynne's soul. That's what's wrong with her."

"Lynne is just depressed," he said in a placating tone.

"I've seen it with Fiona, and with every other difficult case I've had."

She could see the flash of him thinking about the soccer player who'd killed himself before he shook it off.

For that she was glad.

But this was different. She put her hand on his arm. "I know this sounds insane and you don't believe me, but I'm asking you to trust me. I need to find Dermot, and I don't know where to look. Just help me find him."

"And then what?" He shook his head. "Lynne needs to lie down and ice her leg. The swelling—"

"Will go down once I see to Dermot. I have a plan, but I need to find Dermot," Abby interrupted. She stepped into him, imploring him with her gaze. "I believe in your magic. I need you to believe in mine too."

He studied her silently for what seemed like forever. Then he nodded. "I'll take you to him."

41

There was no one home at Dermot's.

Finn got back in his car after he'd helped Abby into the passenger seat. Lynne was in the back, eerily silent, on the drive over. On the floor next to her was a wet painting that Abby had insisted would heal Dermot.

He put his hands on the steering wheel. He didn't know what to think. Abby's story of stolen soul pieces was something out of an old sci-fi movie.

"Where else could he be?" Abby asked.

Finn sighed. "Abby, I want to believe you, but do you realize how this sounds?"

Abby's lips twisted, wry. "Yes, I do. That's why I asked you to trust me."

He thought about it. He studied her—he didn't doubt that she believed what she believed, but he couldn't buy into a theory that somehow Dermot—his oldest friend—could be responsible for hurting Lynne.

"It was a mistake," Lynne said in a disturbing flat

tone. "He didn't mean to do it. We have to help him before he hurts himself."

Finn looked at her in the rearview mirror. "Why would he hurt himself?"

Lynne met his eyes in it. "He feels guilty. He thinks he hurt Fiona too."

Finn jerked. "What?"

Abby put her hand on his arm. "Let's just find him, just in case. To make sure he's okay. Do you know where he would have gone if he were upset?"

He sat back, staring out the windshield. He thought about all their old haunts as kids, but he doubted Dermot went to any of them. There weren't any spots that stood out for any reason.

Except...

He put the car in gear. "I know where he'd go."

The one place in Tullaghan that Finn tried to avoid at all costs: the place where Fiona had been hit by the car.

42

At first, Abby had no idea where they were going. Then her intuition clicked, and she realized they were going to the spot where it'd all started: where Fiona had lost her soul piece.

She looked at Finn. His jaw was set like granite. She put her injured hand over his on the stick shift.

He glanced at her, and the expression in his eyes kicked her in the gut. She wanted to tell him she was so sorry for causing him this pain, but she needed to find Dermot before anything worse happened.

Before something worse happened to Lynne.

As Finn slowed down and pulled over to the side of the road, Abby saw Dermot standing in the middle of the road up ahead.

"What the hell?" Finn murmured, scowling. He quickly got out of the car. "Dermot!"

"Help me out, Abby," Lynne said from the back seat.

Abby wanted to tell her to stay put, but she remembered what Bro Paul had said about Lynne standing on her own two feet, so she forced her protective instincts aside and got the crutches ready while Lynne slowly angled her legs out of the car.

"He means to kill himself," Lynne said as she took the crutches. "Don't let him, Abby. It's not his fault."

"Jesus." Abby made sure Lynne was stable on the crutches, went back inside the car to grab the painting, and headed for Dermot.

He was still in the middle of the road, silent, listening to Finn who was arguing with him.

She had to give him the painting. She just wished she knew what'd happen then.

He wanted Lynne to have her soul piece back—Abby believed that—but beyond that she had no idea what he wanted. Would this healing go bad too?

If it did, Finn would forever blame her for hurting his friend. Well, only if he started believing in "magic," she thought with a self-deprecating chuckle. At least she had his disbelief going for her.

She herself, on the other hand, had no excuse. If this went bad, she only had herself to blame.

She had to take a chance; otherwise, who knew what'd happen to Lynne.

So Abby stepped forward. "Dermot!"

He and Finn both turned to look at her.

She lifted her arm to hold the painting up for Dermot to see.

A car careened from around the bend close to Dermot and Finn. They both shouted, Finn pushing Dermot out of the way as the car barely missed them.

Abby jumped out of the way too, but as she did, the

draft from the car pulled the painting out of her hand. It flew in the air, landing facedown on the asphalt.

They all stood there, mute, staring at the back of the canvas.

Abby went to it first, kneeling down to peel it off the ground where there was a thick smear of paint. Her heart lurched when she saw the smudged mess the asphalt had made of the wet oil paint. She searched it with her senses, looking for any hint of the healing she and Claire had woven into it, but there wasn't even a glimmer.

Lynne came to a stop next to her. "Oh no."

Abby gaped at the ruined painting in her hand. She didn't have words for how she felt. She wanted to burst into tears and scream in anger at the same time. She wondered if she could go grab Claire to do another one, except according to her, she and Sarah were going to Dublin today.

She was fucked.

Out of nowhere, she remembered that her mama used to say, "Trust in the Divine, baby. They always have your back."

So Abby did the only thing she could think of. "Bro Paul?"

He showed up instantly, taking in the scene. When his gaze fell on the painting, he winced. "Well, that sucks."

"I'm not sure what to do," Abby said honestly.

"Remember the last time you and Claire painted?"

She nodded. She'd put that painting that Claire had done of Abby's hands glowing with healing in her room, but she hadn't had time to do anything about it.

Bro Paul got in her face. "Now is not the time to woolgather, Abs. Focus. Did you see the past life scene that needs to be edited?"

"I wish I could unsee it." She shuddered, still feeling the chill of the stone on her wrists before the sword came down over them. "I haven't edited it yet."

"Don't you think now would be a good time?" he asked, not veiling his impatience.

"Just in my mind."

Bro Paul got in her face. "Get your hands back in order or everyone is fucked here. If you don't call that back for yourself, you can't help anyone here."

She blinked.

"It's shit-or-get-off-the-pot time, kid." He patted her shoulder and stepped back.

"Okay." Okay, she could do this.

She hoped.

She closed her eyes and pictured the scene again, only she edited it so that she listened to her intuition and stole away before the sultan asked her to do anything.

Something in her diaphragm clicked open, and she felt her hands get warm.

Opening her eyes, she held her hands up to look at them. They looked like they always did, though her fingertips tingled. She touched her injured wrist and felt a zap shoot up her arm, through her shoulder, and up her neck.

She had no idea what that meant and, as Bro Paul pointed out, now wasn't the time to woolgather.

It was now or never. She'd find out soon enough if it worked.

Facing Dermot, Abby focused on all the pieces of souls he had attached in the spiral around him. She felt each one, pushing aside the sorrow she felt from them.

She pictured what she and Claire had drawn: Dermot and Lynne. As she imagined all the people who'd had soul pieces taken, their souls showed up one by one, until they all formed a ring around Dermot. She recognized the angry man with the emerald eyes from the hospital; his soul nodded at her in respect.

Then Abby held her injured hand out, her intent centered on that multicolored mosaic of soul pieces trapped in Dermot's soul. *Come.*

The entirety of it began to vibrate. But it didn't shake apart.

Then she saw Dermot's soul step forward, away from his body. He reached inside and drew all those pieces out, holding them out and offering them to her, a look of remorse on his face. His soul turned to all the other souls around him and said, "I'm sorry."

She stared at him. *This is done.*

And then she refocused on the multitude of soul pieces. *Be free.*

They burst out, sparkling in the light, a shower of color. For a second, they suspended in the air before they whirled and returned to their respective souls.

Abby turned, waiting to make sure Lynne's soul piece returned to her.

Lynne gasped the second it did, rocking on the crutches. Coughing, she caught her balance before Abby reached her. Abby kept an eye on her, making sure her soul reincorporated it completely before relaxing.

She'd never done anything like that. She hadn't known that it could be done, much less that she *could* do it.

Her mom had died when Abby was eight, so she wasn't able to learn from her for very long, and her soul had crossed over right away so Abby didn't have a chance to even ask her spirit about the way of things. She remembered everything her mom had told her, but beyond reading cards she couldn't remember what her mom could do.

Not that it'd matter. "You can't compare your gifts with someone else's," her mama used to warn. "That's like comparing two apples. Even if they're from the same tree, they're going to be different, because they come from a different stem."

In this moment, she felt like the strength of their tree, every single branch and all the women with them, encouraging her and congratulating her for coming into her own. It was like finding a type of home—her place in the whole scheme of things.

"Abby."

She looked at Lynne. Lynne's color was coming back, and her gaze no longer looked dead. It was like she was back all the way. Abby exhaled in relief.

"Abby!" Lynne screamed, pointing. "Do something!"

Abby turned around and gasped.

She'd had been so entranced by the power and beauty of the soul pieces flying away that she didn't notice Dermot. He'd fallen to his knees and was clutching his chest.

But it was his face that caught her up: with each leaving soul piece he withered more and more.

He collapsed on the ground, writhing.

Lynne screamed again. "No!"

43

Finn saw his life flash before his eyes when that car sped out of nowhere. He had a flash of what it must have felt like for Fiona, but then he set that aside. Med school had trained him to focus on the crisis at hand. He was just glad the car had come from behind him and Dermot and not the other direction, because then Abby and Lynne would have been in danger.

As it was, Abby's painting was destroyed when it splatted on the asphalt. He saw the devastation on her face and felt bad, but frankly, he was beyond relieved she was okay.

But then he heard Lynne scream, "No!"

He spun around, searching first for her and then Abby, but they were both fine.

Then he heard the choking sound behind him. His training had him moving to the sound before he fully registered what it was.

When he saw Dermot, he couldn't believe his eyes. It

looked like he couldn't breathe, so Finn knelt on the ground and checked for a clear airway. "Dermot."

Dermot was incoherent, his hands grasping at nothing. His eyes stared at something they couldn't see. His face was emaciated and getting thinner by the second. His breath gargled in his throat, and he reached out.

Abby skidded to a stop next to him, falling to the ground on her knees.

Finn looked at her. "What's happening?"

"I'm not sure," she said honestly. "I think he's dying. Maybe he couldn't be sustained without the power of all those souls?"

"You know I don't believe in that," he said. Except what was happening before them was undeniable. Dermot was withering, skin sagging over stark bone, a husk of his former vital self.

"Do something, Abby!" Lynne screamed.

"Bro Paul?" Abby looked off in the distance for a matter of seconds. Then she nodded and said, "Okay, I know what I'm going to do."

She reached down and put her hands over Dermot's chest. For a second, Finn thought they were glowing, but he blinked and it was gone.

Then she looked down at Dermot and gasped.

Finn looked down too.

Dermot was breathing harshly, sweat on his brow like he'd just had a longtime fever break. He stared directly at Finn as his face filled in again.

Finn sat back on his heels. "Well, fuck me."

A shadow passed over them. Finn looked up, expecting Lynne.

But it wasn't her.

At first, Finn didn't see anything for the glare of the sun. Then, squinting, he began to make out a feminine form. The more he looked, the more the outline filled out though it was still transparent, until he realized who it was.

He staggered to his feet, his heart pounding. "Fiona?"

She came toward him, smiling, seeming to float. She reached out and touched his face. It felt like the brush of gossamer on his skin. *Now you can believe again,* he heard her voice say in his head.

Gaping, he watched her go to Dermot, who was sitting up now. There were tears in his eyes as she approached him. "I'm so sorry," he whispered to her.

Finn heard her voice in his head again. *Now it's time to forgive yourself.*

Dermot swallowed audibly, but he nodded.

Fiona turned around and smiled brilliantly at Abby.

Again, Finn heard her in his mind. *Sister. Take care of them both.*

And then Fiona's figure slowly evaporated, leaving nothing but the faint hint of coconut shampoo behind.

"Well, fuck me," Finn said again with twice the feeling.

44

Three Months Later

Abby stepped back from the painting she was working on and looked at her subject. It was very different than what she normally painted, but this was a private commission—for her husband.

"Are we done yet?" he asked from where he stretched out naked on the couch. Finn's long body took up the entire length of the couch, and the sunlight streaming in from the windows of her studio lit him up in the most delicious way.

"Almost," she said, pretending to add a few more strokes only because she wanted to revel in his naked form a little longer.

Being able to heal with her hands had freed her artwork to be more expansive. She didn't feel like she needed to do one particular thing any longer, so she explored different styles and subjects.

She had Claire to thank for that. They still got

together for paint dates. Sarah would drop her off and then come back for dinner. Sarah was reserved, but they were on their way to becoming good friends.

She set the brush down and picked up a rag. "I'm done now," she said, walking toward him.

His beautiful eyes sparked with desire, and then his lids lowered in the look he got when he was thinking of ways to corral her back into their bedroom. He swung his legs onto the floor.

No need for the bedroom when there was a couch handy right here. She put her knees on either side of his hips and straddled him.

His lips curved in a smile as he gripped her hips. He ran his hands up her back and down her arms, taking her right hand, turning it over, and kissing her palm.

After she called back her ability to heal with her hands, her wrist had healed almost overnight. It was as good as new now, but Finn was still protective about it. She didn't mind. She hadn't had anyone care for her that way since her mom.

Finn wrapped his hands in the ends of her hair. "Lynne won't be here for an hour."

Abby grinned. "Really?"

He tugged her closer to nuzzle her neck. "I think we should take advantage of my current state of undress."

She laughed low, running her hands up his chest.

That day in the middle of the road had changed everything. At first, she hadn't been sure it was a good thing. Finn kept looking at her like he expected her to zap him.

But they'd talked about it, and her gifts, and his

residual skepticism. Finn liked to talk. He liked to kiss too, and he was very good about knowing when to do each.

But he also listened, for which Abby was grateful. He also respected her gifts in a way that she'd never imagined. A few weeks ago, he'd even talked to her about a patient he had, asking if there was an energetic cause for an injury no one could explain.

They'd gotten married at his parents' farm, a small ceremony with just a few people, one pet horse, and an irreverent Franciscan monk.

At the thought of Bro Paul, he suddenly popped into the room, his hand over his eyes. "You should tell him, kid."

Not yet, she thought. *Go away.*

"Come on. You know you want to tell Finn about the baby." Bro Paul peeked from between his fingers. "If he wants, I'll send him images of her. She's so frickin' adorable."

She was. Abby's heart flopped open every time she thought about her. She knew that she was going to have dark curly hair and purply blue eyes, with her father's pragmatic instinct about life and her love for colors.

"What is it?" Finn asked her. "Bro Paul?"

Bro Paul chuckled. "Aw, man, it's only a matter of time before he cracks open the way Lynne is. Ha ha! Tell him to brace himself. I'm outta here, kid," he said, blowing her a kiss.

She rolled her eyes and then returned her attention to her husband. "Yes, it was Bro Paul."

He ran a hand under her shirt, to her belly. "Did he tell you to tell me you're pregnant?"

She blinked in surprise.

Grinning, he lowered her head down gently to kiss her. "I'm a doctor, love. And I can count."

"Well, hell." Frowning, she sat back on his thighs. "Bro Paul said you were ready to crack open like Lynne. Maybe he's right and you're coming into some gifts too."

"Maybe," he said with an amused smile.

"Are you happy?" she asked carefully.

"How could I not be? She's going to be beautiful like her mother." He pulled her to him and kissed her, a tender forever sort of kiss.

Finn was more intuitive than he believed. She'd seen him interact with his patients, listening not just to their words but also what they weren't saying. He was an excellent doctor, but to her he wasn't just a miracle worker anymore—he was a miracle.

He'd moved his practice to Sligo, about half an hour away from their new home. He'd also limited his hours and only took patients he felt passionate about. He worked from the house at home as often as he could, and when he did, he always paid her a visit in her studio. He had a sixth sense about when she was ready to take a break.

They'd bought the house that he'd taken her to see.

The roses were still in glorious bloom despite the autumn.

"How is Lynne doing with all that, by the way?" Finn asked, holding her close.

By "all that" Finn meant the supernatural stuff. Abby

snuggled in. "She's hanging in there. You see her more than I do. You'd know better than I do."

"When she and I get together, she's mostly cursing me," Finn said in a wry tone.

Finn had performed a surgery on Lynne six weeks ago. She was currently walking with a cane, but Finn felt good about her prospects.

On some days, Lynne was in the clouds. Others, she was less than positive and sure that she was never going to dance again. Abby still believed, but she also knew that Lynne had things to resolve in herself.

She wanted to heal the old familial curse in Lynne's line, but Lynne kept putting it off for some reason. Abby didn't understand it—if you could fix it, why wouldn't you?—but she respected Lynne's choice.

Still, the times when Abby looked at Lynne and she didn't look right bothered her. Abby had come to the conclusion that it was some sort of spirit overlapped on Lynne, but since Lynne didn't want her to touch it, she couldn't do anything about it.

It'd driven a little bit of a wedge between them, and that made Abby sad. Finn knew it, so he did what he could to encourage them spending time together, like tonight when Lynne was coming over for a movie night. They were going to watch *Moonstruck* because Lynne missed Manhattan.

Lynne didn't talk about Dermot.

Dermot had decided to go to the States for a bit. Finn talked to him, asking him to come home, but Dermot wasn't ready yet. Abby reserved judgment on him.

Finn dipped his head to kiss her lightly.

She clung to his lips, feeling some of the worry about Lynne and Dermot fade. When she lifted her head, she said, "Was that on purpose?"

"Every kiss I give you is on purpose. Every kiss I'll ever give you is on purpose." He tugged her hair to tip her head back to look into her eyes. "Are you ready to be ravished, Ms. Angevine?"

"Yes, please," she said with a smile.

He lifted her shirt and tossed it aside. Then he ran his hands down her body, pulling her close, exactly where she liked to be: skin to skin.

It was home.

Her mama used to say, "Love heals the world." Abby believed that. Love *did* heal the world—love and Finn.

THE BEGINNING

I've always danced as if I were deaf. It's no wonder since my mother died because of The Whispers.

The first time I heard them, I was in Jackson Square with my mom. I was four, and I had on a pink dress with a skirt that billowed out as I twirled.

But before I heard The Whispers, I heard the drums and fell in love.

I felt the rhythm of their deep voices vibrating through the square. Their sound shot directly to my chest, their beat echoing in time with my heart. I'd never heard anything so profound; I'd never felt anything so stirring, and I wanted to get closer so I could be surrounded by them.

For a change, I didn't have to beg my mom to go to it. She dragged me to the powerful music like she was in a trance. When we got to the crowd, she pushed our way through the throng to the front.

The performers were all dressed in white, from the men beating the drums to the women who danced.

When I was four, I didn't know what they were doing was called yanvalou or that it was a Voudoun prayer to call deities. I just knew that the pounding of the drums was the most exciting thing I'd ever felt. I knew I wanted to dance like that too, because the truth of their movements was more powerful than anything I'd ever heard anyone say out loud. So I began to undulate, arms raised in joy.

I turned to my mom to show her my dance.

She stood next to me, eyes unseeing, swaying as if she had an invisible partner. And then I heard it—the voice purring at her. *Go join the circle of women. They have power you don't. They'll understand you in a way no one else will. Leave the child...* I wanted to say "No!" but my voice wouldn't work. I stopped dancing and began to cry until she finally noticed and took me away.

That was The Day Everything Changed.

The last time I heard The Whispers was on The Day of Endless Darkness, when I was six. That was also the day I saw a demon for the first time.

I heard it before I saw it, a cold hiss of The Whispers directed at Mom. *Life is hard. This is too much. Wouldn't it be peaceful to leave it behind? It would be so easy to end it all, just turn into the oncoming traffic...* With each seductive murmur, the demon's tentacles wrapped tighter until Mom was gasping for air.

This time, I managed to cry out, but my mom didn't pay any attention.

Then the demon turned to me.

Its eyes were empty, black-tinged and rotted at the edges. Its mouth gaped, and I swore I could see the words seep from the open hole in a sickly cloud.

My mother's knuckles were white from her grip on the steering wheel. She began to turn the car toward the other lane...

When I screamed, the sound of crunching steel eclipsed it.

Mom died, not because of the head-on collision with a pickup truck, or because of bipolar disorder the way the police thought. I knew exactly what had pushed my mom to her death.

That's when I stopped listening, because I realized The Whispers were in everything: in my mom and in music. In a stranger passing by on the street. But when they were being especially pernicious, they were even in my dreams.

When I became a dancer, I used to be able to make up for not truly hearing the music by just following the choreography I was given. The other dancers used to make fun of me—the great Madelynne Broussard, tone deaf. What they didn't know was that I was terrified that if I gave over to the abandon, The Whispers would come at me.

Now, since the accident with Kevin, everything has changed. I can't rely on my talent to make up for my fear, and I don't have anyone to tell me what steps to follow.

On top of that, it's all coming back—the hearing, the knowing. I'm afraid of what am I going to hear, but I'm even more afraid of never dancing again.

Did you know that for every review you leave a fairy gets bigger wings?

Help a fairy out and leave a review for PAINTER OF SOULS.

Will Lynne dare to dance again? Find out in DANCER OF TRUTHS, the next Irish Hope novel.

A lost dream.

The need to put away the past and face the future.

A chance for redemption and love...

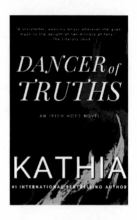

"Highly recommend delving into this magical Irish story!"

— NICOLE

"[Kathia's] writing is fluid, with a touch of sexiness and loads of romance, just what you need to relax after a long, hard working day."

— GABBY

Get DANCER OF TRUTHS.

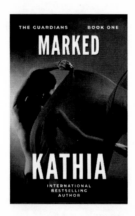

ALSO BY KATHIA

LAUREL HEIGHTS

PERFECT FOR YOU

CLOSE TO YOU

RETURN TO YOU

LOOKING FOR YOU

DREAM OF YOU

SWEET ON YOU

BEDFORD FALLS

UNDER THE KISSING TREE

DANCING ON A MOONBEAM

SILVER MOON SPARKLING

STARS SHINING BRIGHT ABOVE

PILLOW TALK NOVELS

PLAYING TO WIN

PLAYING DOCTOR

PLAYING FOR KEEPS

THE GUARDIANS

MARKED

CHOSEN

TEMPTED

WHIMSICAL NOVELS OF YOUNG LOVE

SWEET ENDEAVORS

UNRAVELED

PROJECT DADDY

For a complete booklist, check out Kathia's site.

LOOKING FOR SOMETHING NEW?

International travel, a matchmaking duo, and everlasting love...

Meet the Merriams.

You'll want to spend your holidays with this family.

———

WILD IRISH ROSE

LOVE AMONG LAVENDER

VALLEY OF STARS

SUNFLOWER ALLEY

A FOREVER OF ORANGE BLOSSOMS

A BREATH OF JASMINE

———

Ava has more books, and they're all fab. Be sure to check out
her entire booklist.

https://avamiles.com/books/

ABOUT KATHIA

With over 6 million books sold (and counting), Kathia's novels have been #1 bestsellers around the world. They've received starred reviews from Booklist, have consistently earned Editor's Picks for Best Romance, and have been featured by *O, The Oprah Magazine*.

Kathia has written over 40 books so far, some translated into several languages, all about hope and dreams and the bonds of friendship and family. She's also written a couple screenplays and various poems (her ode to the color orange is particularly moving).

For more, check out...

www.kathiaherself.com

You can also find Kathia in all the usual places...

instagram.com/kathiaherself

facebook.com/kathiaherself

twitter.com/kathiaherself

bookbub.com/authors/kathia

**DON'T FORGET TO SIGN UP FOR
KATHIA'S NEWSLETTER.**

What do you get?
The latest on upcoming releases.
Bloopers and deleted scenes.
And a front-row seat to Kathia's adventures.

Do it. It's a piece of cake.

www.kathiaherself.com/newsletter

Made in United States
North Haven, CT
28 July 2022

21942612R00226